Praise for *Eggshells*

'*Eggshells* is a work of impressive imaginative reach, witty, subtle and occasionally endearingly unpredictable . . . Reveals an artistic vision which is distinctive in contemporary Irish writing.' —Rooney Prize for Irish Literature Judges

'Charming, and original.' —*Booklist*

'Engaging and humorous.' —*The Dublin Inquirer*

'Inventive, funny and, ultimately, moving.' —*The Guardian*

'Delightfully quirky.' —*The Irish Independent*

'Full of action and humour . . . beguiling.' —*The Irish Times*

Magically delicious.' —*Kirkus Reviews*

'Wildly funny.' —*The New York Times Book Review*

'There's an everyday magic to this gorgeous urban fairytale.' —RTÉ

'A memorable debut.' —*Totally Dublin*

WUNDERLAND

a novel

Caitríona Lally

NEW ISLAND

WUNDERLAND
First published in 2021 by
New Island Books
Glenshesk House
10 Richview Office Park
Clonskeagh
Dublin D14 V8C4
Republic of Ireland
www.newisland.ie

Print ISBN: 978-1-84840-805-0
eBook ISBN: 978-1-84840- 806-7

British Library Cataloguing in Publication Data. A CIP catalogue record for this book is available from the British Library.

Typeset by JVR Creative India
Edited by Emma Dunne
Proofread by Susan McKeever
Cover design by Jo Walker, jowalker.com
Printed by Scandbook, scandbook.com

New Island received financial assistance from The Arts Council (An Chomhairle Ealaíon), Dublin, Ireland

New Island Books is a member of Publishing Ireland.

10 9 8 7 6 5 4 3 2 1

*To Liam and Mary Lally for their lifelong encouragement
and* ara it'll be grand *style of parenting*

The night the census was filled out in Irish homes, Roy was on a bus on the way to the airport. He was counted by nobody, included by nobody, went unnoticed, unmarked. He was not for ticking into a box; his mind was otherwhere than home.

DAY 1

Roy

Der Jeansbügler = man who irons his jeans

Today was Roy's last day on the day shift; he would go back to split shifts tomorrow. He didn't like the day shift. The lines of tourists outside the Miniatur Wunderland formed early; the children in buoyant clumps, the parents keen as mosquitoes. There was an atmosphere of barely contained urgency, like the prescription counter of a pharmacy on Christmas Eve. Before leaving his apartment for work, Roy checked the expected waiting times bar charts on the MiWuLa website. Low red bars showed for today, the highest between 12.00 and 12.30, a strip of oddly sized bollards that would decide how busy his day would be. He wondered again: how could they predict what time visitors would decide to show up?

His walk to work took four minutes. He passed the queue at the front – longer than the bar chart suggested – and walked up two flights of stairs.

'Allo,' the cashier greeted him.

Roy was tall and fair and vaguely Germanic looking but people here still knew he was foreign. His body was hairless, his pot belly taut, his head egg-shaped and yet, despite these rotundities – and unlike the large bowl in the first letter of his name – Roy had no rounded ways. He thought and spoke in a linear manner, all points and edges and measured constructions. Not a syllable was wasted, not a vowel was accidentally uttered before being thoroughly thought through. His name should have started with a K, all sharp angles and lines, and K, if you rotated it clockwise, was like a slightly rickety table. Roy wouldn't stand for rickety, however; Roy would curse and spurn rickety and hire a carpenter to banish rickets and dents and tinges of things that weren't supposed to be there.

He opened the door to the small kitchen used by the security guards and cleaners for their breaks. He nodded to Stefan, his flatmate, and Eric, another security guard, who were both watching a small portable television.

'Allo,' they said in perky unison.

Roy looked at his watch. He was some minutes early for work; he was still new enough in the job to turn up for work early, but he was old enough to not start working until the minute required. He decided to eat his lunch apple now. The cold smack of it, always a shock, and the sweetness. He ate right to the core and unintentionally chewed a pip. It tasted of almonds, of marzipan on a Christmas cake. Roy shook out the remaining pips – little brown teardrops, the dried blood-tears of a saint – and put them in his pocket.

When he got up, Eric and Stefan turned at the scrape of the wooden leg on the tile. Roy beckoned towards the door, they said something, he nodded as if he understood and walked off. He unlocked the door of the cleaning-supplies cubby and saw the orange bucket, loaded with spray bottles and cloths, with his name on it. It made him feel even more foreign when he saw his name next to the other German ones. He said them all aloud, dwelling for extra moments on the bunched consonants, hissing softly the *s*'s and *c*'s and *h*'s. What would it feel like to be fluent in a different language?

Would he think in different ways? He liked to think he'd be more effective or forceful if he had been given the right verbs and nouns from toddler-hood, because learning a second language could only provide him with second-hand verbs. He'd studied German in school and regretted not keeping it up – the guilt of a language learned well and mostly lost plagued him. It surely wasn't his investment to lose.

Roy picked up his brush and dustpan, leaving behind his bucket of cleaning sprays and creams for a quieter time. It amused him that he could clean without need of water, that brightly coloured liquids with throat-tightening scents would take the place of water. Maybe water would become extinct, replaced by more highly coloured, multi-functional liquids in every aspect of life.

He skirted by the historical dioramas with their educational voiceovers inside headphones, the dull, plodding sibling that preceded the glamorous model railway. These large glass cubes told seven millennia of German history, from 5,500 bce to a sudden embarrassed stop at 1942. Roy identified with these underrated tableaux. They didn't get the attention the model railway exhibition got, the high-achieving brother that everyone wanted to visit. He entered the exhibition. Eight miles of track ran through real and imaginary miniature lands in several large rooms over three floors, with no heed to start or finish, top or bottom. Somebody, or a group of somebodies, had decided that Switzerland was a good starting point, but to Roy, it just seemed arbitrary. That was a bother; there should be clear guidelines that let you know the start and finish of something, like going to a football match. It was clear when to stand for the anthem, when to throw your hands in the air and roar with delight, or when to tut and walk out in disgust. Who *gets* to decide starting points? Surely the person who picked where the start was could also pick where the end of the world was.

There were no wrappers or chewed gum-lumps or ice-cream puddles today – there seldom were – but Roy ran his brush gently over the perfectly clean floor. Trying to look busy took as much effort as actually being busy. As he reached the miniature replica of the Alps, the lights began to dim. Every fifteen minutes, the entire exhibition went dark so the exhibits could be lit from within. This was his favourite part. Details that were easily missed in full bright were obvious now: figurines on trains, people dancing in apartment blocks, a man photographing a naked woman on a bed in a loft. But the trains, oh, the trains, the *trains*: the trains carried away the details so rapidly that, no matter how many times he crouched by the Swiss Alps, he never could quite figure out what that woman was doing to the man in the fifth carriage of the plum-red train or why the small boy was tugging at the jacket of the tall man. Even if he could speak fluent German, he felt it would be cheating to ask the engineers what the scenes were intended to mean.

Roy stooped over the train station at the foot of the Swiss Alps. A cave at his eye level was lit by an orange glow; a group of miniature scuba divers was huddled around a campfire inside, their treasure chests arranged around them. There could be no logic to this – there must be some creative free play afoot, the kind of fireball thinking he couldn't thrust his mind towards. The divers seemed to fit right in; they were right at home hundreds of feet above sea level in this mountain cave, warming their hands while they presumably discussed their hoard. There was something too smug about them so he gave a quick glance around to make sure nobody could see, then he leaned over the railings and smashed the figurines flat with his brush before gathering the broken bits into his pocket. There, that'll show them.

He straightened up and shuffled along the rail towards a mountain road scene. An elephant led a steamroller along a miniature motorway. Several large wheels of cheese had fallen out the back of a lorry up a mountain and were rolling down the hill. A wheel of cheese was a really fine thing; it was good to have foods in the spherical, even if wedges were later cut from it in the triangular.

When the visitors in front of him moved on, he too moved along the rail to stand in front of a miniature castle in a miniature lake. A flying contest was taking place at the lake's edge, with all sorts of magical-looking flying machines taking part: a strawberry, still miniature but giant in scale compared to the figurines, a pink glitter guitar, a clog and a giant-in-miniature red pepper. A figurine was just about to fly off the edge; another had already crashed into the sea. Roy put his hands into his pockets. He could feel the apple pips in his right pocket and he dug his thumbnail into one of them. Then he took the pips out, holding them between his thumb and forefinger like he was checking brown diamonds for carat-worth, and laid them behind the red pepper flying machine in a line: one, two, three. They looked like a trail of nervous droppings from the pepper. He moved on to the Lindt chocolate factory as the lights started to come on.

A boy of about twelve was crouched at the hatch of the factory. This control button drew the largest crowd because it cranked up a mechanism that appeared to make a small block of chocolate and deposited it wrapped in gold foil into the lip below. The chocolates looked as though they'd been kept in someone's pocket for too long, all misshapen and covered in lint and finger smudges. Reaching into the hatch for the chocolate was like reaching in for a train ticket or a snack from a vending machine, with the same fear that the goods would get stuck or some creature inside would nip your fingers.

No sooner had a chocolate dropped into the hatch than it was snatched by the child with one hand and the button pressed again with the other hand. The boy remained on his hunkers, unwrapped the chocolate and stuffed it into his mouth, his hand ready to scoop out the next one when it fell. When the boy's hand went to press the button again, Roy walked over. A backlog of several children had built up, waiting to get at the chocolate, too wary of this older child who acted like an adult. Roy tapped the boy on the shoulder. The boy looked up at him. Roy pointed at the children behind. The boy shrugged and got up slowly, peeling the wrapper off the second chocolate, and walked away with a swagger. The waiting children had surrounded the factory and were chattering excitedly, and for the second time in that first hour of work, Roy wished he could understand the code. Learning new languages used to come easy to him, but since landing in his middle years, fresh syllables had remained just out of reach. As he watched the children talking to each other, however, he knew that the language needed to talk to other people had nothing to do with syllables and everything to do with something he just didn't have.

Gert

Das Flugzeug = flying thing = airplane

The airport was packed. I sat on a metal seat and watched the procession of attractive people pulling wheelie suitcases with one hand and holding disposable coffee cups in the other. Their steps were assured, their faces unstrained, and I wondered if their lives were really all that simple. I looked at the different destinations on the screen. Hamburg was beginning to lack the appeal of other places; maybe if I stared hard enough, the perfect destination would become clear. Every new city that appeared on the screen whirled around my mind: I pictured Paris Gert in a stripy top, sipping red wine, but I don't like red wine and horizontal stripes do me no favours. I imagined Milan Gert but again the fashion quivers took me over. Chicago Gert was tempting: a city with plenty of skyscrapers. I feel safest when I know there are people higher up than me, and I surely couldn't feel low when everything was so high.

I boarded the plane at the last possible moment. My bags were so lumpily packed they'd be easy stuffable around the boxier suitcases. Sure enough, as departure time approached, there was an announcement of a delay and I felt smug about waiting to sit down. I organised my heft into the seat and looked out the window at the baggage handlers fecking cases into the hold with almighty force. Funny how it is we pay our holiday savings for a lengthy view of a runway. There were tuts around me: a mother desperately tried to contain her toddler's limbs; well-cut passengers made it clear they were frustrated because they had Places to Be. I was quite content – this was a holiday for me – to just sit and not have to do or sort or make or act.

Hard to know what to expect with Roy. I've done so much worrying about him the past half-year I've had to pull back a bit and assume things will end the right way up. When I fixed him in his job in Germany he wasn't very happy, but getting him out of Ireland was the only solution I had: if you can't solve a problem, get it the hell out of the country. A friendship misconstrued is how I'd put it, an ill-advised friendship with a teenager. The whisperings of an inappropriate closeness only ever reached the shout of *Nonce* from a gang of teenagers on a street corner, but I needed to get him out before the accusations came from other sources. Gráinne didn't know what to make of it so she backed off, and I couldn't take it on then so I exported the problem. My friend Simone lives in Hamburg and her husband works at a model railway exhibition. I begged my way into a cleaning job there for Roy – if he didn't like the job he'd sure as anything like the surroundings. Our parents couldn't bring themselves to mention his name, but Mam put a box of Barry's tea and a multipack of Tayto into my hands, to 'share', as if Roy and I were children planning a midnight feast or I'd get lonesome for Irish foods in the few days away from home.

Allen, thankfully, has gone from a pressing concern, butt-of-a-rifle-type pressing, to a back-of-the-mind concern. Is it that the problems in my life have a habit of waxing and waning like a set dance in full swing, or is it that I can only pour focus on one at a time?

I opened one of the magazines that I bought for the trip, the only time I buy magazines really, pages of ráiméis that they are, telling me that buying this must-have or wearing that signature piece, holding your go-to handbag or wearing your statement skirt would make me stand out from the crowd – but if we all wore what they told us to wear, we'd all look the same; we can't all stand out from the crowd so we'd all be standing back into the crowd. Part of the signature look they encourage us to get is to wear one type of jewellery and be known for it. I'm more of a metal slut, wearing gold, silver or copper as the mood grabs me. Teaming, they go on about too, teaming different pieces of clothes with the right accessories. And teeming it is: teeming with nonsensical horseshit. I don't know where they get such words from, words you'd never use in the supermarket or the pub, words that don't mean what they really should mean. Teams should be about ball games or groups of people all wanting the same thing, not bits of a rig-out put together just so. And the tips on go-to handbags – surely all your handbags are go-to; there's no point having them if you don't go to them. And as for statement pieces, what if you don't want to state anything with your clothes, what if you just like them?

I flicked on through the magazine to the comparisons between expensive designer versions of clothes to cheaper versions for 'ordinary' women. Problem is, on my carer's wage, even the cheaper versions are out of my budget. Their skinted is my minted and I don't know where that leaves me. I once calculated the average cost of the nine skirts the style pages of a Saturday newspaper supplement showed: €327. That's what the style writers thought the average woman could spend on a skirt – and the galling thing was, this wasn't even one of the fancier magazines. And I was baffled by this use of the singular – *Team a red lip with a smoky eye, Pair a cigarette pant with a kitten heel.* If an alien were to read these magazines, he'd think human females were born with one lip and one eye and one leg. There is advice on how to *pull off* the latest trend, how to make something unwearably ugly wearably ugly. But why would you spend your time and money buying ugly out-fits that require such efforts to wear – why wouldn't you just wear what you want?

There was a round-up of the latest BB creams and CC creams – how long till the manufacturers make it to the ZZ creams, having got an entire alphabet out of our purses? When I got to a gardening feature that said dahlias were becoming cool again after having been 'dismissed in the past', I thought, *Ah, for the love of Christ.* Bad enough to be told that your clothes and shoes are gone out of fashion, but when the contents of your garden are outdated, that might be when we need to look at ourselves.

Roy

Der Kleiderschrank = clothes cupboard = wardrobe

He tidied away his bucket and cleaning accoutrements and left the Wunderland at lunchtime. He liked living in a North German city that was almost a foodstuff, and his workplace couldn't have been more suited to his tastes. He hadn't had much choice to begin with. Roy was moved to Hamburg for bad reasons, reasons he had to work to pitch out of his mind last thing at night when things unfinished descend relentless. Gert, the more tolerable of his sisters, had arranged a job through a friend in a city in a country that wasn't Ireland. He hadn't wanted to leave, but he couldn't be doing with hostile untruths on his hometown streets. The job hadn't appealed to him either but the location more than made up for that. Gert was coming to visit this evening. She would stay for six whole entire unbroken days. There would be questions – with his sisters there were always questions – and he would do his utmost to deflect them.

Roy's living quarters, in a converted warehouse in the City of Warehouses, were just behind the Miniatur Wunderland, so he went home for lunch rather than have circuitous conversations on the cusp of two languages with near strangers. Loading canals ran between the buildings, water-gardens dividing the blocks of old warehouses. From his apartment, he could hear the *thuh-dunk* and *kuk-klunk* of containers being moved from ships in the port. He had seen carpets and tea and coffee and cocoa and spices; if he ignored the electronic goods, he could imagine he was living centuries ago.

His was the shabby, as-yet ungentrified block of apartments. It came with the job, a shared apartment with Stefan, the security guard from the Wunderland. They had separate bedrooms and shared a bathroom, small kitchen, and living room. Stefan spoke little English; Roy spoke little German. They communicated in a series of nods and grunts. Neither's food took up much room in the fridge; neither's food took up much space in the cupboards. Neither's things took up much space on the bathroom shelf; neither's things took up much space on the living room bookshelves. They mostly worked different shifts and passed each other like, well, like the trains on the tracks in the Wunderland.

The sofa in the living room was so comfortable it was uncomfortable; the cushions sucked in your whole body until you felt as if you'd been filleted. Roy preferred to sit at the small wooden table under the window. There were two chairs at this table, but if Stefan were to sit on the second chair, life would seem too poky and not worth living. Roy took his book of European train timetables from the bookshelf, one of the few contributions to domesticity he'd made, along with *Bradshaw's April 1910 Railway Guide* to Britain and the German–English English–German dictionary. He settled himself at the table. He liked books that had more index than content – the index was surely the best part, the dark meat on a roast chicken.

The *European Rail Timetable* defied European boundaries and included some timetables for train rides in Asia, South America, and Africa. How did these journeys make it into the book, he wondered, and how did Australia and Israel and Azerbaijan make it into the Eurovision – who decided these illogical inclusions and what was their reasoning?

There were always so many questions, there weren't enough question marks for them. He didn't know who to ask, or even if answers existed.

Roy closed his eyes and opened the book. He had landed on France.

The Bordeaux–Toulouse train would be leaving at 10:47/14:45/17:30, stopping at Marmande, Agen, and Montauben along the way. It would take two hours and fourteen minutes. The precision appealed to him, the joy of knowing when you put foot on the step of the train carriage that, barring engine failure and livestock invasions and track suicides, the train would pull in to your required destination to the minute of the expected time.

His phone fizzed and beeped, a sound so seldom it jumped him. He looked at the screen. An unknown number appeared and he clicked on the message: *Leaving now, Roy, need anything from the airport shops? I'll text you when I'm near!*

From the context he knew it must be Gert: she was a blatant misuser of exclamation marks, a sender of superfluous messages that imparted nothing. He also didn't like the assumption in the lack of signature. Roy hadn't saved any of his family's numbers; it seemed too permanent somehow, or presumptuous maybe. He replied with a terse *Who is this?* and set his phone to Do Not Disturb. Then he got up, went into his bedroom, and opened the wardrobe door. He knelt down and gently took the three smashed scuba divers out of his pocket and placed them on the bottom of the wardrobe, with all of the other figurines (collective noun: a liberation of figurines). He pushed one of the more recent additions towards the others, saying, 'Gunther, meet Anna, Lucas and co.'

He pushed another figurine forward and said, 'Julia, meet the gang.'

Then he pushed the third figurine forward and said, 'Jonas, meet everyone.'

He left them to acquaint their miniature selves and opened his homemade filing cabinet. He took out three matchbox-sized pieces of paper and began to draw up miniature birth certs for his new recruits. This was the hardest part of making his Wardrobe Wunderland: he had to scrutinise their faces and come up with a suitable birth date, then he had to imagine from their clothes what their parents' occupations were. He left the lines for Jonas's parents' names blank; Jonas had the bang of an orphan about him, and he hoped Julia and Gunther would be kind to him. Roy called a cheery 'Have fun!', closed the wardrobe door, and went into the kitchen.

He made and ate a ham sandwich, same as every day, and when he had finished eating, he dabbed his mouth, picked up his keys, and left the apartment. As he was locking it, the couple from the apartment next door climbed the stairs towards him. They held hands and bags of groceries. The girl smiled at Roy.

'Allo,' the girl said.

'Allo,' Roy said, averting his glance.

They seemed so happy it felt rude to look. He let himself out the front door. If there was a back door, it would lead straight to the canal and a gush of water would be the ground-floor apartments. An airbed could float nicely, inflatable pool toys could serve as furniture, and a whole fleet of goldfish could roam freely through the apartment. He realised a fleet of goldfish was probably not the correct collective noun and pulled out his phone to google it. (This was what phones were useful for, not for exchanges of needlessness with your sister.) The collective term was a *glint* or a *troubling* of goldfish. Glint made sense, conveying the flash of metallic bright, but a troubling didn't seem right. As pets went, surely goldfish were the least nuisance, needing only the odd pinch of food and change of water. They only troubled humans when they kamikazed out of the bowl, and even then, they could be binned and replaced without veterinary cost or children noticing.

After lunch, he returned to miniature Switzerland. The background chatter of the visitors in the Miniatur Wunderland was soothing: it was like listening to a piece of wordless music, or the low throb of a fridge. He swiped a duster over the music festival exhibit, where DJ Bobo had sent the miniature crowd wild. Roy struggled to understand the patience required to paint the tens of thousands of figurines attending this festival, but he liked the detail of the large traffic jam going into the festival, and the queues for the portable toilets, and the first aid tent, and the orange-uniformed binmen emptying bins. Away from the crowd, a miniature woman was giving a miniature man a miniature blow-job. The man, like all the other figurines in Wunderland, was two centimetres high, but even on a face no larger than a Legoman's, his pleasure was evident. Roy stared at them from different angles. Some men plant their country's flags on the summit of Everest; others plant their semen in the orifices of other humans; Roy had no interest in either.

He had slept with a woman once, many years ago, an episode that he had not sought out but accepted when it was suggested to him. When they had reached the bedroom, the woman had undressed clumsily, taking off her tights and throwing them on the floor in such a way that Roy's mind was on the mess to be tidied up and the laundry to be done rather than the act that was about to take place. He had undressed then, feeling that there should be a less awkward start to the act, a button you could press, maybe, that would shimmy your clothes to the ground. What happened next was simply a continuation of awkwardness. Parting the woman's legs was like unfurling an artificial Christmas tree, pulling apart reluctant stalks that seemed to fit better together. The rest of the act was little more than a basic repetitive procedure, like sweeping a floor or stripping wallpaper. He hadn't felt any more pride or sense of accomplishment than he had when he'd landed his first newspaper round aged eleven, beating off several keen fifth-class contenders. All the while, the woman had kept up a sex prattle that distracted him. She seemed to be saying the same thing over and over with slightly different words; by the time she had come up with the fourth synonym for his genitals, he wondered if she'd been studying a thesaurus. Her verbs were imaginative but she was limited by a fixed number of body parts, and such underuse of nouns took the horn right off of him. He felt compelled to respond, but it was like a game of chicken; she kept asking for *more more more harder faster,* but bodies age and lung-power is finite, he wanted to say, he had only so much puff in him. He kept promising more, but within the bounds of keeping it physically possible, and by the end he felt he'd run a thankless marathon and failed to deliver all he'd promised. He had only one set of genitals and one pair of hands and one heart that felt as if it might give way under the strain of all she seemed to want, and so he drew to an underwhelming close with a face the colour of an aneurysm.

When they had finished, he had stroked her arms perfunctorily. They were bony with a soft hairy layer, but she wasn't very pleased when he said it was like stroking the furry stalks of tomato plants. Afterwards he'd lain on the bed while she put her clothes back on. It seemed indecent to watch her dress, even though he had seen as much of her as she could show. He had wondered if this was why doctors asked patients to undress behind a screen before conducting examinations that were much more revealing than the discarding of underwear. When she had left, Roy had felt relieved and a small part glad. He could say he had done it; he had tried sex and found it to be as unsatisfactory as making bread in a bread maker or eating a boiled egg without salt.

He looked at the miniature couple again. The man's face was infuriatingly smug. When the lights began to dim, Roy picked up his cloth and looked over his shoulder: nobody was watching. He pretended to spray some cleaning fluid on the cloth, leaned forward, and picked up the girl figure. He put her back down on her knees between some trees, looking as if she was about to suck a branch, and left the man to his smug devices alone, looking incredibly happy with his sunbathing. Then he gave each of them a brief swipe with his cloth.

He moved on to a village fête taking place at the foot of a medieval castle. He pushed the button nearest his hip, and a trumpeter began to play. A father showed his very small daughter how to push another button, but she hadn't enough force to push it all the way. The father put his finger over the child's finger and pushed. She squealed and he wondered if there was a specific word for index-fingernail pain in German. A miniature puppet show began. Roy pushed a button to set off a fireworks display. The father pushed another button to set in motion a ghost train in a cave under the castle. It seemed like a jolly fair day, some place between a medieval English Hear Ye affair with knights on horseback jousting, and an American fall show with pumpkins on display. Roy felt over-stimulated; if there were suggestions of England and America in a scene that was meant to be Switzerland, the rest of the exhibition seemed to hold all kinds of sensory overload and twisted promise. Under cover of the feathers of his

duster he bashed some of the figurines off their feet and scudded them towards himself. This will thin it out, he thought,
there's no need for so many people having unearned fun. He
scrunched the figurines into his fist and pushed them into his
pocket; he'd see to them later.

The small girl near him had begun to whine again so he
moved on, just as the light was starting to dim. He could see
the boy from the chocolate factory crouched down peering at
something – this child seemed to exist on his hunkers. Roy
bent down to look at what the boy was looking at. Miniature
robbers were tunnelling through a wall, just about to reach
the vault of a Swiss bank where miniature armed police were
waiting. Gold ingots were piled high in the background. The
boy turned his head to look up at Roy.

'Heist,' Roy said, pointing at the bank. This surely was a
German word: the vowels were in all the right places. The boy
continued to stare. Roy couldn't decide if he was just being
belligerent or didn't understand.

'Heist,' he said again, before he caught sound of himself.
He had become one of those people who repeats something
in a louder voice to a non-native English speaker in the hope
this will make them understand. At what age do we become
the thing we've always despised? The boy was staring at him
as if he knew more than there was to know about him. Roy
could feel his own cheeks blushing and was glad of the dark.
He smoothed his hair, straightened up, and moved on. He
passed a miniature wedding on the steps of a town hall – he
could see nothing out of the ordinary there – and stopped at
a miniature man mowing the miniature lawn on a miniature
roof garden. This was something he could look at forever:
someone doing a usual thing in an unusual place. Next he
stopped at a construction site. The boy now passed him by,

barely glancing at the binmen or the building work. His lack of appreciation for manual workers annoyed Roy.

'Allo,' he called to the boy. The father of the small girl looked at him, but the boy didn't turn back. Roy sighed. The lights came back up. He walked on. In the Alps, a group of miniature people sat on the back of a flying dragon, casually, as if they were sunning themselves on a beach or sitting in a park. They seemed a little callous, indifferent to the tasks of the binmen and the construction workers. Roy liked the incongruous characters or acts that seemed to fit right in – maybe a practical model-maker had created the ordinary people in a park and a whimsical one had come along and put them on a dragon.

He rounded a corner and walked up some steps. On his left, behind glass, was a miniature train station. Handprints smudged the glass along with small nose-tip prints. Roy leaned closer to stare in. The glass smelt of chemical cleaner and old breath. He took a blue spray from his bucket and sprayed some onto the glass. Then he wiped, slowly, methodically, with a melon-yellow dust-cloth. A mixture of miniature travellers in modern clothes and traditional Swiss dress waited for their train, staring at him. Did they think a large yellow cyclone was coming their way? A rector, or a vicar, was mid-march, in an obvious hurry, clutching his doctor's bag. His hurry was so great, Roy wondered what sort of ecumenical problem could be so pressing. Maybe he was going to alert the authorities about a yellow cyclone coming from a giant cleaner. Who would be the relevant authorities in that case? Some emergencies are more difficult to define than others.

A double-decker train passed through the station, and Roy was almost surprised to see the miniature passengers still waiting after the train had passed. A woman wearing a pink

dress had been knocked flat on her back, her head danger-
ously close to the edge of the track. She looked too cheery to
be suicidal – surely nobody killed themselves in a pink dress –
and anyway, she should be lying directly on the track if that
was her plan. A clock was also lying on the floor of the train
station, flat on a pole like a compass. It reminded Roy of the
millennium clock in the River Liffey that had been installed
some years before the century changed hands, its 120-mil-
lion-second millennium countdown thwarted by river murk.
He had paid 20p for a postcard of the exact countdown to the
millennium. This clock was different though: it was round
and wasn't digital or neon or covered in river scum. Looking
at it lying flat on its back like that made him feel the wrong
way around, like a vertical letterbox or a backwards swim in
a cruise-ship pool.

He picked up his bucket and walked a bit further up
the steps. Dragons were breathing fire under a train and on
a platform, watched by baby dragon chicks in a nest. Here
was the real life-size boy, standing very still in front of the
dragons, watching them closely as if they were liable to take
off at any moment. He looked younger than his face-age,
more vulnerable than he had done at the chocolate factory
or the bank heist. Was he too young to be a latchkey kid,
or was that term even used any more? Roy moved quietly
wide of the boy and walked up the rest of the steps. A train
ran under the transparent step underfoot. He stopped by a
miniature monk abseiling down a mountainside to church.
Superman flew overhead. He could make out Heidi and
Grandpa and Peter and Clara in her miniature wheelchair
outside a mountain hut with goats; they even had Heidi's
loft. There were figurines of women in short dresses – the
creator had lashed fake tan onto the legs, a tan so brown it

looked green, but their arms and faces were pale. Then he saw the same rector or vicar with the same pointy hat carrying the same doctor's bag in a hurry down a street. 'Oh!' he said, more to himself than anyone else.

'Es ist der gleiche Mann.'

The voice was at his shoulder. Roy spun around. The boy was pointing to the figurine of the rector. Roy shook his head. He felt sheepish and muttered that he didn't understand.

'It is the same man,' the boy said, in English accented with American.

'You speak English,' Roy said, unsure whether this was a statement or a question.

The boy shrugged. 'I watch a lot of American TV,' he said. 'Anyway, it is the same man – this priest.'

'Yes, I noticed,' Roy said, 'and he's still in a hurry.'

The boy nodded. He moved closer to Roy to point something out, but Roy jumped backwards, attempting to put an Alp between him and the child.

'I must go,' Roy said. 'I'm on duty.'

He had found himself using stronger verbs with duty inherent in them since he'd come to Germany.

'OK,' the boy said, 'see ya.'

The way he said *see ya* could have been truly American. Roy nodded and walked on.

The day passed like any other. Surfaces that had been dirty were washed and became clean. Surfaces that were clean became dirty and were washed. Muddy shoes came and went, sticky hands grabbed metal bars, noses and mouths and hands rubbed the glass, and lungful after lungful of fetid air – a turmoil of impure air – was breathed into the low-ceilinged room. Roy dusted, he wiped, he polished, he swept, he mopped, he dried. He performed lots of verbs that required no object and plenty that required objects as well. When the silver handrails gleamed and the floors shone, he checked his watch. It was ten minutes until his break, so he picked up his cloth and ambled to a miniature building that looked like a gym. There was a high climbing wall and several climbers in harnesses halfway up. Roy stared at them. He wondered how climbers ever got to see the view when they were staring at brute concrete walls or rock-faces. He'd rather be at the top looking down or the bottom looking up, not in the middle looking at solid grey. The climbers looked so cocksure that a surge of rage rose in his gullet. He pretended to dust the exhibit and waited for the lights to dim again before wrapping his cloth around the climber figurines, plucking them from their harnesses and emptying his cloth into his pocket. They rattled with the figurines already occupying it; Roy had committed his own personal heist. On a corridor on top of the building were two cleaners, a man and a woman, washing and sweeping the floor. He felt as if he had been immortalised on canvas, grateful that someone thinks of the cleaners. He gave the miniature window pane a half-hearted flick of his cloth – the miniature cleaners would clean it better from the inside than he could from the outside. Then he pulled off a scrap of yellow from his duster and left it near the miniature cleaners. This felt like an exchange from another universe, like world leaders swapping relevant gifts from their countries.

He hurried through Bavaria and Knuffingen, and passed through Austria, Middle Germany, and Hamburg. Then he went back down to the cubby. On the gridded sheet of paper on the inside of the cubby door, he signed his name and ticked the areas he had cleaned.

Gert

Das Kopfkino = head cinema = playing scenarios in your mind

We finally took off from Dublin. The woman across the aisle from me took a lipstick from a small tubular mirrored case that looked specifically designed to hold a lipstick. How are other women so sorted that they remember to bring not just the item itself but the box designed to hold it? There surely must be a magazine that can tell you how to live.

I needed to find my phone so I yanked up my bag from under the seat in front. It was bulging lumps like a snake just ate a horror of rats, but I was never one for efficient packing, leave that to the Tetris-players. There were more things rammed into a couple of tote bags in the overhead drawer that would doubtless spill out with any movement. How do those people do it, the ones who lay out their outfits to be packed, packing the right things in just the right order, to wear to just the right place? Christ, who actually accessorises on holiday? Who the fuck has the inclination to bring additional fiddly crap when it's hard enough to dress yourself?

Time was, when I packed a suitcase I experienced a foolish kind of optimism. I imagined everything would be different and I misjudged, miscalculated, ignored all previous experience and packed moisturisers, serums, face masks, exfoliators. I used to bring cosmetic stuff I never use at home on holidays, thinking I'd have the time or the will to use them, but they travelled back with me unopened.

I checked my phone. There was a message from Allen: *Everything OK here, will pick up the kids soon. Safe flight x*

I read the text again and again until it wavered and I knew I was wet-eyed. Might not seem much to most couples but this was hard-got, this level of bland certainty and assumed affection. It felt safe to go, safe to let go, and I stuffed my magazines into my bag and settled back into the seat to nap.

No sooner had the eyes shut than images and memories started banging in, however. It's why I try to stay moving and busy, a small-town shark that will die if I stop. I tried my *one potato, two potato, three potato, four*, but that only got me a few seconds before my mind spun back into its loop, replaying a scenario that was burnt into my eyeballs, that no amount of therapy can delete.

The scene: it's an ordinary enough day, a Saturday. I'm bringing the kids home from a football match. Allen said he'd stay behind and get started on the dinner. After a rough few days, he seemed in better form; there was a serenity about him that I didn't know then to fret about. The kids and I get out of the car in the driveway and I notice some takeaway menus in the letterbox, half-in, half-out, and my stomach plunges. I know something is up: Allen has an obsessive streak – if he was home and in his right mind he'd have heard them come in the letterbox and yanked them out and into the recycling bin. I force a cheery tone into my voice and tell the kids to go back, wait in the car for a minute, that we need milk in the shops and we're going out again. There are grumbles and complaints and I up it to ice cream. 'We'll get ice cream too and crisps, just get back in the car. Now, see who can get their seat belt on the fastest – Mammy just needs to get money.'

I try to put the key in the door; my hands are shaking that much the keys are rattling on the keyring and I drop it, the keyring; finally I get the right key in the lock and my ears, eyes, and nose rev up a gear. From the sitting room comes a whimpering and in I run to find Allen sat on the ground bare-chested, surrounded by broken glass, his arms and chest slashed. I gulp in the scene: there's blood but not enough blood that he's hit an artery; the emphasis seems to have been more on the number of cuts than the depth of them. I bend down to him but he tells me to fuck off, that he's not worth it, to leave, that it would be better for everyone if I left and took the kids with me. I take the phone out of my pocket and call – who, who the fuck do you call in these circumstances? I try to think of an order of importance and I think of the kids, the kids are in the car expecting ice cream. I call Gráinne first, tell her Allen's sick, a kind of urgent sickness has come on him, would she bring the kids to her house. I call an ambulance then because in this sort of mind he won't get in the car with me to hospital and I need someone, just please *someone, anyone* to come and take over and tell me what to do, what to fucking *do* in these circumstances because I'm so far out of my depth I haven't seen bottom for months. I tell the 999 operator to please hurry but that there's no real rush, I don't know what I'm saying or what kind of sense I'm making, I can't be accountable for my words, and I say sorry, I'm sorry I say down the line to the very kind operator who tells me help is on the way, and I try not to cry because if I start crying stopping could be a problem. Once the phone calls are made, I crouch down to lay an arm across him, to comfort him, like, but he pushes me away and puts his hand over his face and begs me to just leave him the fuck alone. Gráinne pulls up then and I rush out and transfer the kids over to her car with a cheery, 'Change of plan, kids, Aunty Gráinne will take ye for ice cream and crisps!' They're confused. Benjy starts to ask where Daddy is and Hazel is looking closely at my face because children can see through false cheer, but I bundle them into the car and hand them cash, euro notes from my pocket, must be large notes judging from their excited faces. Gráinne starts to ask what's wrong. I hiss 'Hurry' to her, 'Hurry them out before the ambulance, I'll call you later.' I go back inside to pick up the glass, promising Allen I won't look at him, won't touch him, I'll just get rid of the glass so as the kids don't hurt themselves. There's a method there, mentioning the kids, hoping it'll bring him back to us, but he just sobs louder and I feel like a right bitch for throwing guilt onto the carpet to add to his distress. The paramedics come in on a woman ignoring the man bloodied and weeping in the middle of the room, sweeping shards of glass into a dustpan, saying 'Yes, yes, I'll follow in the car.' How fucking callous must they think me?

That was two years ago, the first of them, these episodes. It came unexpected – but wait, not really: there had been inklings. He had admitted to being low but denied it was a mental health issue – he had put that down to problems with the relationship, namely, problems with me and what, or who, I wasn't. How readily I accepted the blame: if he was unhappy, it must have been my fault. It deflected nicely from the real problem: let's focus on my inadequacies causing my husband to look outside the relationship, rather than a very real depression that had little to do with me.

No, this first attempt forced a decision, a realisation. Depression denied was finally admitted and medications were taken. Medications were also, subsequently, intermittently *not* taken of an unexpected sudden and moods plummeted and further suicide attempts were made, or maybe they weren't real attempts and who the fuck was I to know whether an attempt was genuine or a cry for help, whether an attempt was *credible* as an emergency services operator asked me on one occasion, and I said I didn't know but the slash-marks on his wrists were real and credible, never mind the purpose of them. That became our new whirligig life until a six-months-long stability that has me tentatively, cautiously optimistic. (If it wasn't for the *cautiously* I'd be horrifically depressed after so many *this time will be better*s and *this time is different*s). Six months seemed a decent amount of time to be not-suicidal, but who's to say that's the case? Last month, I conducted my usual mental triage and decided Allen and the kids were currently safe and Roy was in more need of a visit, long stretch that he's put in alone in Germany. I had managed to put Roy somewhere to the centre back of my mind after I'd got him fixed up in Hamburg, in order to focus on Allen. My brother was a dimly gnawing ache that I didn't let myself think about. But now was the time to move him full forward in this Subbuteo game of family issues. There are only so many problems you can keep concurrently boiling before they come at you in a torrent.

Roy

Der Staubsauger = dust sucker = vacuum cleaner

He went into the break room and Eric nodded to him. Eric had some English but he didn't like to use it when Stefan was around. Roy had six years of German but those years had been followed by many more years without; maybe years spent not learning a language after starting it were measured exponentially.

'Alles gut,' Roy said and sat down in the chair vacated by Stefan. He felt a perverse pleasure in speaking more German to those who had some English than to those who had none. Eric was watching soccer on the portable television. England were leading Italy 1–0.

'Harry Kane!' Stefan gave him a thumbs up.

'I'm Irish, not English,' Roy said.

Eric shrugged as if the Irish Sea was as insignificant as a miniature lake in the Wunderland. They watched the game in silence. Italy scored. There was a computer on the table, which Roy clicked on, set to the homepage of the Wunderland. He logged onto the visitor bar chart – the bars hadn't moved much. Then he opened a search box and keyed in *latchkey kid* to an English–German translator.

'Schlüsselkind,' he muttered.

Eric stared at him. 'Kane?'

'No, no, forget it.' Roy waved a hand in the air. The lack of language to say the things he wanted to say was like somebody putting a sponge to his brain, staunching the words trying to enter. Was it harder to learn a language afresh, with all the excitement of something new, or to dredge up old words for new things he wanted to say? Was the German he learned in school enough to convey his adult mind? He'd rather say nothing than say things that could point him out as all wrong. He checked his phone in a kind of dread-hope but there were no messages.

After break, his task was to clean the gift shop. This was harder work. Visitors who had been so careful not to drop things in the Wunderland were not so careful by the time they got to the gift shop. And the rooting in pockets and wallets and bags for money set free pieces of rogue paper and rubbish and lint and tissue shreds that stuck to the floor and weren't always fetched away with a lick of the brush. Roy hated squatting to pick up rubbish; it was hard on the knees and the dignity. The cleaning he didn't mind, the actual act of rubbing and erasing and wiping, but the tugging of things from surfaces they'd adhered to, surfaces they wanted to be part of, was like writing yourself into a memory you played no part in. Also, the gift shop was where arguments took place. Families that had been so peaceable, joyous even, in the Wunderland turned fractious during discussions about purchasing brightly coloured pieces of tin and plastic. In the Wunderland, Roy sometimes thought he would like a family of his own; in the gift shop, he knew he wouldn't. Watching children in the restaurant argue over their side of the seat reminded him of a suburban gatepost painted halfway vertically: one side fresh-white, one side old-yellowed, the petty boundaries of it; adults were no better.

The mop bucket was blue and made of sturdy plastic, presumably to withstand the heaving and wringing of the mop without toppling and spilling. Roy liked the mop bucket; he liked things that were purpose-built: the enchantment of specificity. One half of the bucket had a conical sieved funnel in which to wring the mop, the other had a slight jug-like spout from which to driplessly pour out dirty water. What was most appealing about the mop bucket was that whoever invented this knew what they were doing. It wasn't a bunch of wafflers in a well-lit conference room (a collective noun for the people who decide things they know nothing about could be a *bluster*: a bluster of suits) making decisions from words and figures on high-quality headed paper; this was somebody who had cleaned many floors.

He swept around the outskirts of the gift shop. Better to sweep than use the hoover; the hoover performed its mechanical duties well, but try any angle as he might, Roy could not get the blasted arm of it to stay upright. He leant it against the wall and it fell, he laid it flat and it tripped him, he flung it in a temper and it goaded him. The hoover was called Henry (why not Heinrich in this country?) with a face painted on the metal body, and there were days when Roy could have kicked Henry's nose in. He had taken to fantasising about a hoover that would stand upright unaided – why couldn't the mop-bucket inventors have set their minds to this?

As he dragged his rubbish bag around the gift shop to do one final pick-up, he passed the shelf of little model trains, so many of them, so uniform, so waiting for someone to take them. And why not – didn't he deserve one as much as any stupid child who didn't even earn their own money? He took out his cloth, let on to dust the shelf, and swooshed one into his rubbish bag, where he gripped it close to the bag's neck;

he'd retrieve it later. He looked around as casually as he could, but nobody was paying any heed to him; they never did. Roy felt a blast of exhilaration – this was new, this was thievery on a larger scale. His confidence had grown when he realised that nobody was watching, that nobody seemed to notice the figurine removals. He patted the figurines in his pocket, half-expecting them to have made a leap for it and legged it, but they were still there. He couldn't wait to introduce them to their former miniature colleagues in their new home.

Roy clutched the model train he'd stolen inside the bin-bag and left the gift shop. He liked trains, he loved trains, he obsessed over trains with a zeal that bordered on mania, but he had no desire to ride in them. How could you see the beauty of the train if you were actually *in* the thing? An old steam train gave rides near his homeplace in Ireland and he couldn't understand why anyone would pay to ride in it – the joy was in looking at it from the outside. Also, trains in real life were imperfect. They rusted, they stank, the seats held leftover coffee cups and spills, chocolate wrappers and stains, detritus thoughtlessly discarded. To Roy's mind, these left-behind things retained something of their owners, some-thing impure, something tainted, something that was not the essence of the train itself.

Visitors were still trickling into the Wunderland when he left. He had given Gert directions to the station nearest the Wunderland. He walked along the cobbles and crossed the water. He still hadn't figured out if this was the main river or one of the canals and it mattered to him, it mattered greatly, whether he was walking over something natural or manmade. Whichever it was, it was the colour of the river at home, bruise-brown tinged with green. He went into the station and looked around, but there was no sign of his sister so he walked slowly up and down the platform. At times like this, he thought he would like to smoke, but perhaps it was too late to start. If your middle years are clattering down around your ears, is it too late to take up a bad habit that should be started in your teens? He studied the street index and map on the platform. It was an A–Z of streets and he was gratified that it began with Abbestraße and ended with Zypreßenweg: it wouldn't feel like a definitive A–Z if either A or Z was missing. He wondered if there was a street for every letter but decided against checking because it would ruin his day if there wasn't. A train, a real non-miniature one, slowed in a diminishing rattle. Roy peered at the carriages. Passengers moved in and out of the train doors crisscrossing each other so naturally it made him wonder how life worked so smoothly for most people. There was no sign of his sister. He felt a flutter of relief that she hadn't made it, he wouldn't have to contend with any invasive questioning. He said 'Oh well' under his breath and turned quickly to climb back down the steps when he heard a shout.

'Roy!'

He turned around. Despite his misgivings about his sister's arrival, it was nice to have someone speak his name in the right intonation. She came bumbling towards him, laden with one medium-sized bag and several small bags where one larger one would have worked better. She moved ungainly, lumpenly towards him; Gert never walked, she hurtled.

'Hey,' he said.

They knew each other too well to hug – he could never understand how family members progressed from sharing baths and seeing one another's nose-pickings to a polite kiss on the cheek or a hug. He looked at her. She was smiling, but despite the cheery expression, it was clear that life had beaten her hard about the face. Her clothes were baggy and shapeless and she was wearing shoes to convalesce in rather than travel in; he couldn't help but think of a scarecrow in the wrong field. She looked creased and unpacked, like she'd just taken her winter clothes from a storage bag under the bed. She was more cream cleaner than miracle spray foam. Roy felt it reflected badly on him to have such an awkward person for a close relation, but she looked at him like he was the person she liked best in the world and that felt nice.

'It's good to see you,' he said.

'Great to see you too, Roy,' she said. 'Are you going to show me your place?'

'My place,' he said, 'let's go to my place.'

Gert

*Trümmerfrauen = rubble women = the women who cleared
and helped to rebuild cities after the war*

He looked tired when I saw him, tired as a wrung cloth, but
he smiled when he saw me so that was a fine start. He looked
familiar and unfamiliar at the same time, as if a man I knew
had walked into the ladies' toilets. I'd hoped he'd give me a
hug or some kind of a fond gesture after the hours I'd spent
on the train and bus to the airport back home and the plane
and the train here. Trains, planes, and automobiles, I almost
said, but he doesn't like it when Gráinne and I talk in clichés
or state the obvious, and he would have pointed out there
were no automobiles in my trip seeing as I got the train two
hundred yards from my house.

'These bags are fierce heavy,' I'd said, and only then he'd
shaken himself a bit, like a dog just out of water, and offered
to take them. Fair amount of time lost between me landing
and him offering but I came here to see him and not to have
my bags taken from me like a duchess. When he leaned over
to take them, I caught the bang of him, like an old car-seat on
a summer day. His voice sounded scratchy, like it hadn't been
used in a while, like he needed to pick the scabs from his throat.

'Christ, my head is melted travelling across time zones,' I
said, more to say something than anything else.

'You only travelled across one time zone, Gert, it's an hour's difference.'

'Well, when a trip into Dublin counts as a major outing, this feels like a trek halfway across the world; let me have it.'

I'd left some of my magazines on the train so a German girl could practise her English and learn all about what to team with what, and by the time I'd sorted out my bags and got off the train, I noticed Roy had turned to leave. You'd never think we were related at times like that, you'd never think he was related to anything human. I'd texted him earlier to say I was on my way and got a 'Who is this' response. Between the last time I'd texted him and today, he'd erased me. I felt culled like a superfluous deer in a city park.

We walked from the station to his lodgings. The cold was the kind of cold that hits you in the nostrils and travels to your bones. The damp at home I can handle – the damp and I are old friends; but this was a dry old cold that made me wish I was twenty years younger. We crossed a river that he said was a canal, but it's hard to tell these things, especially in the dark. Then we crossed another canal and he let us into a building right on the water, as if somebody had dumped a bag of cement in there and it had sprouted into a building. Up the stairs we went and into his lodgings. A man was sitting on the sofa, good-looking in the way of the beast, with a lump of a beard and a pair of downcast eyes. He looked past Roy to myself and paid almost the same heed to me. There are times when you wish yourself a beauty, even an ageing beauty, rather than to be looked on like the worn sole of a comfortable shoe. Hell, I'd settle for *Looks well for her age* or *Well-preserved*, even if it does have a whiff of formaldehyde about it.

Roy had told me his flatmate had very little English so I gave him a wave, a small wave, because anything with large amounts of arms would have taken up the whole room, it was that small. Roy gestured in my direction and said 'Gert' and gestured in the flatmate's direction and said 'Stefan', and that's about the height of the introductions that were made. He got up then, Stefan did, and shook my hand, then he said something in German and went off to his bedroom.

'Are you sure he doesn't mind me staying?' I asked Roy. 'He doesn't seem all that happy.'

Roy swatted his hand backwards as if he was performing some kind of half-arsed aerobics. 'He never seems all that happy, it's fine.'

Now the word *fine* is a curse of a word, it's a scourge of a nothing kind of word, it doesn't tell you anything about what you wanted to know.

'That's grand then,' I said, because if a general word is given to me, I'll give an even more general word right back.

Roy put my bags on the sofa. 'Are you hungry?'

'I could eat a bite,' I said. 'I had nothing on the plane – eating up so high gives me awful wind.'

Roy looked as if his ears hurt him then; he's a terrible man for getting all het up about anything to do with bodies. He went to the fridge and opened it. The bare white of it was a bit of a shock. I closed my mouth before I could ask what he lived on because he goes into a huff if he thinks I'm trying to boss him.

'I'll take you out for dinner,' I said. 'My treat seeing as you're putting me up.'

His face relaxed a bit then. 'OK,' he said.

'What kind of food would you like? Chinese, Thai, Indian, German?'

The German was tagged on at the end, like a multiple-choice quiz on daytime TV for a large cash prize: *Which one of these is NOT in Asia?*

'Or Asian fusion?'

Roy looked mithered by choice. 'I don't know, let's just have normal food.'

'Grand,' I said, wondering what the fuck normal food consists of. 'Anyway,' I said, 'I don't really understand Asian fusion, do you? Local takeaways in small towns that span whole continents in their cooking, it can't be right. Or worse, take in added continents with no apparent link – there's one near us that serves Mexican and Italian food.'

Roy stared at the ground. I felt like I'd kept my umbrella up long after the rain had stopped.

'There's a bar near here that serves food,' he said.

'Right, I'll just get myself sorted and I'll be ready in a minute.'

Any other brother you could say you were going to the toilet, but it's joined-up bodies he thinks we have, myself and Gráinne and Mam, with no orifices or anything going into or coming out of them. If he could delegate his bodily functions, he would.

I took my wash-bag into the bathroom. With two people in such a small place (the size of it!) I thought it'd be fighting for space I'd be doing, but the sheerness of the emptiness hit me, like a hotel bathroom after the guests had gone home. You could tell it was used, but there was nothing except for a bar of soap and a jar with a shaving brush and an old-fashioned stick of shaving soap and a razor, which I presumed was Roy's seeing as his flatmate had the beard. There was a light-switch near the shelves, which I flicked: nothing happened. Must be a switch for a light long gone. I left my wash-bag on the shelf – fine deep shelves they had and no use made of them – and went to the toilet. The flusher needed twiddling – you had to tug it briefly upwards before pushing down. These are the things you remember from visiting a new place – not the landmark cathedral or the paintings in a gallery, but the knack required to flush the toilet and the bockety light-switch. I splashed my face with water. My eyes in the mirror were as red-rimmed as if I'd been sobbing since Dublin, but they'd look a bit better in the dark of the pub. I was glad Roy used soap. I use it at home because it comes in cakes and bars. When liquid soap comes in syrups and ganaches, I may switch. I came out of the bathroom and Roy jumped like he'd been scalded.

'Should I put my bags in the bedroom?'

'Oh.'

He stared at them as if they'd suddenly appeared in front of him and he'd had no hand in bringing them in. I took it as a yes and picked them up. I stood at the neck of the room and looked in. It was barer than the rest of the flat; a neat lonely bare that saddened me to my stomach. There wasn't a book or a picture or a bit of clothing anywhere; I've seen TV programmes about prisoners who had cells more homely looking than this. It wasn't the look of a room that had been cleared for a guest either: it was the look of a room that hadn't seen a living thing for an age. Roy stepped in after me and looked around as if this wasn't his room at all.

'You can put your things on the chair,' he said, 'there's no space in here.' He stood awkwardly in front of the wardrobe, his arms folded behind his back, pressed against it. I looked around. All the furniture was an orange-brown wood with a ghastly sheen: chair, wardrobe, single bed. The bed wasn't the kind of single that could just about squeeze in two people; it was the kind you'd feel a draught on your arse hanging over the edge if you turned too sharply sideways. I dropped the bags on the floor. It had the same dark-green carpet that was in the living room: thin, with a tight ropey texture, and lined with straight ridges. The kind of carpet you'd snag your toenail on and wonder if life was out to get you. Roy's flat had a temporary look about it, like he could run off at any moment. I dumped the bags and turned around to face him. 'Ready, Eddie?'

'Ready, Teddy.'

He smiled at me then, like I was an ad on TV that was funny the first time. He was Eddie and I was Teddy and Gráinne was Freddy when we were young because our parents always seemed to be asking if we were ready. It didn't bother myself or Gráinne that we got boys' names because girls' names didn't happen to rhyme with *ready*. Roy used to fret about what we'd do if we got landed with another brother or sister – we'd run out of names that rhymed with *ready*. He always put the worry before the thing to be worried about.

He was an unrelenting worrier. As kids, when we went to the playground, he worried the swings that weren't used would feel left out; when we had cousins over, he worried they would wear out the delph faster than usual. He worried not just about things you wouldn't think to worry about but about things that really shouldn't ever be worried about. And now, he worries about the wrong small things and disregards the large things, the herd of baying elephants in the room pawing at the ground.

We left the room, left the flat, he pulled the door behind us. When we'd left the building, he hunched over and seemed to close in on himself.

'Where do we go?' I asked because he seemed to be letting me lead the way and I didn't know which way I was headed.

'This way,' he said, pointing back the way we came from. We walked past the station and I got that feeling you get the first day or so in foreign countries when you recognise a building or a street, that buzz of old-newness. We walked across a main road and down a small street. He walked fast, my brother. Even though we've nearly the same-sized legs he seemed to make better use of them and I was near running out of puff when he gestured me in the door of a pub. The pub was small and dark with lots of empty tables. We waited a while for somebody to tell us where to sit, but when nobody came I said feck this for craic and sat down at a table near the window, Roy following me in unease. There was a menu on the table, all in German.

'Will you get some dinner for me, Roy? Anything will do.'

'All right.'

He picked up the menu and glanced over it. His face showed nothing so I don't know how much of it he could understand, but I felt like sitting back and letting him take over. All our lives I'd been setting him up, sorting him out: now he could get some kind of sustenance for me. Snatches of Leaving Cert German kept appearing in my head, but only the questions, which are useless without being able to understand the answers. *Wie komme ich am besten zum Bahnhof, bitte?* Which is the best way to the train station, please? It's not much use seeing as the station is the one place I know how to get to. That's about the height of my German. My default second language is Irish; when I try to remember German my brain comes up with the Irish instead. I find German sentences a right bitch to form – by the time I get to the end I've forgotten what verb I wanted to use. I was going to have to stick with shouting key words and miming on this trip; Roy was in for a treat.

I looked at the menu, trying to pick out words. Maybe I was better off not being able to understand it. I get annoyed reading menus full of pan-fried this (how the fuck else would it be fried?) and twice-fried that, sun-dried this and corn-fed that, hand-reared this and hand-cut that – you'd swear the industrial revolution had never happened the way foodies were ignoring machines and rushing back to manual labour. Their great-grandmothers would be somersaulting in their graves shouting, 'Use the machines, you shower of ingrates.'

A waiter came over with a notepad and pen. He looked aggrieved to find us sitting so comfortably in seats not of his choosing so I smiled at him, a great wide cheese wedge of a smile he'd have been a mean prick not to respond to. He loosened up a bit and Roy stated his order, looking embarrassed to be asking someone for something. I sat back and let the language mist over me; it's very relaxing hearing sounds that you know must mean something but you don't know what it is they mean, picking out the odd familiar-sounding portion of a word. The waiter took the menus and walked off. Roy sat back like a soldier who'd won a fierce battle.

'How's the job working out?'

'Fine.' He leaned forward and rubbed his face with both hands.

I gave him a bit of time but that was all that was coming. 'Are the people nice?'

'Yeah, they're fine.' He was looking around the pub now but there were few enough other customers to latch eyes on so he had to come back and meet mine.

'Is the flat OK?'

'The apartment's fine.'

The tone, the slight emphasis on the word *apartment*, not enough for full-blown italics, but enough to let me know I'd done wrong by calling it a flat. Roy answers questions as if he's interpreting his life for an interview, picking out the vaguest words that reveal the least.

'How are you getting on over here?'

'Jesus, Gert, you've done nothing but fling questions at me – ease off, would you?'

'All right, all right.' There was no glass to drink from, nothing to clutch onto. I stood up. 'What'll you have to drink?'

'I already ordered a bottle of wine with the dinner – sit down, will you.'

I sat back down. I took to staring around as well, and our heads swivelled this way and that way, any ways but not towards each other. We must have looked a right pair. I could think of nothing else to say that wasn't a question, and I don't like uttering a statement about myself, because if he was interested, he'd ask, so silence was the most suitable thing for now. I'd just started thinking about the fact that I'd four more nights of this and how much it'd cost to change my flights, but then the waiter came with the wine and two glasses – long stems holding up great big bowls you could keep small fish in. Red wine. I'd have ordered white if he'd asked; red gives me a sore head and an itchy nose. The waiter said something and Roy nodded and he poured a trickle into Roy's glass. Roy sipped and sniffed and nodded before holding out his glass for more. Who *was* this person, unabashedly judging the wine as if he knew what corkage or quality tasted like? Had this happened since he'd left home or was he just faking it? When I sneaked a peek at his face, though, I could see the bottom lip half-chewed in agitation: he was playing a part but couldn't fully maintain it and that gave me some ease. Nobody wants their younger sibling to hotfoot it into sophistication without them.

The waiter poured both glasses halfway – what good the size of the glass when they half-fill it so mean? I felt like part of a couple on an ad for fancy flats (sorry, *apartments*) or glamorous honeymoon destinations. I took my glass in hand and held it out to say cheers, but Roy's was already to his mouth. Small things that mean so much to the rest of us, he can't bring himself to partake in; basic rituals are like poison to him. When he was a teenager, he wanted us to move our family Christmas to New Year's Day because all the presents would be cheaper in the shops and we could buy discounted cards and decorations and Christmas food in the sales. There was such a decent, firm logic to it, it was hard to argue – but the sense of occasion had got mislaid somewhere along the way.

'Cheers,' I said, thrust my glass into the air in front of me, and took a great big gulp. The wine clawed at my throat like a hot wasp, but it felt good and warm on the way down my gullet. I could feel Roy looking at me sideways; but better to be looked at sideways than no ways at all.

'How's Allen and the kids?'

'Hazel has an eye infection,' I said. 'She's all pink and puffed up with it. She got tablets but I don't know if they're doing any good – the puff isn't going down any. I asked the doctor for an eye patch or something to stop her picking at it, but he said let the air at it to heal. Air, I ask you, what help air when you're red-eyed and blinded with the crud from the scratching? It'd be easier if she was a dog and you could put one of those plastic cones around her neck to stop her. And Benjy, he's got – Roy, hey, Roy, are you listening to me at all?'

He looked at me then, face on him like he'd sucked petrol fumes from an exhaust pipe. 'Yeah, I'm listening. And Benjy?'

'Well, Benjy's been in and out of the doctor's with a throat infection that won't lie down. They told me he'd get better as he grew up, but it's worse he's getting. I have him gargling salt water, aspirin in water, water hot as he can bear it – Christ, I'd try water with a dose of bleach in it if I thought he'd get better.'

Roy's lip curled then and I knew I had him. He can't bear the idea of pain to the kids; it's my way of seeing if he's listening.

'How's Allen?'

'Grand now, he hasn't been in at the doctor's in a good many months. I think they're all delighted by my absence these few days.'

Roy grinned, a kind of disloyal grin when I think of it; he's on the side of my husband and kids rather than his sister. 'What's he at these days?'

'He went back to the job in the county council – he had to. Pension, benefits, stability, you know yourself.'

Roy nodded.

Every time Allen recovered from his latest bout of depression, his mood would rise and he'd take a sabbatical from his county council job to *find yourself in meaningful work, follow your dreams*, as his counsellor suggested. The counsellor held no truck with money and seemed to think any financial worries put forward were projecting or transferring or distracting from the real problem. And maybe if I was a counsellor, I too would project away from money talk and onto deeper problems that would need many more eighty-euro-an-hour sessions to solve.

When he got to a certain mood high, Allen would come up with various career projects that seemed like wonderful ideas; he would spill over with enthusiasm and it would be up to me or the credit union to piss on his dreams with practicalities.

A couple of years ago, he wrote a business plan for a restaurant selling only Christmas dinners all year round, aimed at returning emigrants and soldiers who'd Christmassed in war zones, but our town doesn't produce enough of either. Then he wanted to open a warehouse way out rural in which the broken-hearted could come to smash cheap plates. He had visions of the righteously wronged hooking up after, riled into a frenzied froth from their flingings, but either the dumped weren't angry enough or the angry weren't dumped enough and the credit union decided against funding yet another of his schemes. He gets low when these ideas are quashed and is quick to lash blame in my direction, so I've learned to stay back and wait for the high to dissipate and the idea to naturally fall sideways, or for the credit union to play bad cop. I can't play mammy to everyone in my life; I have to sit tight and play savvy sometimes.

'So, tell me about the place you work.'

'There's not much to tell. I clean different parts of it every day, and I get two days off on a rota every week.'

'Are you off the next few days to show me round?'

'No.' He made a fist and ran it over his hair. I kept quiet, on the hope for more. 'I couldn't get the days off, they were short-staffed.'

'In February?'

'Yeah.' He stared at the table throughout, as if the words were printed on the varnish sheen. I didn't know what to say to that so I took another sup of my wine. 'I'm working split shifts from tomorrow so I can see you between them.'

'All right.' I don't know what I'm feeling sore about. I came over to check he was settling in well and what better way to check than to see him at work. 'Will you be able to show me around the Miniatur Wunderland one of the days?'

'I don't know, they're pretty strict about work. And I don't know about getting you in for free.'

I turned to look at him. Mostly I don't look because he's shyer about speaking when I look. I treat him some ways between a feral animal, *softly softly*, no sudden words, and a teenage boy, no eye contact, feign disinterest or casual interest at most. Sometimes it's like he came from a different set of parents, from a different species entirely, from parents with metal for organs and wood for bones and set concrete for blood.

'I might drop by tomorrow or the next day, see these trains.'

Now he brightened, now he sat up, now he looked as close to comfortable as I'd seen him yet. 'There are more than a thousand trains running over fifteen kilometres of track. And the lights go down every quarter of an hour so you can see them lit up inside.' He smiled at me, a genuine smile with the bang of actual happiness in it. How rare, how lovely. 'I like the trains best of all. You might like the figurines best, Gert – there are 260,000 of them, give or take a few.' His grin turned mischievous, a kind of energy I hadn't seen in him in years.

'I look forward to seeing it,' I said, trying to put in as much enthusiasm as seemed warranted.

He probably could have gone on for hours about trains and tracks and miniature figurines, but the waiter arrived and set a plate in front of each of us. A large white plate with a slab of breaded meat and three small, yellow boiled potatoes dotted sparse with herbs. Something about a peeled potato makes it look powerless and undignified, like it's been stripped before changing into a prison uniform. Roy's plate was the same. He took up his cutlery and got going on the food immediately. I ate more slowly. The food was fine but the taste was bland.

'You'd get better food in hospital,' I said, giving him a small nudge with my elbow. His knife clattered onto the table and he looked irritated. I didn't know how to go about reminding him this was the way we went on when we were kids. This was the way we skitted and sneered at any kind of new food that was put in front of us, any holiday that saw us in a restaurant, especially a foreign restaurant, making faces and making mock of the cuisine. It felt like he had chosen a foreign city over our childhood.

'Grow up, Gert, just eat it.'

Being told to grow up by my younger brother was disheartening, like I'd missed a stage of development somewhere along the way. It felt like Roy was more part of Hamburg than of our family; maybe I shouldn't have acted so hastily to send him away. As a child, he'd wanted out of our tribe. He always looked to other families: their food was better, their cars were newer, their birthday cakes shop-bought.

I gave up on my plate; Roy had stolen the appetite from me and I had mind only to drink now, to hell with the itchy nose or sore head. He ate the rest of his meal in silence too. Silence between siblings is generally comfortable – everything has been said at least once one way or another – but this one stung. His life had become something that mine had no part in and he resisted every effort I made to participate in it. I supped my wine, half my face enclosed in the wine glass.

'This would be great for steaming Benjy's face in – you know, when his sinuses are at him. You could put hot water with a drop of brandy in, his face would be totally covered, then when he was finished I could drink it back.'

Roy looked at me, not sure whether I was joking or not. I wasn't sure whether I was joking or not. His posture unknotted a bit. 'There's a crossroads nearby with a Hamburger Street and a McDonald's on the corner,' he said, and looked at me expectant.

It took a few seconds for me to realise he'd made a joke; this was his version of a food-related joke. I guffawed, too shrill and obviously insincere but he didn't seem to notice. We finished our wine, I asked for the bill, and the waiter asked if we wanted two bills. What a country, the details they think of! Roy looked a bit angsty and I said, 'No thanks, one bill,' and paid. Thank Christ for euros – it's hard enough foostering with the bill at the end of a dinner without trying to translate back to your home currency in your head. Roy looked horrified by the way I stuffed the pristine five-euro note I got back in change into my wallet any old how – to join the fivers already there ragged to ripping point – but I horsed into a conversation about the weather so I didn't have to listen to a lecture on how to handle currency. We walked back to his apartment. Stefan was in his bedroom, but a slip of light came from under his door.

'I'll just get my things from the room,' Roy said.

'Are you sure you'll be all right on the sofa?'

'I'll be fine.'

He moved ahead of me into the bedroom and took an uncovered duvet and a pair of flannel pyjamas from the chair, a neat pile that had been made with care. The uncovered duvet bothered me a little, all I could think of was sweat and old skin and pubes, but there was more I could be worrying about than new stains on old things.

'You go on and use the bathroom,' I told him, 'while I get sorted here.'

'OK, goodnight, Gert.'

'Night, Roy.'

He stood by the door for half a breath longer than necessary, but no move was made on either side to say more than that or make gestures that might not be reciprocated. When I heard the toilet flush and the bathroom door opening, I went into the bathroom to brush my teeth. I tiptoed back through the living room to get to the bedroom and Roy pretended to be asleep and I pretended to think he was. I ignored the contents of my suitcase, pulled off my clothes, and got into bed in the nuddy. It gave me a snigger to think how disgusted Roy would be if he knew.

I turned out the bedside lamp as soon as I'd gotten into bed. I had a book with me, but it felt wrong to be reading a book in English about Ireland when I was in Germany surrounded by German speakers. Sometimes it feels like travelling is just bringing your book to read in a different country: same words in the wrong language.

As I lay in the dark, my eyes getting used to the blackness, I heard noises from the flatmate's bedroom. The bed creaked rhythmically, there was panting building up to a stifled crescendo; Stefan must be giving himself a treat. I often think that if it weren't for the persistence of women, mankind would eventually give up on womankind and wank itself into extinction. I don't like bearing witness to something I shouldn't, like seeing the joke-shop-funny magnified teeth of a friend through the bottom of a glass of water as they drink. I thumped a cheek-hole into the pillow and tucked my shoulders under it as if I was hoisting its featherweight on my shoulder in a parallel vertical world, stuck my finger in my up-facing ear, and closed my eyes.

Try as I might, however, no matter how hard I scrunched them shut, the same bleak reel played on the inside of my eyelids. Even in a different country there was no escaping the grims and my mind took me back home.

One day years ago, prior to any kind of self-harming incident, before I realised something more serious was afoot, I asked Allen why he recoiled when I touched him and why he slept as far as possible from me in the bed, and while we're at it, why he was so down in himself. After a lot of pretence of tiredness and work stress, he said: 'There's something missing.' I instantly thought of missing laundry and had to drag my mind from the sock-swallowing Bermuda Triangle in the washing machine.

'Missing, how?' I asked, buying time.

He said, or maybe he didn't say, maybe I goaded it out of him in different sets of words, maybe there was no defining sentence but the meaning of it, the ultimate gist was: there's something missing in our relationship. He told me he'd *fallen out of love* with me, to use his words. I felt sheer disbelief. The whack to your ego that does is like a slap in the cunt. How do you just stop being in love? When exactly do you stop? Is there a single point, a final farting, belching, slurping, tooth-picking, sex-refusing, snoring nail in the coffin? *Falling out of love* sounds so active, but surely it was more passive than that. If I was honest then, I'd have retaliated with, *I'm not sure I'm all that in love with you either but we're in this fucking thing together, mate, suck it up*. The more I thought about it, the more it seemed downright foolhardy, reckless even, to base the stability of a family on continuing sexual attraction. What fucking *idiots* were we?

He'd started looking elsewhere, he'd said. I asked him why. 'I feel like I'm missing out,' he'd said. 'Fuck's sake, we're all missing out,' I said. 'You don't see me getting the ride off Matt Damon, do you?' He'd looked surprised then, surprised that it was possible I had urges beyond him.

I didn't want to ask how far the concept of *looking* stretched for fear of the answer, but I knew the woman in question. Over the years I've learned Allen's shorthand for when he fancies someone: *she's sound* means a good-looking young woman who listens carefully to him and laughs at his jokes. Sound, is it. Women his own age who look bored at the same jokes aren't quite so sound. So this woman, the sound woman, was someone Allen worked with. I'd met her previous at a work do. She was someone you'd take to dinner; I'm someone you'd eat crisps over a pint with. She wore an event of an outfit, all structure and poise and dry-clean only. A lot of brush-strokes had gone into giving off her natural look. She giggled at his jokes, a well-placed hand on his arm, tilting her head at his sage pronouncements on life. It was such a cliché I couldn't even be jealous, but I was annoyed at him for believing the final package. He gets irate at me for running a brush through my hair before we leave the house; if he only knew the time and effort that went into her *natural* look.

I was off kilter for a while then, found myself overthinking my gynaecologist's friendliness, laughing a little too hard at my dentist's moth-eaten jokes – but surely most women fall a little bit in love with their dentists and gynaecologists. It's how we reconcile them rooting around inside us. The more I thought of it, though, the more I believed there was something more amiss than our relationship. He was down in himself, not just in us, despite his insistence that *us* was the problem.

I tossed around in the prison-like single bed, trying to find ease, but no sleep came. My mind took me back home, back to the pastel-painted room of a relationship counsellor, with pictures of soothing mountain scenes on the walls and a box of tissues on the low table between us, a single tissue half-pulled out, primed for tear-duct action. I had suggested he should talk to someone to try and figure out what was wrong. If it was some form of depression, a therapist would surely figure that out. When he insisted it was the relationship that was the problem, I shifted position: marital relations turned to martial rules of engagement in that instant. All right then, I said, we'll try relationship counselling. He was so lethargic I couldn't see him upping and leaving us, but something needed doing – he was half-in half-out and we needed him all-in. Allen was unwilling to attend until I emotionally blackmailed him, using the kids as props: think of the children, they need happy parents. I was relieved he agreed to go, however unwillingly. Maybe he recognised there might be more to the problem than me.

I assumed the counsellor would see hints of depression but no: she was charmed by this public version of manhood in the beige easy chair in front of her.

Scene: the counsellor, a woman in her late sixties wearing comfortable clothes; me; Allen.

Counsellor, head tilted towards me, an expression of compassion mixed with understanding on her face: 'Have you considered picking things up in the bedroom?'

Me, thinking of rogue socks and dirty clothes shed on the bedroom floor: 'You mean upping my game?'

Counsellor, nodding enthusiastically, smiling as if her slowest student has just cottoned on: 'Exactly. Make more of an effort.'

Allen: silent all the while.

Me, thinking: why the hell does the responsibility of improving our sex life lie solely with me? Is it because Allen declared his dissatisfaction first, or how did it come about that I was to blame?

I felt I had to prove my sexual worth, not just to him but to her, in the reports back. I also felt deliberately sidetracked from the main issue, that Allen needed medical assistance for a mental health problem. Between him and the counsellor, they seemed to think if I just put more effort into the relationship, he'd feel better about me and better about himself and better about life in general. I was baffled by the obliviousness of the counsellor, but too cowardly to speak up.

The accusation that something was missing in the relationship, specifically our sex lives, felt unfair. Unbeknownst to me, a sexual performance evaluation had been established, with my prowess or actions being judged. *Performance*, they say, it adds to the acrobatic expectation of it.

If I had known, I'd have put more welly into it, but he hadn't seemed keen so I'd backed off. And once you tell someone they're lacking and imply their performance needs improving, self-consciousness creeps in. I'd never thought previous of how I was rated in bed – I had thought being good in bed was like being a good parent: if you just show willing you're doing all right. But I upped my game. I asked male friends with younger girlfriends, I had a gawk at some porn, and turns out Allen was right, I had dropped the ball somewhere along the way, somewhere between fumbling in the back of a car when we first started and snatching quickies around the kids' waking hours and his moods.

I did my research and conducted every textbook fantasy. I was Allen's slave, his matron, his teacher, his maid, his nurse, his waitress, his nanny. (Why do we reduce sexual fantasies to one-nouned traditionally female professions – where's the sexy role-play for office-bound technical writers and economic statisticians?) Since most of my real-life roles involved serving or caring, my sex life had turned into a busman's holiday. I had to up my game in the uniform department too. I couldn't reuse my carer's uniform for the nurse fantasy; the navy slacks were too functional, the tunic too baggy: even my job wasn't up to scratch and needed tweaking.

I was one great big action verb in the bedroom those months; but wait, not just the bedroom, because that counted as boring. I needed to Spice Things Up, which involved taking it to the sitting room, kitchen, bathroom, hall, stairs, and landing. I was like a nympho estate agent or a sex-crazed interior designer demonstrating different ways to make use of all the rooms in the house. I couldn't always stay focused, though, and sex in the shower had me eyeing the salmon-pink tinge to the grouting, wondering whether a nailbrush or toothbrush would be more effective to get rid of it.

Needless to say, none of this worked. I gave him my all but my contemptibly familiar forty-two-year-old's all couldn't compete with an unfamiliar twenty-four-year-old's.

There's a quiet sadness to prove-yourself sex, the sadness of a teddy bear in a hospital shop. It should be fun but there's something desperate about it: too much noise, too much action, too much thinking and worrying and analysing if he's liking it enough, if I'm doing it right, if the glare from the landing light highlights my lumpy thighs. My own needs were secondary; never was I completely honest about what I wanted. And anyway, I'd gone so long without considering my needs I couldn't have told him what they were even if he'd asked.

After weeks or maybe months of this new regime, I asked him if he wanted me. He said, 'I want you as much as you want me.' *That means everything and nothing*, I thought.

As well as being an acrobat in bed, I was meant to be severely groomed, honed, and tweaked and pruned and desperately reduced. And so, I worked on myself; I worked on becoming what apparently I should have been all along.

I attacked all traces of body hair with a zeal I usually reserve for removing nits from the kids' hair. I exercised voraciously to remove all traces of a life lived large. I shopped furiously to try to beat ageing, as if getting older was something that could be beaten into submission with bottles of gunk. Skin grooming had moved on from when I first learned to Cleanse, Tone, Moisturise as a teenager; there was now double cleansing and oiling and priming and seruming and hydrating and filling and correcting to my face before I even started on the make-up. The make-up itself had layers and layers of products and required sculpting and contouring and highlighting, Michelangelo's David had nothing on the effort that went into my appearance. My face was thick with all manner of shite and it seemed like Polyfilla thinking: pile on enough muck to fill in the cracks. The upkeep was horrendous and it wasn't entirely successful. The light in the bathroom is better on one side of the mirror so my right eyebrow was plucked more accurately than the left. I covered my hair-greys with a home colour that made me more homely than coloured: I used an empty plastic tub from a ready meal to mix the colour and my hair smelt of lasagne for days.

There were verbs of subtraction – losing weight, plucking, shaving, lasering, waxing; there were verbs of addition – applying lipstick, putting on fake eyelashes, adding smoothing underwear to the parts of my body I had failed to subtract.

In one appointment, our counsellor drew our life on a flip chart. She used permanent marker, which I took as a good sign; she would surely use temporary marker for the couples who look like they wouldn't last. The counsellor said we needed to make more of an effort to get out of the house. The implication was that Allen's depression might be cured if I wore a dress once in a while and we went on date nights. Date Nights. Since when did we have to take all our dates from the Americans – the kids go on play dates, their parents go on date nights. What happened to just playing and going out? Why do we have to noun the fuck out of everything?

So, a dress. If I put on a dress, she said, and take him outside the house – because the house is associated with practical matters – and we talk about things that aren't related to the house or the kids, that would put the spark back in our relationship. *The spark.* I don't want sparks in our relationship, I told her, there are more than enough sparks and explosions already; it's the steady even flame I crave. And besides, if we're not talking about the house or the kids, we'll be talking about suicide and that's what I'm looking to get away from.

I put up walls, she told me. Well, dry rot has set into these walls, I told her, they're fit to collapse.

I use humour as a defence mechanism, she told me. I couldn't come up with anything witty to say in response, which surely proves I don't.

I was torn between wanting to please her by agreeing with her and wanting to rip into her bullshit. If I agreed with everything she said, she'd call me a codependent people pleaser and advise me to consider my own needs. If I argued with her, she'd tell me I was defensive and resistant to advice. I opted for a middle ground; I nodded at some parts and looked perplexed at others, as if I was considering seriously the shite she was proffering. When she got me to explain my role in this clusterfuck, she implied that I knew what I was letting myself in for when Allen and I got together, that I knew what was in store. She told me I *got something* from the carer role, that it was fulfilling some kind of need in me. After a while, I grew to resent paying five hours of my wages for fifty minutes of nodding and how-does-that-make-you-feels: for that kind of money I wanted a mended life. I ended it abruptly, cancelling my last session by voicemail and wondering if counsellors look up RIP.ie for troubled clients who suddenly vanish from their books.

I didn't hate her, though. She was just doing her job, which unfortunately didn't collide with my needs. During one session, I noticed the label sticking out from her cardigan, which endeared her to me – especially when I pointed it out and she swatted away the remark without bothering to fix it.

My mind took me back to the present, to the sleep that wasn't happening. I opened my book and tried to read; there was little to be gained from going over terrible times.

DAY 2

Roy

Der Spaßmacher = fun-maker = clown

Roy unlocked the cubby and took out his bucket. He had an urge to initial the box beside his tasks before he completed them to disrupt the order of things. He had an urge to smudge the clean lines and turn some of the numbers on their heads and erase the rest. As he was getting his cloths and sprays in order, Inge walked up to him. Inge had been working at the Wunderland for years and, even though she was a good bit younger than him, Roy got the sense that she'd lived through centuries more than he had. Every part of her face seemed to turn downwards, her head slumped into her shoulders, there was no neck to speak of. Her shoulders sloped down and the whole body seemed to morph into one jaded unit; even her hair seemed weary. None of this posture worked with her height; even though she was tall, she gave off the impression of shortness. Roy looked closely at her face and tried to see if she resembled any of the figurines in the Wunderland.

'Morgen,' she said, pulling the hanks of hair nearest her forehead down over her face.

'Morgning,' Roy said. He had decided on a hybrid of English and German for some words. It wouldn't make him feel as if he was losing ground, even if it did sound like he couldn't speak either language correctly. He took his things from the cubby so Inge could get in, and he set off to the miniature land of Bayern with his bucket. It was almost 5 a.m. At home, he had worked office hours, starting at nine and finishing at six. He had sat for his work then, sat in front of a computer screen and carried out virtual tasks on projects that he couldn't see, whose point he couldn't see, for whose ultimate benefit he couldn't see. This cleaning work was hard and the pay was lower, but the satisfaction was immediate and the results plain to see. Also, he hadn't been sleeping well, and likely as not was still awake at three even if he didn't have to work, so this suited his circadian ways. And he liked being up when others were down and down when others were up. He enjoyed working split shifts, where each shift had the same times on different sides of the clock. It was as if the day was handed to him in two parts. Other people had five days in their working week; Roy had ten short days.

He had a long duster that could reach all 260,000 figurines of people and animals from some point in the exhibit. He had spent the first couple of weeks figuring out the best vantage point for each section of the Wunderland. Start at the top and work down, he'd been told; like someone who'd inherited a business then frittered it clean away.

He brushed the duster over a cave with stalactites and divers and nuns, wondering why there were so many scuba divers in the Wunderland and what hold they had over the designers, but he came up against mortar in his head. He dusted the fairy-tale castle and the house with miniature towels out to dry on the balcony. For him, the wonder of the Wunderland was the mundane things made small, the glorious efforts made to miniaturise a laundered towel on a railing, rather than miniaturising an obvious thing like a castle. Roy reached over and picked one of the tiny towels off the balcony, sniffed it for freshness, and put it into his pocket. He dusted the figurines at a street festival and the tiny tankards of amber beer, thinking about how miniature drunkenness would manifest. He moved to the mountains and swiped at a deer about to leap across a canyon to the fairy-tale castle. The deer looked confident, cocky almost; that's why Roy despised nature: animals doing what they were supposed to do and looking most at ease with the doing of it. He dug at the deer with his brush and sent it crashing to the valley beneath. *Fuck you, nature.* While his mind was in the animal trough, he pulled out his notebook to examine his favourite animal compound nouns in German:

Stinktier = stink animal = skunk

Faultier = lazy animal = sloth

Schnabeltier = beak animal = platypus

Tintenfisch = ink fish = squid

Fledermaus = flutter mouse = bat

Nacktschnecke = naked snail = slug

Schildkröte = shield toad = tortoise

Schweinswal = pig whale = porpoise

Seeschwein = sea pig = manatee

Stachelschwein = spike pig = porcupine

Seehund = sea dog = seal

Gürteltier = belt animal = armadillo

Murmeltier = mumbling animal = groundhog

Trampeltier = trampling animal = camel

Menschenaffe = human monkey = ape

Roy looked at his list. He wanted to find a way to bulldoze these animal names into conversation, but conversations seldom seemed to veer into zoological topics. Maybe he could create a table quiz round which gave the literal translation of the compound noun in English, and quizzers would have to guess the animal. That would require having friends in fours to fill a function room, though, and that's where his idea disintegrated.

Roy lived happily among the collections of German nouns that forced new nouns, the logic of Hand + Shoes = Gloves. He'd gone on a dictionary hunt and found Glühbirne = glow pear = lightbulb, Drachenfutter = dragon fodder = apology gift for spouse. Trying to put nouns together to make compound nouns, nouns that usually don't go together, was difficult in a notebook; the pen resists and insists on spaces, but the keyboarddoesn'tseemtomind. He liked lumping nouns together into words that would sound unwieldy in English; he liked the logic of German, even if he held no truck with the gender of nouns. He imagined German could be *his* language – at first he thought that he might be able to say things in German that he couldn't say in English, but now he reckoned that if he translated German back into English, *this* might be his tongue: the right language the wrong way around.

He took delight in learning words the likes of which he would seldom use in English or the combinations of which he'd never seen before, and enjoyed forcing them into conversation in German. His colleagues at the Miniatur Wunderland had been at the mercy of conversation starters involving sidings and belfries, pince-nez and bellows, semaphores and aqualungs (so much the better if he didn't understand their English meaning).

He put his notebook back in his pocket and moved his duster down to a cave under a mountain. A woman in white stood beside a white horse lit by a ghostly blue lamp. This must be some reference to a myth or fairy tale he didn't know, some belief or way of living that he knew nothing about. If he knew all the myths, legends, folk tales and fairy tales of a country, surely he'd find a way to live adequately there?

Roy moved to a small alcove on the other side of the mountain. In another cave, men were carving huge statues of rabbits and a bird, which seemed wonderfully pagan and primitive and pointless. Miniature nuns were walking up and down the mountain to church. He brushed the duster over them, only then noticing that interspersed among the nuns were penguins of diminishing size. Nobody would notice an absconded nun or two, so he thwacked his duster over a nun-clump, pulled them off their feet and into his pocket. Now the penguins outnumbered the nuns and several pairs of ghostly amputated feet remained.

He went on to dust each tiny flower outside a large house, swiping a couple into his pocket with a quick look for security cameras. As far as he was aware, from his time spent in the security room, there were pockets of the Wunderland that were free from cameras – and even where there were cameras, if there was limited night staff, he was safe. He did the majority of his figurine liberations when the lights dimmed; darkness surely hid his worsts.

A miniature goose sat in a tin bath and he gave it an extra tender dusting; he liked creatures not behaving as they should and acting out of context, out of sync with their species. They were less smug this way and theirs was an awkwardness he could get behind.

Now he moved into a more traditional pocket of Bavaria. Miniature men blew long horns; ladders and wooden bridges closed distances across gullies; goats speckled the mountain. The figurines here wore traditional clothes and carried knapsacks and looked so wholesome he wanted to punch them. A miniature couple was kissing beside a grotto to the Virgin Mary, and with a sharp dig of his duster, Roy flattened the two of them to the ground but, oh no, now they were on top of each other and he was trying to discourage things from going any further, not goad them into worse acts, so he turned the duster around and hacked at them with the narrow hard handle until the glue came unstuck and they fell apart. They didn't quite come unstuck the way he had planned: the man's head was still attached to the woman's by the lips, but his body slid down the mountain. Maybe he would join the deer at the bottom – the visitors would think there was a fairy tale or legend about a deer and a headless man they should know of.

He heard footsteps behind him and turned around. Inge was looking at him like she wanted to say something but had misplaced the words.

'Yes?'

'Do you have a spare cloth? Amerika is very dirty today.' She gave a turn of the mouth that was on track for a smile. Roy started. She had concealed her English well until now.

'Sure,' he said, putting down his duster and reaching into the bucket for a cloth. He handed it to her and she smiled again.

'What time do you finish today?'

Her perfect English unnerved him. He wanted to make some gesture, some nod towards German, but there was no one word that would do, and forming full sentences were still a problem for him. 'Ten. What about you?'

'Same. Once Amerika is clean, I work on the shop.'

'Ah, I have to do the control room after Bayern.' He found it hard to say Bayern without saying Munich after, but if he called it Bavaria, he got a thirst for beer. Inge was still standing there, tugging the curtains of hair into place on either side of her face. Roy was unnerved; women didn't usually come undone in his presence. He picked up his duster again and inhaled loudly. 'Right,' he said.

'Richtig,' she said. It came out like a military command in her language, but when he looked at her she was smiling, then with a wave of her hand she was gone.

He ran the duster over Leonie's fifth birthday party; the miniature child had a pool party with balloons and sea-lions on a waterbed. There was an ice-cream cart, a barbecue, and clowns. Roy hated birthdays; birthdays were terrible days fraught with false promise, the only guarantee was disappointment. And as for clowns: clowns were a scourge upon scourges – he hated their uniformed humour and dogged focus on fun. What kind of person laughed at a clown's slapstick stupidity? Roy dug the duster into the clown's face and, when he was knocked flat, smashed the head and body in, dug the heel of the duster handle into the clown until he was nothing but clown-dust. He shook out the duster, leaving a miniature pile of former fun behind. Could there be a German noun for rage-against-clowns? Then he examined the miniature children and found the figurine he thought was Leonie, the one in the flounciest party dress holding the presents. He leaned over the exhibit, ripped Leonie from her glued standpoint and flung her face-first into the swimming pool. The ripples caused the sea-lions to bounce on their waterbeds. The child bobbed a little and was still.

He moved on to one of his favourite scenes of the exhibition. Miniature men were at work around a house, and when you pushed the button, a man cut down a tree onto the roof. A woman came out of the house shrieking in a man's voice. He had listened to it over and over but still couldn't make out what the voice was saying. The adult visitors often laughed and lingered at this exhibit, which made him curious as to what the words were, but it would feel like cheating to ask a German speaker. He liked the reversibility of the screw-up: the tree that fell onto the roof stood again after the scene had played out, with the potential to not mess up another time.

He dusted around a miniature swimming pool, peering at the swimming-togged figurines, looking for Inge's likeness.

Then he moved his bucket and accoutrements to the show-jumping ground and swiped his cloth at the horses and the miniature piles of horse dung, wondering if dusting piles of miniature shit was the most useless task he'd performed.

He put his duster in his bucket and walked back to the cubby. The hoover was still in the same position, looking innocent, hose curled like the snake in a pharmacy logo, but Roy knew what a vicious sneaky beast it could be.

There were so many faces in the Wunderland, so many faces to be cleaned and dusted that they weighed on his mind, took on a dose of reality, becoming almost as real to him as faces in old family photos. These miniature plastic faces were his work colleagues, his audience, his friends. When he was out in the life-size world, after work, he searched people's faces for similarities to the figurines in the Wunderland. A group of young people he saw on the U-Bahn one evening on their way to a concert took on the look of the miniature festival-goers in the Wunderland, and he had found himself searching their faces and clothing to identify which figurines they were based on. He had stared at the faces of the figurines this morning to see if any of them resembled Gert, or if she resembled them. So far, he hadn't found her plastic likeness. Roy started putting his cleaning accoutrements away and thought about his sister's visit. It was good to have her here, yes, but she upset the routine in ways he hadn't countenanced. She had read far into last night, and even with the door between them, the pages turning in the dark were like knives at his ears, her throat-clearing the sound of an old car revving up. She said she was here to check in with him, which suggested an equality of meeting, but he saw it as more of a checking up on him, the way a doctor might do with a patient, an inequality of dealing that rankled. Her good humour was corrosive; too much trying and smiling on her part was trying and unsmiling for him.

Also, Gert's talk veered between the various ball- or fruit-shaped growths and tumours of the mothers of their friends or the friends of their mother's: people he didn't know or had forgotten if he ever did know. She had no interest in the benign tumours, but the malignant ones brought her particular relish. She chronicled every medical mishap and misdiagnosis of distant acquaintances, the ones that were the most serious, rarest, never-seen-the-like. He had no interest in this misery-grabbing, trying to write herself into a tragedy she had no part in.

Gert's obsession with fruit-shaped growths was like their mother's obsession with tortured martyrs. When they were growing up, their house was full of pictures of various martyrs and saints in all manner of agonised postures, and since they had moved out, the pictures had taken over every piece of wall space. Their mother ranked her martyrs in order of quantity of pain and originality of torture method: St Matthew was a particular favourite because he was flayed alive, Bartholomew came a close second, being skinned alive. St Isaac Jogues had his fingernails pulled off – that was another good one; he was the saint she prayed to when any of them caught a finger in a door. St Peter was crucified upside down, so he was the patron saint of headstands and acrobatics. St Erasmus had his intestines ripped out, and St Hippolytus was torn apart by horses. St Blaise was flayed with wool-carding combs so she prayed to him when knitting. St Lawrence was grilled and roasted alive, so she prayed to him while doing the Sunday dinner. St Ignatius of Antioch was eaten by lions at the Colosseum in Rome so he got called on when they went to the zoo. St Agatha of Sicily had her breasts cut off, and he didn't know when she prayed to her. Roy liked their specificity; his mother held no truck with general saintliness and that made sense to him. And he liked the sense of certainty that came from the saints and martyrs, the assumption that there was a right and there was a wrong, no matter false accusations.

Gert

Mundraub = mouth grab = stealing from someone's plate

He came back to the house as I was eating my breakfast, creature of the night that he is. I never met a man more suited to unsociable hours. His morning shift ended as my morning holiday shift began. He drank a cup of coffee with me, and I ate some bread and butter seeing as that's all there was in the cupboards.

'Will we go to the supermarket,' I said, 'get some food in?'

He looked surprised at that, maybe he didn't think there was anything amiss in the bare shelves. 'If you like,' he said. 'There's one around the corner.'

Roy rooted in the cupboard under the sink, pulled out a couple of reusable bags, and off we headed.

'Did you ever think we'd all be bringing bags to do the shopping – when you think of how it used to be?'

He looked surprised again, this brother who could have been a stranger. 'It's better for the environment this way,' he said. 'The plastic isn't—'

'I know well what the plastic is and isn't. I'm just remarking how easy you get used to one behaviour after years of accepting the other behaviour as normal.'

'I suppose so.'

I'll take his supposes if they're all he'll grant me. We walked the rest of the way in silence.

Sometimes, when I venture into the city at home, I go to Asian supermarkets to wander the spice aisles. Regular supermarket spices don't interest me so much: no, these are large packets, possibly aimed at restaurant chefs, large plastic bags of spices that make me think if I used them I could be an entirely different person who would home-cook every night and not have a husband with his head in the coffin, oh no, this way I would be safe and my family would be safe and we'd eat home-cooked and life would be perfect. Times I've loaded my basket with every kind of spice, spices I haven't heard of, spices that smell so strange and strong and different they're reassuring, they tell me there's a whole other way to live out there. But somewhere between the spice shelves and the till, common sense creeps in and I remember myself and my limitations and I skulk back to decant my almost-purchases onto the shelves.

Times I walk nights, when the house can't contain me, circling around the neighbourhood, tangenting off at the roads with the nicer houses, the ones that keep their curtains open. All the dinner parties! All the plates of nibbles that look like they've been crafted and assembled and not just fucked out of a packet and onto the nearest clean plate. The bowls of flowers and vases of fruit make me wonder when the hell did we switch containers for fruit and flowers – didn't it used to be vases of flowers and bowls of fruit? And how did all these people know there was a receptacle switch and why didn't anyone tell me? All the sitting rooms I've peered at that look like they've been thoroughly cleaned, with no clutter or shite crammed behind the furniture. Sometimes I linger outside a house and stand on tiptoe to see if the gap under the sofa contains stuffed toys and papers, and it never does. How do some families organise themselves so thoroughly, so completely, that there is space for empty space? Surely we can't be the only family eating TV dinners on sofas seething with old crumbs and lost coins and Lego pieces.

Those nights I walk, I walk the legs off myself. I'd rather be off out on the toes than tiptoeing around unwanted in my own home.

This supermarket was a discount brand that we have at home. I knew the layout before I hit the aisles: cereals and breads and cakes in the first aisle, with produce halfway down. I like that this supermarket doesn't ever change its layout; there is surely a special place in hell reserved for whoever decides to switch the layout of a supermarket, violating your automatic pilot and unleashing a ferocious aisle-rage. I assume it's in an effort to make you buy more, but what a low way to go about such things. I was drawn to the middle aisles, the section that sells different discounted items every few days, random things you'd often think might have fallen off the back of a lorry. Like the make-believe lands at the top of the Magic Faraway Tree changing, you don't know what will come next: a lucky dip of a shop.

'Don't you love the stuff in the middle, Roy?'

His lip curled up a sneer. 'You mean the useless tat that clogs up Mam and Dad's house?'

I bristled, as I always bristle when he treads over our family disloyal. 'It's not all useless, some of it's very useful. I love the randomness of it – how do they choose what to sell each week?'

'I don't know, it's probably based on what they think suckers will fork out for.'

I ignored him, even though it seemed a terrible waste to spend so much of a six-day trip ignoring the person you came to see. I picked up a small box of cereal.

'You can't buy that – they don't eat cereal for breakfast here.'

'I couldn't give a fuck what anyone else eats. I eat cereal and I'm buying it.'

I put the cereal into the basket with more force than my appetite actually was for it, and then I reached back and took a second box of cereal from the shelf, just to spite him. Roy picked up some dark bread and put it in the basket – of all the foods in the shop, I'd swear he was picking out the most foreign ones to spite me. I put in a loaf of brown bread and on we walked, matching each other's basket fever, item for item, local for foreign. The chocolate prices were cheaper so I threw in a few large bars – handy gifts for Allen and the kids.

'You're going to eat all those in five days?'

'Yes,' I said, 'I'm going to sit in your flat – sorry, *apartment* – and stuff every ounce of these bars into my mouth, then I'm going to rub my gooey hands all over your sofa and maybe your bed.'

He looked as if he was trying hard not to show disgust in his face, trying hard to pretend he was OK with the idea of stains from my body. We moved on.

'Do you eat jam or marmalade?' I asked.

'No.'

At the produce aisle, I picked out a melon and a punnet of grapes, a couple of punnets of strawberries. Roy looked dubious as I loaded them into my basket, maybe wary he'd start growing a fruit tree from a mis-swallowed pip. We curled around the corner to the dairy section. I picked up some milk and cheese – lots of cheese, because it seemed he only eats pale-coloured foods.

'Crisps?'

'All right – ready salted.'

Christ, the vanilla of crisps; I wanted to get the hottest tortilla chips I could find and force-feed him them to see a reaction.

Instead, I put some ready salted into the basket; red packaging, magnolia contents. I gave up soon after that and skipped the alcohol aisle; that would have resulted in conniptions or worse.

We got to the check-out. There were two people ahead of us; the woman waiting in front of us had left a large gap behind her but hadn't put up the metal divider. I put my basket onto the metal part of the conveyor belt and started to unload my groceries. The woman turned around and hissed something at me. I turned to Roy. 'What the hell did she say?'

He looked embarrassed then – not angry at the woman for her rabid hissing, embarrassed about *me*. 'You're supposed to wait till the person in front of you puts the divider out.'

'Oh, for fuck's sake, is it really that important?'

Roy looked away. He mustn't have had the German to talk to the woman, but if he did, I knew whose side he was on. When it came to my turn, I packed my bag slow as I could. Roy was almost snatching food items from the cashier's hand and firing them into his bag, but when his bag was full, he had to stand and watch nervously as I plodded, slug's pace, picking up each item, examining it, and putting it in my bag. The paying then became another intentional fiasco. I spent a while rummaging for my purse, and when I found it, I decided to give the exact change. The person behind me in the queue didn't look too pleased, but more importantly, Roy's face was blotched with rage. And then it hit me – what is it you've become, Gert, flying hundreds of miles just to antagonise your brother?

We walked back to his place in silence, up those steps and into the flat. Stefan was sitting on the sofa, but after nodding at us and saying *Allo* in a subdued tone, he scuttled off to his bedroom. It's a curious thing to see a man after you've heard him masturbating; you wonder who – or what – the final spurt was aimed at. We unpacked the groceries; I laid them out on the table and Roy put them away. He eyed the melon as if he didn't know what to do with it, so I made up his mind for him. I took a knife from the drawer and sliced it in two – if only life were so easy cut! – then took a spoon from the drawer to scoop out the seeds and stringy phlegm. The next obvious step was to slice it into boats but, I thought, the world has seen enough melon boats; let's try something new. I hacked and I cut and I sliced and I sheared and, soon enough, there was a puddle of melon juice and botched pieces of fruit all over the counter. Roy stared and stared – the kitchen probably hadn't been used as much since he moved in.

'Melon?' I asked.

He shook his head slowly. I took a fork from the drawer – it's a grand meal when you've used a knife, fork, and spoon to prepare it – and I ate half of it and put the other half in the fridge for later.

'It's a bit disappointing that the flesh isn't the colour of the skin, isn't it?' I turned to ask him, but he was staring out the window as if the water-gloom held some kind of cure-all.

'What would you like to do today?' I asked him.

He got this pained expression then; Roy could patent these expressions, he has such a range of them. This one was like stepping into a bath and the too-hot water hitting the crack of your arse.

'I don't know, what do you want to do?'

'Well, you could show me around a bit.'

'All right.'

He wasn't exactly brimming with enthusiasm for a tour guide but he'd have to do. I put my bag over my shoulder and we headed out the door again. Well, for a man who wasn't keen to start with, he took me the length and depth of the city. He took me on and off the train (which he insisted on calling the Ooh-Bahn), he walked me down the port and up a viewing point to see the city, up roads and down roads, up street escalators and down street escalators, to the town hall that looked like something from the Pied Piper. He would have kept going, too, if I hadn't stopped him a couple of times for a cup of tea or a bite of lunch.

'Will we eat some Chinese food?' I asked, as we passed a restaurant. Best way to avoid another bland meat-and-pota-toes meal – I'd enough of that at home; I wanted to feel like I was out foreign even if the foreign food I ate didn't match the country I was in.

'Sure,' he almost shrugged, but it seemed to be too much effort to do even that. Once he slows down or stops, my brother shrinks back into himself.

We went inside. I looked at the menu, and even though I knew I should be trying some new food in a new country, I went for the same thing I always do: chicken balls, sweet and sour sauce, rice.

'Boiled or fried?'

'Boiled, please.'

Roy winced and sneered, his whole body acurl.

'What's wrong with that?'

'Gert, have you ever tried *actual* Chinese food?'

'Roy, you can go and shite with your chow mein – do you think the *actual* Chinese are eating chow mein in Beijing right now?'

'Well, there's more chance of that than them eating spherical chicken nuggets in red sugar-sauce.'

'Ah, just fuck off and leave me have what I want. Seldom enough I get to eat out.'

A low blow, do we pick it up in the maternity ward these martyred manipulations? Hard to come back from it and, sure enough, his lips were twitching, voice itching, but he said nothing. We waited in silence for the food. There was a small child in a big chair at the next table, his head almost in his plate, another child chewing a bun case to get the last of the dough out, an expression of pure concentration on her face, and I panged for my two. There was no wine; I had only tap water to ease the discomfort this time and I was slow about gulping it in case he'd get annoyed by the toilet stops later – especially if they were in a café and I went on to buy more coffee which *just serves to perpetuate the toilet cycle*, he would tell me. I didn't see him go to the toilet once; Christ, the *control* of the man. The food came; hard to sulk when there's good smells and hot food in front of you. Mine was a particular brand of neon orange-red that whets my hunger more than a subtler sauce would.

Roy cleared his throat as if he was about to pronounce on something important. 'Isn't it strange ordering food in a foreign language that's not the language of the country you're in?'

'What?' My head was in my not-yet-bit-into food.

'The waiter isn't German, we're not German, but we're meeting in the middle with English. We're at an unfair advantage, though – it might even things out if we all spoke German, then it'd be mutual pidgin.'

'A kind of double confusion instead of a triple,' I said. It's important to encourage him, even in his brain-frying oddness. 'Do you want to taste?' I asked.

Roy leaned over, stuck a spoon into the sauce, tasted it, and grimaced. 'If food could taste ugly, this would,' he said, working his tongue as if he could erase the sauce-memory.

This was my brother partially returned to me. It wasn't the funniest thing that has been said but I laughed to keep this fragile conversation afloat. I dipped my fork into his noodles and watched his shoulders rise and his mouth clamp shut. 'What?'

'I don't like people touching my food,' he said. 'It's unhygienic.'

'Unhygienic, my arse, I'm family.'

He didn't look convinced, in fact he looked even more disgusted by the fact of being related to me. 'And it's theft.' He said this triumphantly, as if he'd found the definitive reason for me to keep my fork to myself.

There were so many things I could have said, so many things I wanted to say, but I kept quiet and dug my unhygienic fork into my ugly food. When I finished eating I tried to get at the threads of meat between my teeth with my tongue but they were well welded. I took out a packet of chewing gum from my bag and sawed the foil wrapper between my teeth.

'You don't have an empty crisp packet, do you? They give a sharper clean.'

He looked at me in disappointment, like I was a hot-water bottle gone cold. 'I don't,' he said, in a forced voice like he was straining for a shit.

It doesn't take long for my habits to get in on him, and maybe my habits weren't doing a great job of keeping themselves under wraps. I was going from one difficult relationship to another – I should probably use the careful tread in this one too.

Roy was impatient to get going again after lunch; the food stoppings were inconvenient wastes of time, not things to be enjoyed in themselves. It's very hard to enjoy a cup of tea when your companion has downed his in a matter of gulps and is staring at his watch, twitching to get moving.

'What rush is on you?' I asked him, when he looked like he was going to burst his skin with impatience.

'It's important not to waste time, that's all.'

I didn't have the words to have that discussion with him. All this stuff you hear now about mindfulness and savouring the moment, meanwhile Roy is mindfully rushing through the things that could be enjoyed to get to the things that should be rushed or tolerated.

'What do you usually do in your time off?'

'I nap sometimes, or I read my book.'

'The train timetables book?'

'Yeah. It's not the most recent one, but the timetables are likely the same, most of them anyway.'

'Are you going to take a trip?'

'Not yet, but I can plan one.'

'We could take a trip together some day?'

His face was a panic then. 'No, no, I have to work – you need to give lots of notice to book holiday leave.'

'OK, OK.'

There is a time to go gentle and a time to go hard, but now was neither; now was the time to go home.

When Roy left for work, I got into the bed to stay warm more than anything and decided to lie down for a nap. I tried to shove positive thoughts into my mind, I listened for Stefan's rummagings, I tried to think of anything but home but it didn't work.

Allen only began to suffer with his mind years after we'd tethered together. It came as an almighty shock to me: we'd gone through years of trying for children and every test and intervention imaginable and he'd been even-tempered throughout. Only long after those yearned-for children arrived did he come undone.

We go back long, Allen and I. If we were American, we'd be called childhood sweethearts – we started seeing each other as teenagers – but the phrase *childhood sweethearts* gives me the creeps, makes me think of child beauty queens slapped in taffeta and lipstick, simpering and gurning at the cameras adult-like. We were nothing so precocious; Allen asked me out for a spin. He took his da's car to pick me up and we parked down by the lake. We were spotted one evening by a friend of his da's who winked at Allen next time he saw him and asked who he was girlin' with, and that, it seemed, was that – the inevitable chain of engagement, marriage, children was begun. Sometimes it's easier to do the things other people think you should do than invoke their questioning or wrath if you don't. Marriage seemed to be the direction we were heading and that's where we ended up. Friends who had chosen other ways, or had other ways chosen for them, suffer the constant questions (*should I buy the hat, when will you give us a day out, anything stirring, you don't want to leave it too late to have kids,* etc.)

Aside from the slumpings so low he's hard to leave with the kids, and climbings so high he's a danger to himself, Allen is the best of fathers. Some of my friends have husbands who need nagging to do the usual household or childcare chores, chores so routine you'd wonder how they could require nagging. These men seem to think the odd bout of tickling or kick-around of a football constitutes fatherhood. Allen is different.

The morning after a suicide attempt – they usually take place at night, as if the darkness unleashes some kind of mind-demon – the world as I know it halts. It's put on pause, indefinite pause. I ask Gráinne to take the kids: to school, to her house, to the park, anywhere that's not home. These stretchy days are not carved up by mealtimes, school drop-offs and pick-ups, homework and hobbies. Routines are botched; things you thought needed doing suddenly no longer need doing: why shop for food or cook when neither of us has any appetite? You marvel at how you took such things as making a meal or hanging out a load of washing for granted and you despair of ever doing them again.

When you could do with your day being filled by rigid regime, time stretches heedless, hangs thick and sluggish. These days feel unreal, as if they belong to someone else. I struggle to understand how other people can be living through the same hours as myself but mine stretch infinitely longer.

Allen, hospital-discharged – drugged, bandaged, stilled – is mostly in bed the day after. They have no place for him in the hospital, they tell me. If he won't go willingly (and he won't) there are many steps to be gone through before com-mittal is possible, necessary steps after so many unnecessary incarcerations in this country's recent past, but too much for me when I'm not even sure if this is the best solution. The problem is, his own bed doesn't seem to want him either. I'm vigilant downstairs, a guard-dog, ears flaring, nostrils quiver-ing at the slightest movement, or a small-town meerkat on high alert, eyes roving, head slicing side to side, listening upstairs for him to breathe. If he gets up to go to the toilet I'm relieved he's still alive but feary he'll find something sharp in the bathroom to do damage with. Knives are easy to hide, but I could overlook a small pair of nail scissors or a glass jar that could be smashed and sharded. My nerves are like shrapnel.

The contradictory combination of intensity and timeless-ness is unsettling. It feels like a play being broadcast on television: there isn't much movement or change of scene but the emotions are extreme. It's hard to pinpoint exactly what's missing.

I can't sit, can't concentrate but something takes a hold of me, a desire to stay healthy for the children, so I take vitamin C in its most vigorous state: effervescently. I chase the tablet around the water with my finger because I need to feel some kind of power over something and I don't want to kick a dog.

Depending on the risk level (as I assign it – who's to tell me what colour danger-code we're in? I make the decision and try stick with it – after panicking in work one day and leaving a patient half-washed and half-dressed to sprint for the car and rip up the road home convinced from a lack of phone response that he'd gone and finally done it), I call one of the women I work with to ask them to switch shifts with me. I owe so many favours to people who have no idea what their good deed has done. If I was in charge of those prayers, the Beatitudes, I'd add a *Blessed are those who perform kindnesses unquestioned.* But these last-minute requests begin to wear thin; the matron is losing patience with my apparent fecklessness.

Those loosely coiled days, I chew gum like a football manager on the side-lines; it's the only thing that soaks up my nerves and I chew the good right out of it .

I don't pace, I sit rigid, afraid to breathe too loud for fear of what I won't hear. And all this in secret. This vigilance, this hyper-watching, is all done unbeknownst to Allen, unbeknownst to the kids, unbeknownst to everyone. It's the loneliest thing in the world.

Meantime I age ferociously, his every suicidal night branded into my forehead furrows. I feel like a creature from mythology, four hundred years old inside, forty years old on the outside. My neck seizes up after the worst bouts. *Episodes* we've taken to calling them, like a night-slice of soap opera. And that's what it feels like sometimes. For someone who avoids drama and prides herself in getting on with things, it's a horror to find myself in the middle of a scene from an *Eastenders* Christmas special.

If Allen was depressed in Germany, the word *Schwermütig* (melancholic) could be used for him and maybe, just maybe, he wouldn't be so ill here.

Roy

Quasselstrippe = jabber string = chatterbox

Roy's scalp was sweating. His ears felt fried and coated in a batter of words. Of his two sisters, Gert was the one he could tolerate the longest, but Christ could she talk. He believed walks were for silence and observation, but Gert seemed to think they were for filling up with words. In shops, she was never still; she stroked jumpers, squeezed footballs, poked sponges, smelt soaps, turned over egg-timers, pushed buttons of toys and gadgets she had no intention of buying. She unfolded jumpers and T-shirts, failing to notice that people in Hamburg refolded clothes perfectly after unfolding them. He couldn't believe his niece and nephew were only seven and five years old; he had surely heard octogenarians' lives' worth of illness and disease. Could those children really be so afflicted with all the sicknesses Gert claimed? They both looked so pink-cheeked and hearty when he saw them, but maybe it was a diseased shade of pink. He pulled out his notebook containing the list of German translations of diseases he'd made when they'd got home last night. If Gert didn't continue to corrode his good humour then he'd present it to her; she might like to know how sick her kids would be in German. He read:

Blinddarmentzündung = appendicitis

Schwindsucht = consumption/tuberculosis
Blutarmut = anaemia
Gicht = gout
Ruhr = dysentery
Quetschung = bruise
Geschwür = ulcer
Herzklopfen = palpitations
Lungenentzündung = pneumonia

He wished his nephew's name wasn't Benjy; it sounded like a dog's name. And Gert's glutting piggishness was disgusting; her mind never seemed to wander far from the next meal or snack. She needed to take a sup or a bite so often he thought she must have some kind of disease herself. *Worms*, their mother would have said. *Refuelling*, Gert called it, and yes, she was like a small butt of a car with a nifty engine and a whole lot of noise. She ate as if a stopwatch was being held to her mouth. He had to look away when she did that; he was disgusted by her and he didn't want her to see his disgust. These were kindnesses he could never get credit for. *Offer it up*, their mother said about small inconveniences, and he'd always imagined small piles of problems packed into a chute and shoved upwards, as he'd seen cashiers do with tubes of banknotes in supermarkets.

He'd left Gert napping in the apartment while he went to the Wunderland for the second part of his shift, and he was part glad of the time alone. He had gotten used to the quiet, slow rhythms of his own mind, no matter the background noise of the Wunderland during visiting hours, and Gert's constant jabs on his attention jarred. He only needed four minutes to get from his apartment to the Wunderland, but he had left early to gain extra silences alone. He walked to the edge of the largest canal, the one that looked wide enough to be a river. He stood at the water's edge and looked down. What did he expect to see there; what did people ever expect to see in a large dark clot of water at night?

He went into the Wunderland. There was no queue now and he climbed the steps slowly. He nodded to the receptionist, walked through the gift shop, gathered his cleaning equipment, and headed for the control room, where rows of screens zigzagged images from the exhibition. The two guards inside nodded briefly at him and went back to their watching.

Cleaning the Wunderland while people were working or visiting was bitty and unsatisfactory. Roy preferred to get a run at a room on his own, with no grimy hands or grubby foot soles immediately spoiling his hard work. Emptying bins was a simple, routine task that involved a lot of bending and stooping, and much as he tried to remember to bend at the knees to spare his back, Roy often forgot, to the horror of his spine. This part of his job was so endless and thankless compared to physical scrubbing; every time he thought he'd caught all the bins, he found one in the corner or behind a door. He was supposed to change the bin-liner every time, but today, he tucked the dirty part under the clean part to hide his lack of thoroughness. He didn't usually nip so many edges off his job but Gert had rattled his brain and mithered his routine. He snuck multiple peeks at the security screens, behind the security guards' backs. The images were vague and imperfect, the visitors' movements jolty and unnatural. When the lights dimmed in the Wunderland, there was little to see. Roy was relieved; his figurine liberations would surely continue to go unnoticed.

He damp-dusted the surfaces and flicked out his duster every so often, dropping clumps of dust to the floor, which looked like malformed miniature mice. He worked slowly;

today's areas were to be thoroughly cleaned, spring cleaned they called it. Roy went to the computer in the control room and sat at the stool. He half-heartedly ran the duster over the keyboard, sprayed some cleaning spray at the screen, and wiped it off. Then he typed the words 'spring cleaning' into the search box. According to Wikipedia, the origins of spring cleaning possibly date back to the Persian new year, which falls on the first day of spring. Iranians today apparently continue the practice of *khooneh takouni*, which sounded like a theme tune from a Disney film but translated as 'shaking the house'. *Shaking the house*, he ran the words through his mind. If a house could be packed into a canvas sack and shaken by a large hand from above, it would rid the place of cobwebs and rot and decay. He liked the idea. And he liked the sound of khooneh takouni. Performing khooneh takouni made the process seem more meaningful and made it easier to put some leg into it, to give it wasky as his father would say.

He wondered what state his father was in these days. Gert hadn't mentioned their parents, and Roy hadn't prodded the subject. He presumed from her silence that nothing had changed in their attitude towards him, that he had no place in their home, that his name was still sewage to them. If he had done something wrong, he could better understand their rejection. The lad was a friend. They had things in common, trains for one thing. He couldn't understand why Gráinne and his parents could have turned their backs on him. He didn't have the puff in him to defend himself; some things are impossible to deny, but he'd hoped that the people who knew him best didn't believe the rumours. It's hard to stay somewhere you're not wanted, hard to work up to a defence when the assumptions are against you. If he had been listed in his parents' house as their son in the census, surely they couldn't have disowned him so readily. Sometimes he day-dreamed about travelling to every country in the world on their census nights, checking into hotels and being counted elsewhere, or manywheres.

He pushed his forefinger into the cloth and dug it into the corners of the screen, then ran it all around the rim. It came up satisfyingly grey, so he pushed his finger into an unsoiled part of the cloth and repeated the process until it came away clean. Khooneh takouni; shaking the house.

Gert

Verschlimmbessern = to make things worse and to make things better = to make things worse by trying to improve them

I spent a good part of the evening while Roy was at work in the bed reading and napping. The day had turned damp, a sly skulking rain that felt dishonest and sneaky.

Time hung pendulous without the children. I hadn't been away without them in years and I felt I should be doing something for myself, but I was wore out from walking earlier in the day and I felt jaded with new things. The break in routine was discombobulating, the days had grown extra legs, and I found it hard to peel myself out of the fug of nap-sleep, threaded through with the strangest of dreams. When I wake from daytime naps I'm mithered in drool and I don't know where I am or who I am or if I am. I needed a steer. I needed sturdy hours filled with concrete plans; this timelessness did me no favours after all.

The things Roy decided to show me were not the kind of things I'd go abroad to see, but I couldn't think of what I did want to see so I stayed in the bedroom instead. I'd never travelled far-flung, properly foreign, to Asia and Africa and the like – it always seemed too much like work – not like some of my friends who left home to travel for a year around faraway places. *Backpacking* they call it, a strange word – I don't call the kind of travel I do *suitcasing*. Those friends who used to bore me with travel tales (it was the biggest! best ever! most amazing!) now bored me with their children stories (it was the funniest! cutest! most advanced); I'll get my revenge after this trip. I'm not sure if I like travelling or if I just like imagining myself describing the experience to someone after. I'm not sure if I like sight-seeing or if it's something I feel compelled to enjoy, like Christmas food: do I really like turkey and plum pudding or do I just like the tradition of it? I mostly deny it, despise myself for it, but I dislike difference. I have to stop myself seeking out and reassuring myself with the same shops and café chains we have at home.

Years back, I worked a carer's job in New York. The smugness I felt of getting to know another city's way of going on, the superiority when I compared my home city to the new one, quieted after a while into acceptance of the faults of the old country when I began to see the flaws of the new. Roy had little of the pride or confidence of mastering a new place; he navigated his way easily but didn't have the ex-pat swagger.

Stefan had been moping around the apartment earlier but he'd gone off out now. There was something mournful about lying on a single bed in a strange apartment in a strange city while it rained outside, and I knew I should be making better use of my time. If I was doing the same thing in my own house at home, the pressure wouldn't be on me to be enjoying myself. I felt low-level glum, regional-news kind of glum, with their constant tellings of house fires and car crashes and the occasional farm accident. I got up, thinking at least if I was vertical I'd be spending the day in some sort of right shape. I looked out the window at the drizzle falling on the canal. The drops were so light I couldn't see each one hit the water and it gave off the effect of a dusty surface, a grey uneven dust that needed to be swept clean. I decided to ring home. Allen would be in from work with the kids; the tea would be near ready. I dialled the number: it felt more deliberate to push each number-button rather than mind-lessly scroll through my contacts.

'Hello, Gert,' he said.

'Hey, how's it going?'

'Grand, the kids are fine. How's things over there?'

'It's hard going. He's not in much form to talk, hasn't asked about Mam and Dad or Gráinne at all.'

'Well, it's early days yet. And he's probably afraid of the answers. I wouldn't worry too much. You're doing mighty just to be over there with him.'

I got a bit wobbly then. Allen and I are not the kind of saps for whom soppy is their way of getting on, but when you're told what you need to be told even though you didn't know you needed it, well, that's enough to cramp my voice with tears unspilt. 'How are the kids doing?'

'Great.' I could hear Benjy laughing at the TV in the background. 'We've just ordered a pizza and we're going to eat it in front of a movie.'

'That sounds fun.' I felt even more mournful then, that I wasn't there with them, that they didn't seem to miss me, that Allen got to be the fun parent while I served up balanced meals that took an age to prepare but didn't taste as good to small tongues. The tedium of cooking uninspired meals on rotation is mine not Allen's. When Allen is away and I'm alone with them, it feels like a lack; when I'm away and Allen's alone with them, it counts as fun. I could hear the pair of them squabbling in the background then and I knew I was far from their thoughts.

'I'll put Hazel on.'

There was a rustling and muffled words and then a 'Hi, Mam' from a bored-sounding voice. How does a seven-year-old sound so jaded already?

'Hi, pet, how was school today?'

'Fine. Mrs Moriarty was out sick so we got put into Miss Murphy's class. They're ten so they were doing really hard sums but we were allowed to do drawing.'

'Oh, that's even better.'

'Yeah.'

I flung some more questions at her but the answers were getting more meagre. Trying to knock conversation out of a child on the phone is like trying to squeeze sunshine out of an Irish summer. I ended with reassuring Hazel that I'd be home soon but it was more myself I was reassuring. 'Put Daddy back on, will you?'

And before I had a chance to say bye to her, Allen's voice came down the line. 'You got all the news then?'

'Such as it was. Miss me?'

'Course I do, especially when it's bedtime and they want a story the way Mammy does it.'

I smiled then, I allowed myself that. We said goodbye and hung up before the moment demanded anything heavier. I felt emptied out, like the skin of a sausage after the meat has been squeezed out. It's a sad thing to know that the part of the world you created is carrying on just fine without you; it foreshadows what's to come.

Allen had sounded cheery, but not worryingly so. Even-keel cheer is what I'm after, the name of a mellow low-alcohol beer maybe. I let out a breath I hadn't realised I was holding. The doctor has reassured me he's currently stable, but when your go-to mode is watching, scrutinising, analysing behaviours and speech patterns or lack of behaviours or speech patterns for signs of deteriorating mental health, it's hard to switch off and go back to normal, if I could even remember what normal was. I wonder if we'll ever get back to taking things at face value, to one of us saying something and the other reacting only to the thing that's just been said, without dragging years of mental-health history, de facto patient and carer relations, into the fray.

I had resisted the urge to ask how Allen was, other than a brief pleasantry at the start of the conversation. We can't talk about the things that need talking about so we talk about meals that have been consumed or need to be purchased. We talk in deliberately light-hearted tones about the final scores of the games our children play (*they beat them to the ground, that's our girl!*) and the new shoes that need to be bought (*their feet go up a size overnight!*) and the pick-ups of children and the delivery of briquettes. Minutiae repeated is the tedious wrecker of some marriages; it's the saviour of ours. Less an elephant in the room, more a landmine that could explode if somebody stepped on the wrong topic.

The shift in the rules of engagement happens so slowly. If somebody had told me twenty years ago that I'd be living in a relationship of pure avoidance, of begging for affection scraps, of locking small loaded rooms in my mind, I wouldn't recognise myself. Where is this person who used to believe things worked out, who used to believe happiness was a choice, was under your control? Happiness is the big thing now in this no-problem-left-unturned therapy culture; we're all supposed to be on the seek for happiness. Christ, the *naivety* – are other people's lives so abysmally easy that happiness is the only thing they're after? Happiness! Maybe start with stability, money, the ability to leave the house without worrying what you'll find on your return. *Flourishing*, that's another state we're supposed to aim at; I'd settle for coping, myself.

And as for the Ten Steps to Happiness and Tips on Achieving Inner Peace you see in magazines – for fuck's sake. The assumptions made in those pieces are astounding. That you have spare time and a spare room in the house to create a meditation room, that you have money enough to throw at various health professionals and not-so-professionals, that you can take yourself off on solo trips to meditation resorts and spas that cost more for a weekend than our annual family holiday. And those uplifting posters in friends' kitchens – I get the most intense urge to tell those people to Live! Laugh! Love! their Best Lives without me in it.

There's a one-hour time difference between home and here but there should be more, to properly signify the difference. My phone automatically changed to German time, but I hadn't changed my watch; it kept me fastened to the mealtimes and school times of home. I got an urge to send a postcard – to buy, write, stamp, and send a postcard home, even though I'd be home before it – because that seems a more honest way of signifying how out of step I am with home than a phone call in real time. But it seems a strange thing to send a postcard from one grey mizzly place to another. While I'm at it, I might as well send a parcel of souvenirs: tat sent with a handwritten address is surely more appealing than tat handed over unceremonious. If I could be bothered dealing with post-office bureaucracy, I'd wrap a parcel of keepsakes in brown paper and tie it with twine, and while I was in the post office and in the nineteenth century, I would send a telegram. To whom or to say what I don't know, but it seems like something that should be ticked off a bucket list. It's like the occasional hankering I get to keep a diary, to document my life in some way, but I'd feel like a gobshite writing to myself.

The rest of the evening weighed down ahead of me. I didn't feel like a tourist with a list of must-dos, more a guest with a list of must-don'ts. I had no desire to go out in the damp and no notion of what to look at if I did. I wasn't in a capital city so I didn't feel compelled to sight-see; it would be more of a sight-*seek* because there were no obligatory tourist attractions. I hadn't really considered that they made guide-books of cities that weren't capital cities. When I'm in a city that other people have been to, I feel it would be a misstep not to visit the Eiffel Tower or the National Gallery, in the same way that it'd be rude to pass through Thurles and not knock into Auntie Breda, but I'm off the hook in a smaller city. Capital cities get all the big museums – they own that country's past; the smaller cities have to divvy up bits of local history between them. If this was Berlin, my sight-seeing would have to take in more war and politics, the obvious wheres and the logistical hows and the bewildering whys of it.

I took a Hamburg guidebook from the shelf and flicked through it – it must have been Stefan's because Roy's books only involved trains. Now that I knew what there was to see, I'd feel bad if I didn't visit these sights; I'd feel my trip would be incomplete if I didn't take the time to see them. At what point does travelling just become another thing to tick off your list and put yourself through the guilt-wringers? The best things to see in Hamburg, according to the guidebook, were the warehouse district (the oldest in the world), the port, and the Miniatur Wunderland. I felt smug that I was unintentionally in the thick of the must-sees. The guidebook mentioned the Elbe Philharmonic Hall, which was open till midnight. Apparently it was controversial for going way over time and budget, so I decided to stay away; I wanted peace from my trip not visits to conflict. But the port, oh, the port,

Hamburg's port, a fine example of the hubbiest of hubs, this is what I want to see. I want to see things moving and progressing not tensions stalled.

Walking a new city makes me feel exposed and unmoored, like the first trip into town alone after childbirth; I'd forgotten how to walk without a bump or a buggy, how to dangle my arms, where I fit on the footpath. I live in a town near the outskirts of a city recently swollen. Soon it will be joined up if the housing estates tentacle further. We seldom go into the city proper, we shop in outlying shopping centres with familiar chain-stores and permanent traffic jams and convince ourselves this is living. Winter hangs heavy in our parts. We have neither the drama of a coastal area nor the convenience of a city. Our chippers close by ten.

I got up from the sofa then; I got up because I should do something that's not with Roy and not with Allen and not with the children. I put on my raincoat – I wouldn't be caught out in a rain-spewer of a city – and left the flat to a cold damp dark. I still called it a flat in my head to retain an internal victory over my brother. I had the keys but I was under vigorous instructions not to lose them. Roy told me that keys are like deeds of a house here, that there'd be rabid fury from the landlord if they went missing, that I was to watch them like they were my own children.

I headed for the port. There weren't many people walking. The smooth parts of the footpath were slippy underfoot so I made for the joins. Nearer the port, there were roadworks underway. It was a potential lawsuit of a footpath, all cracks and lumps. I walked along the edge of the water. It was all so doubled up: the pissings of rain from above, the lappings of water from below. The water came up quite high; it seemed as if a large boat could send a rogue wave lapping at my feet. I could hear clanks and thuds and metal grating on metal from the ships and cranes. The sounds reverberated inside me like a dulled MRI scan – they felt part of me, like they were coming in at my whole body. Roy hates when I say things like that to him; to say them aloud is a damage to his ears.

I stood and looked out at the lights across the water. Ports fascinate me – they have such a system to them: procedures in place, certain things that happen at certain times, crates to be delivered, lorries to collect, men to bring items from one place to another and load them onto different vessels. It must be nice to be part of a large chain of events, rather than paddling around lonesome in your own shallow pool. Ports also frecken me: the logistics of these massive enterprises; who oversees all the cogs? Twenty years ago, I went to college in Dublin and lived in digs near the port. When I returned from nights out in the small hours, I'd see lorries pulled in on quiet streets, the little curtains drawn across the cabins. It looked cosy, Bosco's-box kind of cosy and miniature, an exciting way to live a life.

I passed a sign for the Alter Elbtunnel. I liked the idea of a tunnel running under the river, and walking would give me a right sense of underneath. I followed the green dome and entered an arched door shaped like a giant cartoon mouse-hole. I was a giant mouse scurrying southwards. The building was grey-beige drab; it gave no indication of the magical underworld beneath. I paused to read the information sign. It feels as if I haven't visited a place properly, or *seen* it or *done* it, until I've read a piece of text explaining it. The sign said it cost ten million Goldmarks to build, and I was glad Goldmark was one word: it made me think of a very expensive greeting card or a gilt-rimmed birthmark.

Inside there were metal staircases and lifts and cranks and shafts and metal latticed balconies and an abiding sense of brown gloom. I decided to take the stairs, ignoring the screams from my knees; it's the down movement that's a killer. The second staircase was free-floating; it gave me an eerie feeling in the pit of my belly – my head was still at upper ground level, my body had plummeted down. If this was a James Bond film, the bad guy would be running down the free-standing staircase and Bond would slash it, the camera panning in on the bad guy's expression on the dangle before the fall. When I reached the bottom, my feet were relieved to be on the flat, my knees praised the gods, my stomach thanked the heavens. A sign said this was twenty-one metres under high water. *Hochwasser* is a lovely way of saying high water: it's like the surname of a sea king. I walked the tunnel, echoey, cosseted, and warmly dark with glazed carvings along the wall-sides. There were shells, fish, snakes, monstrously toothed fish, rats gnawing an old boot; I was glad they didn't sanitise the rivery goings-on. I came out the other side. I looked across the water and took in the city-span. I was next to the cruise ship *Aurora*, so big up close I'd be hard pressed to recognise the sum of its parts.

I passed shipyards and jetties and boats; I followed the river, or what I thought was the river, to a construction site but I got slightly misplaced. I tried to leave the site and find a canal to guide me, but I couldn't keep up with what bodies of water were natural or manmade and which one I should be following, so I made my way back to the tunnel. It was a relief to be on concrete again after losing my way among waterways.

After I was spat out from the tunnel, I sat for a bit. The phone call home had unspooled me a little. I'd rung home to check if everything was all right without me, hoping on one level that it was, hoping on another level that it wasn't quite all right. I felt like a plant that had been awkwardly repotted, or an instruction booklet for a device long since thrun out. Any mammy-shaped lack had been filled with fast food and fun. *What's wrong with you, Gert?* I thought. *You've wanted this for so long, to be able to trust that Allen's head is well enough to leave him with the kids for a few days. Now you have it would you cop on and enjoy it.* I shook my head and threw my body about a bit to ward off the dreads and raise a mood that had slung low. Times I live in my head and it takes over my legs and I rouse myself to find whole hours have passed while I've been on the mull. I'd want a slap in the face sometimes.

I looked around me and realised where I was with a start. This wouldn't do; my body shouldn't be in a foreign land while my head was stuck at home. I checked my phone. My house keys and work swipe card were still in my bag and it was a jolt to see things that were significant in my home life become completely useless here.

I got up out of my mullings and walked to a bridge. It was heaving with love locks and I read some of them, but it was like reading a very repetitive diary. Someone always loved someone and it was usually going to be forever. I left the bridge before the cynicism took hold of me. It was the first bluff of love that made Allen marry me, but if it was put to him that day twelve years ago what I'd be like today, I've no doubt he'd run like a man possessed. Which of us wouldn't? I ask you. What man would want to keep the woman who's seen him at his worst, when he could start afresh with someone who'd see him at his best? That's what I think was behind his flirtations with the sound woman. And when that wife has seen the unfunniest things behind the jokey exterior, well, who wouldn't be tempted by the fantasy identity? I don't believe it went beyond fantasy; and if it did, I'm not sure I'm best placed to judge.

As I walked away from the bridge, I noticed a woman standing very still near me. I'd thought she was looking at the love locks as well but she was looking some ways beyond them and then to either side. She was dressed in black with a short skirt – the kind of skirt that wouldn't look out of place at home on a weekend night, but here in a more casual city, and with sheeny tights, I could see she was looking for clients. I was the only other person around and I smiled at her. She gave a bit of a smile back. Hard to know what way to arrange your face when you feel sad for the thing the person has to do but you don't want to do them the condescension of pitying them. I walked on around souvenir shops that were closed. There was a large piece of graffiti on a faraway wall saying 'Kein Mensch ist illegal'. Strange how the bit of German from school comes back to you: *No person is illegal.* It's a grand sentiment, the kind of thing worth remembering, so I took out my camera for it. It didn't come out well in the picture – the light was too faded. Never mind, I don't need to show anyone, I just wanted to feel I'd remember it by making the effort to take a photo – and maybe months later when I got round to looking at the snaps, I'd remember what I was trying to capture. A group of tourists, fresh off a boat by the looks, turned to see what I was photographing and did likewise, fear of missing out getting the better of them. I kept an eye for more photographable German writings; I was holding out my hopes for a graffiti-ed FÜCK.

I was glad the tourists in Hamburg seemed to be mostly homegrown or Scandinavian. I begin to despise English-speaking tourists after a while. I have mixed feelings about tour groups – on the one hand I despise their flock approach; on the other I envy the amount they stuff into their schedules with no transport effort on their part.

I walked by homeless men, tucked into recesses of buildings, so neatly blue-bagged – the same colour sleeping bags as homeless people at home – and it saddened me that a country with a reputation for efficiency could have the same social horrors, couldn't just sort it out. If Roy lost his job and his apartment, there wouldn't be much between him and a doorway for a bed. I shook the thought out of my head and walked myself out of these gloomy thoughts.

Roy

Taschenwelt = pocket world

He knew Gert was out seeing the city, whatever she was seeing, so on his break he rushed back to the flat, knelt down in front of the wardrobe and opened the door. He wanted to check if she had discovered or disturbed his figurines; it was a risk letting her stay in his room, but he'd presumed she'd be too preoccupied to notice. He brushed aside the trousers and jackets he had hung to hide his goings-on and peeked in at his Wardrobe Wunderland. He had nothing new to add today, but he counted what was there: twenty-two figurines in total, thirteen men and nine women. Roy leaned in and arranged twenty-one of the miniature men and women in a circle, spaced out and hostile, putting one of the men in the middle of the circle. Some of the hands and fingers of the figurines were already pointed in accusation at the man in the middle, but when Roy tried to bend another miniature man's hand to organise his fingers, the fingers broke. He picked up the tiny broken fingers and smashed them to crumbs with the butt of his phone; it would be nice if you could smash human accusers in the same way. He left the crumbs in a finger-puddle at the miniature man's feet, closed the wardrobe door, and tore back to work.

Gert

Die Naschkatze = a cat that likes to eat sweets = sweet tooth

I walked back in the direction of Roy's flat. I couldn't coun-
tenance the idea of returning to that grim chunk of shared
brick, and I didn't want to interrupt Stefan's solo pleasures,
but I needed to get out of the rain. I seem to be always trying
to escape different weathers on holidays, getting out of either
the heat or the cold or the wet. Are we ever pleased? A bus
passed with the same number as the bus I used to get back
to my digs in Dublin; I felt the ache for home and a simpler
time in my life. Stop, I told myself again, stop drifting back
to the familiar and focus on the now.

Opposite the station where Roy met me my first night
there was a café. I went inside and said hello to the girl
behind the counter. She had the kind of serene, placid face
I wanted to goad into a reaction. It's times like this I feel
my foreignness worst. *Right slobbery day*, I wanted to say to
her, but where would I begin to find a translation for that?
There was no point in finding a translation for *It's raining
outside*; conversations aren't built by stating the bald obvious
in dictionary-bland words. Behind the counter, there were
steel tubs displaying a large assortment of ice creams in hot-
water-bottle colours. It wasn't ice-cream weather but I needed
to mark my holidays somehow, so I pointed to one.

'Erdbeeren,' I said. 'Bitte.'

Strawberry, I remembered from school; literally, earth-berry. If she had perfect English, this girl, I'd have asked her why they chose strawberry for earth-berry; surely they're all earth-berries because they all arise from the earth?

I paid for my ice cream and brought it to a seat by the window. From this angle I could watch people spewing in batches from the U-Bahn station. They entered in trickles and exited in spurts. It was a comfort to watch people go up and down the steps in great hurries – they all had such places to be, it felt like the world was sorted. People-watching is talked about as if it's a valid activity, but it's just pure nosi-ness, and I didn't think I was seeing the city right when I was watching it from behind glass with a spoon in my hand. I had a gnawing feeling that there was something I should be doing or something I should be getting out of my away-days that I wasn't. Like when I tried yoga once, for easing stress, and felt fury when I came out of it more stressed than I went in, trying to remember all the moves in the right order, bending myself into a stiff knot in an effort to get myself into the right position. All those classes I did trying to find the right hobby, all those ten-week stints in under- or over-heated rooms with other people either pretending you didn't exist or panting to be your best friend, and what did I come out of them with only an aversion to echoey school buildings at night.

I felt a gradual fret come on me. Something about the bare trees here gave me melancholy, and because I was only seeing the city in winter, it made me think Hamburg only ever experiences winter, a kind of German Narnia. When I'm on a hot-weather holiday, life grows convex. I feel heightened, expansive, reckless, like I could do anything, like I could take up a language; hell, like I could *make* up a language. But with Roy in northern Germany in the cold, I felt tightened into myself, huddled, reduced, cut to size. I acted the helpful big sister when I was around him, but alone, I retreated into myself. I was trying to exist somewhere outside of his stress and, lord, have I experience of that.

If Allen had had his way, in the worst of his illness, he'd be out. He'd have left the relationship, left the family, left home, left life, but I clung. I clung, not to the relationship or the need for his parenting involvement, such as they are, but to the past idea of him that could come back again. Those superhero films, the ones in franchises of threes and fours that are titled *XXX Returns*: that'll be Allen, I think; *Allen Returns*.

Before my world imploded with this thing, I had never thought beyond him. Before all this happened (but *happened* is such an inadequate verb; nothing has actually *happened*. Apart from hospital records of small-hours slashings, there is no real proof of anything having taken place, and so few know about it that it might as well not have happened), my mind circled around Allen and the kids. In a wider circle were friends and family, job, et cetera, but the inner circle was complete. No longer. A crack appeared in the join and I've had to pull back in order to keep going. When I realised that I wasn't the problem, that our relationship wasn't the problem, part of me emotionally opted out of it. He wants me in the trough with him, but I have to keep that bit of myself back to cope with the childcare and husband-care. To an onlooker, Allen seems well and we seem like a nice couple, but so much water has gushed under that bridge that our life is a pent-up tsunami. Though if you were to judge us from the words spoken and the behaviour currently exhibited, we seem fine.

Eventually, after a slew of counselling sessions pissing about with the mechanics of our relationship, it became clear

even to Allen that a deeper mental illness underlaid his dis-
content. He agreed to go to a doctor, which led to another
doctor, which led to a psychiatrist, which propelled us into a
regime of medicine and therapy.

(I've always preferred the word *medicine* to *medication* or
meds; *medicine* sounds like it's for a short-term, curable condition, like a teaspoon of Calpol setting the kids to rights;
medication sounds long-term and indefinite; meds has a familiarity, a suggestion of long-term dependence, that daunts me.)

In the two bouts we've had – although *bout* implies a bed-
bound burst of flu that lasts a week rather than a year-long
grapple with an unseen all-impinging gargoyle – anti-depres-
sants have operated slowly. I hadn't realised that when you
have the right medicine in the right dosage to treat one batch
of mental illness, the same medicine in the same dosage won't
go near the next batch of depression a year on, like a different
strain of flu not responding to the previous year's vaccine.

In the public health service, you see many different psychiatrists. None of the tilted head-nodding and soft-voiced
schmooze of private health care; these public medics don't
need to purchase your sickness to fund their golf member-
ships. They are stiffed by the clock; they have only minutes
to burrow inside a patient's head and retrieve a square-shaped
diagnosis to fit into a small box on a file. He's in The System,
I was told. There's no need to worry. The System, turns out, is
a *fight fight fight* tooth and claw to get to see a public psychiatrist every month or so.

If private psychiatric care is within your financial capabilities, and private stays in carpeted psychiatric hospitals,
your mental illness will run a softer path, your experience
will be gentle with slippers. If it isn't, you may go to hell in
a sidecar. I wished that I'd had the balls to bullshit my way

up a profession, any profession, to a rung that would have tipped us into the middle class and given us the trappings that many people don't realise are extras. If we could afford decent health insurance and had the disposable income for several-hundred-euro-an-hour psychiatrists, Allen's slide downwards would at least be coated in fleece not outlined in steel. His hospital stay was the pits, not just unhelpful but from an entirely different dictionary to the word *helpful.* They're saints, we hear, the overburdened medical staff in public psychiatric hospitals, and so they are – but even saints cannot perform miracles in wards rammed to the ceilings with the sickest of patients. And if the system fails the sick person, it sure as hell fails the well, left to provide care we're unqualified to deliver.

Financially, Allen and I are one big sob story. Together, we earn just enough to put us over the threshold of qualifying for medical assistance from the state, and that's when I start to hate. Hate wealthy people not for their cushioning but for their wilful obliviousness to their cushioning, the convenient explanation of positive attitude and hard work to explain wealth and success when inherited connections and purchased opportunities are forgotten. I hate politicians for their assumption that everyone has a bank account full of savings that will take care of eventualities. Allen's life in recent years has been such an eventuality. Times I favour the ostrich policy, head in sand, *ignore ignore ignore.*

Anyway, there were lots of diagnoses. At times, the medics seemed more intent on naming the problem than fixing it. In the beginning, I went along. I thought: in order to kill the beast you have to name it, and this could be the way out. I had no words for what was happening; I didn't know what to call this thing.

But when too many labels were handwritten into forms to be typed up later and slotted into files, the misnaming became more of a problem than the thing they were trying to name. Depending on the day, his mood, whether he was pre- or post-episode, low or high, he was variously diagnosed with: borderline personality disorder, major depression, mild depression, moderate depression, manic depression, bipolar disorder, schizophrenia.

Some of these conditions overlapped; some were new names for known illnesses; some were original. Few were helpful. I turned to the internet every time we had a new diagnosis. He would invariably fall under some of the symptoms of that disorder, but not others. I didn't know where that left us. If he had fallen cleanly under one diagnosis, he might have a better chance of getting the right treatment.

Fortunately, in the way of these things, my life those years wasn't so much a shitstorm as a constant slurry-stream of problems. No sooner had I convinced Allen to see a doctor and he'd righted himself with drugs and counselling, no sooner had we attained some level of stability, than the Roy trouble started. If they knew Roy, if they only knew my infuriating irritant of a brother, they'd know what way that friendship went and wouldn't have suspected worse of him. I chose to believe my brother, I believed him, I did, but with so much having gone on at home I couldn't take another tense relationship. More doubt was something I could not bring myself to handle.

I forced my mind back to the present and ate some ice cream, drawing out each spoonful as long as I could. I looked up the names of berries on my phone to see why strawberries are earth-berries, to keep me someway tethered to the present with trivial facts. When I typed in German, *Erdbeere*, I saw a list of berries with their German translations, including ones I was less familiar with: *chokeberries* and *cowberries*, *cloudberries* and *bunchberries*, *farkleberries* and *thimbleberries*, *salmonberries*, *wineberries*, and *dewberries*. The word dewberry brought back the smell of the nineties to me. My first perfume was a cheap Body Shop dewberry scent but it smelt like sophistication to me. I sprayed it all over myself before dances – the bedroom I shared with Gráinne would be reeking of dewberry and smoke for days after. We had a power of fun getting ourselves ready, but Roy never came to the dances with us; he'd stay in his room and shout through his bedroom door that he'd better things to be doing than flailing his limbs around in order to lure a mate. He made us out to be animals, myself and Gráinne; feral creatures functioning heedless, driven by base urges.

I looked around the café. There was one woman sitting reading in the corner. I was glad I wasn't the only one left in the place; if it was just me and the girl who worked there, it would be like a small dinner party with a counter between us. Another customer came in for a takeaway coffee. The harsh rasp of the coffee-maker sounded like a hoarse robot hawking up phlegm.

I looked again at the German berry translations on my phone. It was daft to be studying German words for berries I didn't even know in English when the words for *Can I have the bill, please?* would be more useful. I gave up and put my phone away. The café seemed to be about to close for the evening; the girl behind the counter was covering the ice cream. I got up slowly and said goodbye. Then I walked to Roy's flat. You'd be hard pushed to call it home.

In the flat, I checked my watch, remembering to add an hour to the Irish wrist-time. Roy would get out of work soon; if I went to meet him I'd feel useful and necessary. We were going to a local sauna that night so I'd save him going home first. I brought my swimsuit and picked up his bag – packed perfectly with hours to spare – and left the flat. Roy came out of work looking forlorn and not as pleased to see me as I'd have liked.

'Hey,' I said.

'Hey.'

'I walked the Elbtunnel today.'

'Oh.' The tone was flat, not a hint of a question mark.

'Have you been there?'

'No,' he said. 'It was going to be a suspended railway but they made a tunnel instead. I can't agree with that.'

'So you're boycotting a tunnel because it isn't a railway?'

'I'm not boycotting, I just don't want to go.'

'Jesus, Roy, I've never heard of anyone sulking at a tunnel before.'

We went back to silence; it was our natural habitat by now. As usual, I cracked first.

'You should have seen it, Roy, it's like something from a Bond movie – it'd be ideal for a chase scene.'

'You say that about everywhere you visit, Gert. They should hire you to scout locations around the world.'

He's a canny fucker – he syruped the barb with a low-flying compliment I couldn't get pissy about. I did what I always do, with Allen, with Roy, with the kids, with my patients. I took the topic to neutral territory, never mind my sore feelings. 'So, the sauna then – have you been before?'

'No, I looked at it from the outside but I've never been in.'

Could be Roy's life motto, I could have it etched on his gravestone. He led us down a side street and into a nondescript building. If he hadn't showed me, I wouldn't have remarked it, the sauna was that hidden. We were handed towels at reception, and then we separated and I headed to the ladies' changing room. Well, if I wasn't mithered by German before this … Not being able to read the signs about clothing put an almighty confusion into me. Some baths you were meant to be naked, others you had to wear togs, some you had to bring towels, others you had to leave towels outside, some were mixed-sex, others were not. The confusion was immense. I was shouted at and stared at and I inadvertently flashed my bits at Roy when I opened a door to the pool in me nuddy. Good lord, any relaxation that was supposed to be happening backfired hugely; I was sweating German signs by the time I left. Swimming in the pool, then, I wondered the etiquette of it: when myself and Roy were breast-stroking away up and down the pool and seeing each other every length, should we acknowledge one another or ignore? There was nothing new to say. Roy didn't seem to have this dilemma: he just stared straight ahead of him as if I was a stranger. Maybe I could learn from him; maybe there is nothing to be gained from talking and circuiting endless words in loops and gaining no new mouth-hold.

When I did get the right togs and towel combination and was sitting comfortably in a steam room with Roy, I snuck a peek at him. He was wearing baggy shorts down almost to his knees – definitely not togs but I understand the fear of going full-flesh with your familiars. Strange seeing your adult brother with no shirt on; I hadn't seen it since we were children. We sat parallel and stared straight ahead.

'Your feet,' he said.

'What about my feet?' I stretched out my legs and wriggled my toes. They're the feature I like best, or maybe I hate least; everyone's feet are ugly so it levels the playing field when mine aren't disproportionately so.

'They're like old tree roots, the kind of roots that spread and take over the garden.'

'Fuck's sake, Roy,' I said, 'yours aren't exactly works of art.'

He stretched out his legs and shrugged his shoulders. 'I never said tree roots are a bad thing. Actually, I think they're aesthetically pleasing.'

A compliment so far hidden it could easily be overlooked; I'd take it. I sneaked a look at him. He was sitting with his eyes closed and I was desperate to know which way his thinking went. This would be a good way for a Bond villain to die, trapped in a steam room with the steam being turned up, a face pressed up against the door slowly slumping down. But maybe I've seen this done, maybe my murder methods are derivative. I opened my mouth to say it to Roy but I'd already been chastised for mentioning Bond movies and I didn't want to be accused of being unoriginal twice in one day.

The steam was clouding and fuzzing around our ears and it felt cosseting and safe. I prefer the damp, swampy heat of the steam room to the dry heat of the sauna, but I'm heat-happy either way. My spit felt cool in my mouth compared to the heat outside, like when you're about to vomit. I thrun a look at him and his face was the closest I've seen to relaxed.

'Are you happy here, Roy?'

'What's happy?' he replied, pushing the toes of one foot into the ankle of the other.

'Happy like content, happy like wanting to stay a while.'

He changed position, dug the toe of the other foot into the wall. 'I didn't think I had a choice.' The tone was defeated, the look of him hunted.

'We'd agreed you'd lie low here for a year or so, till the rumours ebbed at home.'

He shrugged. 'Whatever. You're the one who organised this.'

'Yes, Roy, yes, I fucking well did because nobody else was stepping up, were they? What other plans did you have?'

He shrank and shrivelled back into himself, his bare shoulders curling inwards. I closed my eyes and tried to calm myself. *One potato, two potato, three potato, four.* What fucking use being in a sauna if your heartrate is rising from stress and not heat.

'I'm not looking for thanks but could you stop with the attitude? I'm just trying to find out what it is that you want.'

He shrugged again. 'Here is fine.'

'And would you like to stay here?'

'Yeah, I suppose.'

I gave up then. Here was a stonewall I couldn't smash. I'd need to chip, chip away like a needy rodent. I stared straight ahead but soon I could feel him sneaking glances at me. 'What? What are you looking at?'

'You look like you're going to keel over – your face is cruel red.'

'Fuck off, Roy, you're not exactly looking fresh yourself.'

But he has added to my vexation. I wish I was one of those women who looked like they belonged in watery surrounds – part mermaid, part Bond girl – or even just someone the make-up women at department-store counters wouldn't ignore. I wish I was one of those women who could just sort it out.

DAY 3

DAY 3

Roy

Wurzellosigkeit = rootlessness

This morning's cleaning patch was the airport, Knuffingen Flughafen. Roy liked the German way of starting their nouns with capital letters, and he liked the old historical English documents that capitalised the first letters of nouns and adjectives and some verbs too. He'd never got a hold of the reasoning behind which words were capped and which weren't, but it seemed like a Shout from Another Century. Occasionally, he passed the same homeless man begging near the station, his handwritten cardboard sign read *Ich habe Hunger*. Roy admired that attention to detail; regardless of the man's predicament he still capped his nouns.

No sign of Inge today. He checked the rota. She was in Bayern – he might see her on the way to Knuffingen. The airport, with its miniature planes taking off and landing, was the top attraction for most visitors, especially the men. When the visitors were from somewhere outside of the European continent, somewhere you had to fly from, he wanted to point out the strangeness to them of spending hours in an airport and on a plane only to pay to look at the same thing in miniature at their destination.

The number of photos people took was astonishing. He hadn't yet grown accustomed to it. Roy's thoughts veered unpleasant;

he despised amateur photographers – what would they *do* with all their images? He couldn't understand what people were looking *at*, looking *for*, through their phones or cameras. Did their lenses have a kaleidoscope or a carnival mirror that meant they saw something more interesting than he saw? He reserved his absolute contempt for those who took photos of him as he worked, some with hushed squeals of 'Look, the janitor', as if he was a rarely spotted creature in his natural habitat being photographed for a David Attenborough documentary.

Roy held no truck with the plane-spotters – the most interesting parts of Knuffingen for him were the secret tunnels and dungeons under the airport which held all sorts of strange things. He took a yellow cloth and glass cleaner from his bucket, crouched down on his hunkers, and began to clean the glass panels in front of the scenes where miniature figurines went about their magical business. An elephant pulled a block of stone, a man rode on a dinosaur's back, a giant meerkat (twice as big as the elephant) stood watching. The proportion was so thoroughly skewed it was hard for Roy to keep his bearings. When he'd wiped off the last of the cleaning spray and got up a blinding shine, he moved onto the next panel. Miniature figurines were painting the wood of a large paintbrush in different colours while others chopped it. Roy liked the idea of painting a paintbrush: it would be like cleaning a mop or feeding a fork, an activity doubled. He sprayed that panel and imagined himself small as a figurine: perfectly still, unseeing, unthinking, placed in position and told how to act; it seemed an accurate representation of how this version of life was being lived for him.

He straightened up, his thighs grumbling from the first heave, and ran his duster over the runways and a parked plane with miniature passenger faces inside. They looked so hopeful;

and they *were* hopeful – they were just about to go on their holidays. Things never ended well; didn't they know that? Whenever he saw a family in a car with a Christmas tree tied to the roof, it boiled him up something vengeful – the sheer guileless, gullible, *stupid* hope that things would work out. The things you thought could never happen often did happen, and not the kind of lottery-winning, fortune-inheriting kind of things – the worst things you could imagine were shouted at you by teenagers and then put to you by your sister in brute law-speak before she had you banished and there was nothing you could do. Roy had come to realise that the problem you think you have is mostly not the biggest one you have, that when you take your eye off the general nature of things, another problem announces itself – like when you've done too much hobbling on a gammy ankle and the hips swell up in protest.

Gert had asked him if he was happy here, the kind of question that missed the point so thoroughly it was hard to know how to even counter it. Happy was something for other people; he aimed for getting through and trying to forget. He aimed at not thinking beyond the Wunderland: this was where he could send his energies. Gert's asking him about his plans had made him see how perilously temporary this whole set-up was – everything could dissolve in a miniature heartbeat.

He shook himself and leaned over the bar to the nearest plane but it was just out of reach. He moved to the opposite end, reached in, and grabbed a China Eastern plane. This was a big one; it would bring maximum fatalities. The plane wasn't glued as so many of the figurines were – it was supposed to move when everything was in motion. *Taxiing*, that was the word, the plane would taxi down the runway. Why did some things have to layer confusion? To say a plane taxis is like saying a bus planes or a lorry ships.

The plane tipped over onto one side and he picked it up by the nearest wing, like a boomerang or the neck of a bottle. He looked over his shoulder to make sure no one was watching and smashed the nose of the plane into the ground twice, hard. He smashed it again and again until it could balance on its sunken nose. Then he replaced the plane on the nearest runway, nose-down, arse in the air. The miniature passengers were held in place, suspended by glue, their expressions still happy as if they didn't realise they were in trouble, gormless fools that they were. Didn't they know that happiness was the fleetingest thing, that it was the most foolish state to be in, that they could only be brought low?

Roy considered the different lands in the Wunderland, trying to remember where the miniature emergency services were. Miniature Hamburg had a major fire, with lots of firemen and illuminated hoses. He walked quickly through Austria and Mittel Deutschland, nodding at the older lady cleaning there, wondering if people who lived in the Irish midlands would prefer to live in Middle Ireland, which sounded like a different time period. The lady didn't seem to have any English so he knew he was safe from questions. He walked slowly into miniature Hamburg, looking out for any cleaners, but there was nobody around. He made his way to the building near the port which was surrounded by firemen. Several fire engines were connected to the road by magnets, and he picked up two. Then he dislodged two firemen with hoses – any more and they might be missed – and slipped them into his pocket.

He walked quickly back to the miniature airport and set the fire engines and the firemen around the crash site. The runways were large and flat and easy to clean, but the work was dull and he hurried on to the multi-storey car parks. He flicked the duster around some people racing their luggage trolleys. One miniature woman looked particularly happy with herself – she seemed convinced she was going to win – so he gave her a couple of thunks with his duster to floor her. Her feet didn't come unstuck, so she lay footless next to her trolley, her two feet standing beside it as if they had the power to push it themselves. He picked up her footless body and pocketed it.

His favourite scene was a group of punks arguing with a skinhead while an enormous bird stood in the skinhead's open-top car. Roy wondered whether the skinhead had stolen the bird from the punks or whether they objected to the skinhead's treatment of the bird or whether the bird had anything to do at all with their argument. He liked observing tension in miniature; it made his life-size awkwardness more bearable. He moved onto the town of Knuffingen. This was a completely imaginary land. He wasn't sure which he admired more: the invention of a country from scratch or the insertion of magic into cities and countries that had already been invented, whether greater creativity was involved in creating from nothing or adjusting the mundane to the magic.

He cleaned a wild boar peeking in at a boy on the toilet in a hut in the forest, wondering if you could accuse an animal of perversion, then grabbed the boar and punched its miniature snout a few times before pocketing it. He ran the duster over two monks leering at a woman in a miniskirt bending over a car. The same monks cropped up in other lands, leching away at various miniature females. He tore a feather from the duster and licked his finger, then he slicked the feather onto the mini-skirted miniature, shielding her from the monkish gaze. As he pulled up the monks, their feet came away from the glue. Either they hadn't been glued down properly or they were pulling themselves unstuck to prepare for the Rapture.

Roy turned them around, so they were facing away from the girl, and moved on to dust a palace with a maze in front. He scrabbled around in his bucket and came up with a bottle of cream cleaner. It was white and gloopy and could be dripped from the bottle. He unscrewed the lid and carefully, carefully, held the bottle over the maze and dripped the escape route in cream cleaner onto the fake grass. Good, it wasn't soaking in – now the figurines could find their way out.

In a river that flowed with real water, a blue P sign floated along with a mermaid. A bride sat alone on a rock, maybe a jilted one or a widow-bride looking for her lost love. A car was being winched from the river – who knows what kind of calamity had befallen it. *Winch* was a fine multipurpose word, because where there was winching there was probably also an injured person wincing. He looked in the water for bodies – none – and poked at the car, pulled the winch until the car plopped into the water and slowly sank.

He ran his duster over more mundane miniature activities and items. Roy liked the satellite dishes on the houses – even miniature people liked to watch miniature programmes from miniature satellite. A man was painting a naked woman – and there! The same two monks were watching – watching the man painting the woman or watching the woman, he wasn't sure which. It seemed like a chain of perversity and Roy didn't know who to blame: the woman for posing (surely she could see the monks?), the man for drawing her, or the monks for watching it all. Or should his ire be directed all the way back to the creators of the figurines, the life-size people he worked alongside? He looked at his duster; he'd be all out of feathers if he kept covering the figurines' modesty with them, so he leaned in, picked up the woman, and tossed her into the river. She landed face-up and, worse, tits-up, so he turned her over and put her under the car he had thrown in. Now the monks were watching a man paint a naked woman from his imagination, which wasn't quite so bad, but even still, he pulled feathers from his duster, licked them, and put them over the eyes of the monks. 'Monk see no evil,' he muttered, and it felt good. It felt good to speak aloud into the neon silence words that made sense only to him. There was too much spying being done, prissing and peeking and poking in on other people's lives. That was bad enough but it was the part that came after, the assumptions made based on all the spying, that really spoiled things. Didn't people know enough to know that they didn't know anything about what went on in private? Why was it that people thought they were speaking truths about happiness and feelings but they hadn't the courage to deal with facts and realities? Roy scrubbed the metal bar surrounding the exhibit until it shone with mirrored fury, and when that wasn't enough, he sprayed some polish on a cloth and scrubbed the fake grass until it clumped and uprooted, the landscape looking like the aftermath of a climactic tumult.

Gert

Fingerspitzengefühl = fingertip feeling = tactfulness,
an intuitive flair

He came out of the Wunderland with a sour expression on him. If I was my mother I'd be saying 'Take that puss off you', but I try not to turn into her with the same words in the same contexts. I catch myself doing it with the children especially, using expressions I thought were long dead from disuse until they emerge in a conniption.

'How was work?'

I could have slapped myself for asking. It's the same thing I ask Allen every day he comes home. Sometimes I wonder if there's anything new to say in the world, any new way of asking the same thing that has been asked for centuries, and if there was, wouldn't it be cheaper than marriage counselling.

'Fine,' he said, and we walked slowly.

I suppressed the urge to pester him with questions. His mood goes up like a cloud and down like a brick, a plum that goes unripe to rotten without ever being sweet, no matter the 'Ripen at home' promise on the supermarket label. He's like a particularly moody teenager, or one of the more cantankerous patients in my nursing home, making things difficult for the sheer sake of it. I've one patient, Monica, who takes delight in mimicking every word I say, every word all the carers say. She does it with the skill of a child and it's out of pure badness. You start talking and she follows, one word behind you – a great skill it is to be able to listen for the next word while you're saying the previous one, smile on her like a burnt turkey.

'Where will we go to today?' I asked.

'Into the city,' he said, 'we can go to the art gallery.'

'Great.' I didn't want to add too many syllables that would frighten him like a coloured rag in front of a horse, but I was glad that this art gallery was in the Top Ten Sights in the guidebook. We walked to the U-Bahn, the same station he'd picked me up from, the same station I was watching faces from the previous night. I watched the faces closely again but no sign of any overlap. We stood on the platform to wait, and because there were no words between us, I smiled as pleasantly as I could to show people this was a comfortable silence. The silence continued when the train came and I gripped my lips tight together to prevent me making some inane comment like *Isn't it great the way the trains come on time* or *Nice to get a seat, isn't it.* Working with senile people has me reduced to remarks on the physical here and now.

I sat opposite Roy and we both looked out the window. There were lots of cranes and I began to wonder what was being built but I stopped myself. Such curiosity is pointless; it's not relevant to me what they'll build after I leave. It was hot on the train and the seat must have had a heater under it because my arse was boiled. At the next stop, a man with a dog sat beside Roy. The dog was small and portly with a squashed face, the kind you can't help but smile at, but Roy looked on it with disdain. I felt mildly grateful that I wasn't the only disdained creature in his mind.

The silence grew and I didn't want to fill it with asking how many stops we were going because that would no doubt be construed as needless communication. I was feeling more and more uncomfortable, and even though I likely would never see these passengers again in my life, I wanted them to know there was no badness between us, no fight, this is just how Roy is. It reminded me of an argument I'd had with Allen before bed recently, a hissed argument while the kids were asleep, about something small that grew larger and more important with each hiss. He was well enough in his head that I felt able to argue as equals, without holding fire to protect him as I usually do. But when he played me back to myself, I was shocked at how hideous I was in his words, which sat with me like a tea-scald on the roof of my mouth. He didn't see the tiptoeing, eggshell-treading, tenterhooking I was doing around his moods or his perceived moods: he saw only my lack. When it came time to sleep, we pulled away from each other. I hadn't known a double bed could feel so wide. Roy, sitting opposite me, had his feet pulled in as far from mine as possible, his arms folded across his chest, his body turned towards the window, a similar study in standoffishness.

When he shifted his legs outwards, I knew it was time to get off. I'd become adept over the years at reading his smallest movements and predicting his next actions, at reading the movements of Allen and the kids and predicting *their* next actions, preparing for them unthanked. We left the main train station and crossed the road to the art gallery. We paid for our tickets and started to walk in, but a woman behind the desk called me back.

'Excuse me,' she said in English.

'Yes?'

'Your bag is too big.'

I stared at my bag. It was a shoulder bag, smaller than a rucksack.

'It must be within the A4 limits,' she said, picking up an A4-sized sign and pointing at it.

I gave her the bag and took a tag. I went to join Roy. His lips were pursed together.

'Jesus, that's a bit finicky, isn't it?' I said.

'They're the rules,' he said. 'She's just following the rules.'

He walked on slightly ahead of me. The Roy of our childhood would have sniggered and mocked authority figures along with me and Gráinne, but there was always a side to him that relished seeing someone caught out by a teacher in school. He'd stop just short of ratting you out but the urge would be there. Roy shuffled through the metal detector with the air of a man with something to hide, a look on him like the breath of an apology.

We wandered through an exhibition of clothes that I had no real interest in, then onto some paintings. Some of the text describing the exhibits was also translated into English and I found myself drawn to the pieces with chunks of English text beside them, but I was so busy reading the text I sometimes forgot to look at the exhibits themselves. What was this desperation for familiar words, the frantic hunt for an explanation of the exhibit, the relief when there were English translations of the text, when it's words I should be getting away from?

There was a painting of a group of people tightly huddled together watching something or someone, and I couldn't help wondering how the people in the middle would get to the toilet if they needed to go – too much experience of small bladders in the back seat of the car has sent my brain down that direction.

'Roy, how do characters in action movies go to the toilet – on chases, when do they stop to eat and do the necessary?'

He looked at me like I'd stopped Christmas.

'Never mind,' I said and walked on, past another picture that looked so natural it was like it came with the canvas. I led the way to the exhibition Roy wanted to see, by an artist who makes microscopic sculptures on the head of a pin or the eye of a needle. There were benches set up in a room with microscopes, like a science lab. I walked up to the first microscope and looked down. Inside *Weiße Katze*, a white cat was perched on the head of a pin. It was astoundingly small, so finely wrought and unmistakably a cat, yet when I tore my eyes from the lens and tried looking with my bare eyes, I could only see a small blur on a pin. The sheer enchantment of it. I looked over at Roy. He was looking through the microscope beside me, and when he emerged from his miniature world, there was a look on his face of pure something – happiness, maybe? No, too simple, it was more an ease with the world that I'd never seen before. Hell, I'd barely seen him smile since he was a child.

'Magic, isn't it?' I whispered, afraid of breaking the spell.

'Magic,' he said, but when he met my eye, his expression returned to commonality.

'Swap,' I said, and we changed places. I looked through the lens at a female hand grasping for a male finger in the eye of a needle. It was so exquisitely, ferociously perfect, it almost made me dizzy. I liked *Wippe* best, two girls on a seesaw in the eye of a needle. *Aschenputtel* – a wonderful word for Cinderella – and her three ugly sisters fit into the eye of another needle. If I had eggs enough for another child, Aschenputtel would be a great name for it, but maybe it wouldn't be the best set-up if they thought they'd have to skivvy for the rest of the family. My child-bearing days were probably over, but if I was to go again, I'd like to have a child in May and call her June if she was late hatching, or April if she was early, or November if she looked particularly glum. But screwing with people's expectations might not be a good enough reason for naming your child.

It almost made me weep, these crazily perfect tiny worlds, existing alone in and of themselves, but who knew what happened when the lights went down. In the next room, there were famous buildings on pinheads – the White House, the Taj Mahal, the Colosseum; postcard buildings. In another needle eye stood a polar bear on a melted block of ice, the emblem of our global warming shame. My children have been so brainwashed by that bear that every time I leave the tap running for a few seconds, Hazel will dramatically run to turn it off shouting 'Mum, the *polar bear*'. How is it that the humans you bore inside you can make you feel the worst inside? When I heard on a nature programme that two-thirds of the world's polar bears would be gone by 2050, I calculated what age I'd be because only then was it relevant to me: the ego of me, surely that's the selfish attitude that has cocked up the world six ways from Christmas.

I haven't figured out how to shield my children from the worst of the world but still let them know how lucky they are; I haven't found the balance. I've erred into compensating for home stress with more and more stuff, games and clothes. I've likely given them too much ease. Ruination, my parents call it. My kids think grapes grow seedless and fish swim boneless – I want life's easier things for them but I'd like them to know how good they have it. Why, though? Is there a touch of the heroic martyr to that – the need to have them know their life is good because I made it so?

A poster on the wall gave the life story of the artist, Willard Wigan. If you're an artist, it's a good thing to have such a catchy name. He apparently uses an eyelash for a paintbrush and a diamond splinter for a chisel. The poster says he does the delicate work 'in the one and a half seconds between two heartbeats, the pulse in his finger he uses like a jackhammer'. This control of the body fascinates me, this superhuman slog to make minuscule worlds, and for what? According to the text, since he inhaled Alice in Wonderland by mistake, he also controls his breathing, calling this process 'dead man working'. Christ, Willard. The poster said he had dyslexia as a child and withdrew into his own world, starting with building housing for ants, furniture, and equipment. Roy never had dyslexia, or any other known condition, he just withdrew. Myself and Gráinne have memories of him engaging with us as young kids, but somewhere along the way he lapsed into himself and he hasn't found his way out again. This business of the friendship with the child, I don't think there was anything sinister to it. I believe Roy found a friend with a similar obsession with trains and he latched on, a bit too keenly, to this lad who was on some kind of emotional parity with him. All the fuss that caused, what twisted nonsense. Other people's expectations were a lot more sordid than the truth of it. The lad himself saw no problem with the friendship, his parents weren't worried – it was just empty gossip that wouldn't lie down. Times I wake in the ice-quiet early hours with a gnaw of a what-if, but I quell it quick with a hush now, don't be daft, it's all fine, of course he's innocent. He's a fuck-up of a brother, a cock-up of a human, but he's not *that*, and seeing him accused of that makes me feel protective and defensive, both of which Roy would object to.

I started; I felt movement beside me. Since having children, my antennae are on hyper-alert for the presence of others. When Hazel or Benjy tiptoes into my bedroom with a bad dream that needs swatting away or a thirst that needs slaking, I can sense their small needs before they say anything, while Allen sleeps bear-like beside me. Roy was now standing beside me, reading the biography.

'Wow,' I said, 'small enough for you?'

He looked perplexed.

'It's just a phrase,' I said. 'You know, like "Cold enough for you?" when it's cold out.'

'I understand it, I just don't know why you'd say it.'

I sighed. I understood how Cain felt, maybe Abel was a nit-picking pedant of a brother. He draws me back inside, Roy does. What's the point in speaking words when they're sent back to you with red pen all over them? I felt patronised and misunderstood, like when they put subtitles on a person with an accent in a TV documentary.

I walked on through the gallery alone, stopping at small things that interested me or large things that were only of interest because they were large. When I'd had enough, I left through heavy glass doors and headed into the gift shop. Such pretty things laid out so nicely, but I have so many pretty things laid out so clumsily in my house that adding more belongings won't improve the look. I sat on a bench outside the shop and waited for Roy, next to a rack of free postcards and brochures of tourist attractions. There was a time when I would have swivelled the stand to its limits, gathering one or more of each item, stashing them in my bag. That was when I thought time was infinite, that there would be opportunities to do all the things advertised to do in the world. I shut my eyes. The voices were echoed and reverentially hushed, and I imagined I was in an ancient cathedral. No sign of my brother yet. It was daft to depart speaking terms with someone who wouldn't even notice, but I wouldn't ring Roy, I'd let him come find me. I'd let him start conversations or prolong them but I wouldn't let him finish them.

Roy

Heimweh = home woe = homesickness

This evening's task was to clean the historical dioramas, the part of the Wunderland he identified with most. This was the overshadowed section that only the truly nerdy spent any amount of time in; most of the visitors were pulled harder to the glamour of the trains and magic. There were enormous quantities of facts piled into miniature scenes in Perspex boxes, no screwing with history or proportion that he could see. He could only get part-ways in to polish up half a shine while the visitors were around, but he'd get rightly in when they'd gone. Roy picked up his cloth and sprayed some glass cleaner on it, then started on the Neolithic diorama. It frustrated him that he couldn't get at the figurines – he could do with some of them for his Wardrobe Wunderland. In the Neolithic diorama, there was a scene with 'delinquent members' who'd offended the community being banished across the ford into impenetrable forests. Roy took up a fit of the shivers – there was something so lost and lonely looking about the banished figurines. The punishment seemed unduly harsh, and try as he might, close as he looked, Roy could not make out from the scene what it was the exiled figurines had done, or were said to have done. He gave their side of the glass an extra-gentle polishing and moved on to shine the Early Middle Ages diorama, fascinated by the scenes of torture and violence, interspersed with endless scenes of varied hard labour. This was the grim cousin of the Wunderland and Roy approved of it. There was more honesty in hard work and pestilence than unearned leisure and fun. He gave a quick swipe to the Late Middle Ages box, which seemed to show scenes of endless plague deaths and general religiosity, then he moved onto the Baroque period scenes with their hangings and violence. He heard footsteps and looked around. Inge stood watching him, a sly-curious expression on her face.

'How are you, Roy?'

'Grand, thanks – I mean, good.' *Grand* didn't translate so well; *good* worked better, even if it didn't suit his mouth.

'I saw you with a woman yesterday?'

'It's my sister, she's visiting.'

'Oh, I didn't know you had a sister.'

'I have two.'

'How lovely she came to see you. Is she staying long?'

'A few days.'

Inge nodded. 'Are you having fun with her?'

Roy shrugged. 'She eats a lot. And she wants to talk a lot.'

Inge laughed. 'And that bothers you?'

Roy stared at her. If it wasn't already obvious that these things were irritants, there was no point continuing the conversation. He held up his cloth and said, 'Well, better get back to it,' and Inge waved and walked off.

He quickly cleaned the Perspex surrounding the boxes up to the twentieth century, plentiful scenes of disease and violence and unrest, followed by an early twentieth-century box of depression, poverty, and war. The last one covered 1933–1942 – well, if the previous ones weren't bleak enough, this was the start of it all going so terribly, terribly wrong. Roy sprayed and shone, sprayed and shone, hard as he could, as if sheer brute strength could undo what had happened and redo history the right way. It was utterly incongruous but he liked the sight of the leisure boat sailing down a river, with passengers militantly sunning themselves on deck, ignoring the horror around. He had learned from the headphoned information on his induction to the Miniatur Wunderland that this was a *Kraft durch Freude* (strength through joy) boat, making middle-class pursuits available to the masses. Roy approved of their determination to ignore their awful surroundings and put all their focus into pursuing leisure; there were times when no amount of dealing with the current situation was helpful and the best you could do was ignore it.

Gert

Mutterseelenallein = *mother souls alone* = *extreme loneliness*

I was that tired after dealing with Roy in the gallery that I couldn't leave the flat after he left for his second shift. He'd been acting odd, even by his standards, hovering in my room and sidling along the wall to the wardrobe, but when I'd asked him if he wanted something, he'd scuttled out muttering to himself. I took to the bed, to hell with this holiday. Shocking waste of an evening, but when the mood plunges so low there's no hope of recovering it, you're best placed to indulge it. I ate some toast standing up in the kitchen and wrote a note for Roy that I had a migraine and was in bed. Nothing spooks my brother more than a woman with a medical problem; he'd stay as far from the bedroom as he could. I'd left the evening's entertainment for him to plan and I knew he'd be relieved he wouldn't have to think of something and then do it with me. I gathered myself under the covers, willing sleep to come on. Hard to go from one house you're not entirely wanted to another; how did it come to this? The minutes became hours became insomnia and I was no sleepier than I was when I first went to bed.

Here's how to sleep: a hot bath, warm milk, warm bath, hot milk, lavender salts, lavender oil, Epsom salts, gentle exercise, camomile tea (hot), cool bedroom, warm bed. It's all in the heat-related adjectives – this thing must be cool, this must be warm, this must be hot. Then you've to put your screens away and write down your worries – but what if your worries take up so many pages and set you aweeping so deeply that sleep is a long time fetched? When you're not sleeping because of stress, it's not the quality of the sleep that counts, it's the act of sleeping, or the non-act of sleeping, a time of unconsciousness, of not thinking, not having to think or act or decide. My fantasy these times is an induced coma, a voluntary unconsciousness; when I wake up it will all be OK.

Sometimes I feel so lonely I want to fling myself bodily into a crowd just to feel a connection. The only person I bother with the story of Allen's depression is Gráinne, and only with the sheerest of facts. I need her to know for practical purposes, to take the kids at short notice when things get bad. There are things the people closest to you should never be told, to protect their night-sleeps. Even before Roy's troubles emerged, he would have been useless. He can't handle imperfect realities that might require something more of him. Mam and Dad were too old to be given worry about something that may never happen. They know Allen's a bit quiet in himself on some visits, but we say that's down to his long work hours, little telling the work is in keeping him from the rope. They might think he's selfish for not showing up at every family event, or, if he does show up, not sinking pints and laughing heartily at everything that sounds like it could be a joke, but they put that down to him being a Protestant. My family must wonder why they're rarely invited over, why they're taking the brunt of the hosting. If things are bad, having people over feels like one more cage I've got myself trapped in, the first guest ringing the doorbell like being strapped into a rollercoaster and starting slow; there's no way out now.

We made the mistake of asking for help in the past, of telling certain people a certain amount of the story, and it was worse than nobody knowing. I was handed all the clichés by well-meaners. *Things could be worse. Worse things happen at sea. Think positive. Chin up.* The worst of clichés is not just that they're horseshit, but that people think they're being original, like when you have a new baby and they tell you to enjoy every minute.

Turns out most people don't understand suicidal depression. They assume Allen is going through what they feel after a botched job interview or a fight with a friend, like people saying they've a flu when they have a cold, or saying they're coeliac when they have bread-bloat. Malingering, they thought he was. So, if they think Allen is suffering what they've suffered, small wonder they tell him to snap out of it and look on the bright side and put his best side out and just get on with it.

Consequently, I was told by friends to get a divorce and find a mentally stable man. (If Allen had a physical illness it would be regarded as callous to end the relationship but mental illness was apparently a justifiably dumpable offence.) I was told by a doctor to watch him '24/7'. I was told nothing by his family. His family took useless and added worthless to it. When he was at his lowest, the absolute lowest he could be this side of an overdose, they called on him to fix things or drill things or lug furniture around. Maybe they thought being dragged into endless DIY projects would cheer him up, make him feel useful, or maybe they didn't give a fuck and just wanted the work done. Oh, but could they talk, and did they talk! If ever I needed anything they were at the other end of the phone and they'd hop in the car and be over in jig-time and jiffies. We were all in this together and they were there for me, like a nineties TV show theme tune.

Turns out their version of being there for me was as fictional as the TV show it came from. All I wanted from them was to just show up when they were needed, not when it suited them. It's hard to ask someone to come when you're not *certain* he'll kill himself. In those tight sharp hours one night when I asked his family for help, their logic for not turning up was that he had threatened this before and he hadn't done it. And that's just it. He has a 100 per cent suicide failure rate to date, so they presume the best. It is very hard to convince someone there's a threat of something that you know may never happen and you can't even calculate the odds for – where would you even start?

Crying wolf his sister called it, but we know how that one ended.

She was right, though; he didn't, he hasn't.

No: we tell nobody. Sometimes talking about it is just rehashing old agonies, leaving my head astew. Friends tire of hearing the same misery, especially when their lives are going well. When I told some friends during the first bout of depression, there was temporary satisfaction to be gained from being mired in other people's pity. I was the tragic heroine coping saint-like with it all, but that got wearying fairly quickly. In my sainted wife and mother roles, I wasn't supposed to be drinking or cursing or rearing up vengeful on the delph cupboard – I was supposed to be demure and accepting, forgiving and offering it up. Offer it down to fucking hell, I say – I'd sooner make a pact with the devil than with God. I can't be doing with the cult of suffering martyrs; the lack of scope in the role is galling.

Also, when I tried telling people how Allen's depression manifests itself, I had very few words to throw their minds onto it. It's like trying to explain your version of childbirth to someone. I know from their questions they had notions of us sitting in a low-lit room looking gravely at each other, with melancholic piano music playing in the background. In this scene, I would attend to him in the solicitous position of a nurse or waitress. I would place a firm but gentle hand on his shoulder when his eyes sank to the floor in sadness; I would leave a cup of tea on the arm of the sofa and look on with a furrowed brow as he refused to drink it. I would hold his hand and nod understandingly as he spoke in hushed undertones of his secret sadness.

There's a dignity to this scene that we lacked. It's the unpredictability that's the worst of this thing. The quiet sadness was the easy bit: I knew where he was and assumed he was too lacking in energy to kill himself. Our reality involved more unrest and turmoil. Our reality is: when he's ill, I have no idea what he'll do next; he has no idea what he'll do next.

No: I tell nobody, it's simpler that way. Better to live a lie honestly than to have expectations that can't be met. Waiting for people to step in and help is like seeing those yellow diamond-shaped road signs with a warning-promise of lepping deer – when they don't appear you feel let down.

Telling nobody also means I can cock things up in my own time, in my own way, with nobody to judge my lack of martyred heroics. The choice is not a great one, though. Keep quiet and risk being thought of as a weirdo, running out on things, cancelling last minute, or showing up brittle and flit-eyed, ever-watchful of my phone. Or tell people and be pitied ferociously, given advice from those whose woes only ever ran to the trivial.

I got up out of the bed and took a few gulps from the bottle of whiskey I'd spied earlier in Stefan's side of the cupboard. He might never notice, or if he did, he'd probably blame Roy. I hoped it would knock me out.

DAY 4

Roy

Morgenmuffel = morning grump

When the alarm belted out, Roy sat up on the couch and tried to arrange his consciousness. His head felt as if it was being pulled upwards by a chain that lugged animal carcasses to a hanging position in abattoirs. He got dressed quickly and pulled on his work boots. His father had worked as a mechanic, and he still wore boots like these, worn the way they should be worn, for hard manual labour. His father never showed his anger through his boots when they were children; he showed his disappointment in Roy later through his eyes. His father had got the wrong son.

Roy could hear Stefan stirring in the front bedroom so he hurried up the laces and left the apartment. The cold stabbed his eyes, drawing tears. He tried to remember what was happening today. Gert was going to visit the Wunderland. He yawned up the stairs to work. Inge was leaning against the wall outside the cubby, looking like she was waiting for him. It was as if she had been stuck to the walls of the Wunderland with figurine glue and hadn't left since last night.

'How do you do it?' he asked.

'Do what?'

'How do you not look like you're cut into pieces by tiredness? And how do you speak a different language so early in the morning?'

She shrugged but she looked pleased, her whole face alive with wrinkles when she smiled. 'It's not so bad. You get used to it.'

'I don't know, it's getting worse not better for me. Or maybe I'm getting older.'

'We're all getting older, Roy.'

She sounded so playful it was vicious. He would have shrugged but he was too tired. As well as mastering perfect English, Inge went running before work. Some people seemed to be given more than twenty-four hours in their day.

She leaned closer to him, her eyes wide and expectant. 'Did you hear about the damaged figurines?'

Roy tried to look nonplussed. 'No, what's happening?'

'Apparently, someone has been breaking figurines – nobody knows why.'

'And does anyone know who's doing it?'

'No, but we must all be vigilant and watch each other.' She looked silently at him for longer than he felt was decent.

'Right,' Roy nodded and tried to look purposeful, 'I'll be vigilant. I'm in Austria this morning – where are you?'

'Amerika.'

Roy picked up his bucket and shuffled off in his clompers of boots. His heart was thudding but he tried to look casual. They only knew that figurines were being damaged; they didn't know who was doing it. He felt a slight thrill; it just meant he would have to be more careful. He couldn't stop now, not when his Wardrobe Wunderland was really getting going. He had high plans to conduct a miniature census next month and he'd need a lot more figurines in his wardrobe population to tally up. Roy strode through yesterday's lands, feeling like a giant able to complete Switzerland and an imaginary land in less than a minute. He was like those people he despised, people who went travelling and spoke of having 'done' a country. He couldn't help but imagine a *Debbie Does Dallas* type of porn movie in which they fluted their way through all the locals of whatever country they'd *done*.

He put his bucket down in front of a prison, where a group of miniature prisoners played basketball in the yard. Some were escaping up a mountain. He shuffled his duster along the tops of the prisoners' heads until Inge passed by on her way to Amerika, then he reached over and plucked several of the basketball-playing prisoners from their game. The duster was bifurcated, to get around things like banisters, and it reminded Roy of the leg-spreading of the woman he'd slept with. He should probably have sex one more time so he could have two experiences to compare. Maybe, if he could find the right German to ask politely, he could see if Inge wanted to have a drink and some sex.

Most of the prisoners came away with a sharp tug; a couple came without their feet – the four ripped feet in the basketball court looked eerie, as if two people had drunk an invisibility potion and it had begun to wear off. Roy moved some of the figurines from the back to the front of the prisoner pack, leading the way for this grand escape, and pocketed a couple of others. Roy looked again at the miniature prisoners traipsing up the mountain. What had they done, what had they been accused of doing, that was so awful? They might not have done those things they were accused of; they might be suffering under false complaints; how were accusers so *sure* that the accused was guilty, how could people be so cement-certain?

He moved on to dust an island containing monks and nesting birds – what was it with monks in this place? There had been a crash in a mountain stage of a miniature Tour de France, and miniature men and bicycles were scattered over the road like hay spilled from the back of a trailer. A kangaroo on a bicycle took up the rear. It looked quite content to be last in the race, as if it didn't notice it was a different species to the rest of the competitors. Roy picked up the bicycle holding the kangaroo and moved it through the air, like E.T. and Eliot, before placing it at the front of the race. Then he yanked up the leading cyclist and placed him at the back.

'The last shall be first and the first shall be last,' he said quietly. He would have liked to round off his statement with an authoritative 'Luke 2:10' or a 'Matthew 1:2', but he wasn't as sure of his Bible as that.

His phone beeped. It was Gert saying she'd gone out for breakfast and would see him later. Roy checked his watch. He checked and checked until the moment for his break came, then he walked quickly to his flat and into the bedroom. He tried to ignore the mess and opened the wardrobe door, placing the prisoner figurines with the others. Then he looked at the figurines, took one of the prisoners out, and placed him on his own, arranging the others in a circle facing him. He opened the matchbox filing cabinet and took out two tiny blank pieces of paper and wrote Heinrich on one and Wilhelm on the other. Heinrich looked more sensible, so Roy gave him 1980 as a birth year, while Wilhelm got 1982. He quickly scribbled more details of birth dates and times and parents' occupations and looked at the figurine formation, set up like an attack.

'Be nice,' he whispered to the other figurines, 'he may not have done anything wrong.'

Gert

Auf der Kippe = touch and go

I walked to the train station. I wanted to take the rectangle-shaped yellow line with a stop called Schlump on it. I wanted comfort and it would be soothing to ride an enclosed line, not to be able to understand the noise of the ads or the mess of the announcements. I also wanted to see Schlump, a suburb that sounded tired and hunched in on itself. The screen on the platform said 2 Minuten. Long after the two minutes passed, the screen still said 2 Minuten. Small wonder the Germans have a reputation for punctuality when they fuck with time like that.

When the train pulled into the station, I walked towards it. As I was moving forwards, the train was moving sideways in my vision, causing severe body bewilderment. I got on and chose a seat away from the other passengers and sat backaways so the sights were a surprise. From there, I could see the train on the next track going up the slope while we went down, joining alongside for a brief instance. I felt like I was in a race that I badly wanted to win.

A man got on with a squeezebox and gave the length of the carriage a sweep of his eyes. He spent a short while foostering and it occurred to me that those few seconds before playing must be the scariest bit. I'd likely lose my nerve and just hold the instrument like a shopping bag, letting on I'm bringing it for a walk. The man played either terrible music well or good music terribly and ended on a horror of a high note to silence in the carriage. What must it be like playing to silence? If I finally got round to starting I would never stop playing so I wouldn't have to endure it. He got off at the next stop, unpaid but seemingly undaunted. Another man got on who carried himself like Allen which panged me, not just for my husband but for my husband as he was before everything disintegrated. Even though he's stable now, the disease could flare up with only the subtlest of warnings or none at all, like a botched bomb warning from a terrorist group.

I looked out the window and found my mind drifting to a session I had with a counsellor. She told me, 'Take it one day at a time.' A day, Christ, is a luxury I can barely fathom when things are bad. I deal in hours; when things are exceptionally bad, I resort to minutes. I go someplace else in my head during Allen's episodes and count out the seconds as if I was performing CPR or calling a free-phone number: 1-800, 2-800, 3-800. I have never got beyond 82-800, but even 82 seconds of your life being upended, one flung chair at a time, feels like 82 hours. If those 82 seconds were better put, if they were used to the good, our lives would be a different thing. The image I have of myself in these instances is: phone in hand, trying to decide whether to call an ambulance or the guards, then whether to call 999 or 911, finger on the 9 but never getting further than that, my head fucked left and right thinking the correct decision would save us, but knowing if he made a lunge at the guards in his rage, our predicament would be so much worse.

It's inwards his rage is directed, but it's still a terror to watch.

When he's ill, unpredictably ill, I return to the house in dread. That first suicide attempt caught me on the hop, but

I'm better prepared now. Since then, when he's ill, I turn the key in the lock and sniff: after all the cutting and slashing and minor league stabbings he's been at, I can smell blood at ten paces. No rotting-metal blood smell means he probably hasn't slashed his wrists. I glance around the house quickly. From the hall, if I stand on tiptoe, I can just about see the bathroom door. It's open, probably a good sign – surely nobody would slash their wrists in a bath without closing the door first. (I follow a warped logic but it's all I have to go on.) I deal in probablys and hopefullys and maybes. My gaze takes in the scope of the house then: no body hanging from the landing or the door frames or the sturdier ceilings. No body slumped on the sofa in the living room from an overdose (a method I don't really suspect him of; it's too calm and gentle a way to die – his would likely involve rage). All of this looking and seeking and not-finding is done quickly, but the children are meanwhile standing outside wondering why their mother is taking so long to let them into the house. That's what they'd take from this. If the rumours reach the teachers and they're questioned about what goes on at home, here's what they'd say, from their small standpoints: their mother opens the door a narrow chink and sniffs furiously before opening the door a small bit more, wide enough for her to slip through, before narrowing the gap once more so they can't follow; then she darts her eyes all over the house and leans forward to peer into the front room before opening the door and letting them in. The only possible conclusion is that their mother is quite mad, and who's to say they're wrong?

I shook myself and looked out the window. We were pulling away from an unfamiliar stop. I couldn't remember if this one came before or after Schlump and I couldn't be arsed checking the route map in the carriage. The sky was gunmetal-grim; it was a right schlump of a day. We passed rows of allotments; I'd noticed them on the way from the airport, small patches of tended-to land that give me a bit of hope – so many people tending such small pockets of land can only be a good thing. The allotments with children's Wendy houses, swings, or a trampoline look like their miniature already, a small garden city. The announcer on the PA was one step behind; the stations and announcements of stations didn't match, but she kept valiantly calling out the previous stop before falling into an extended silence, as if she'd been told by a well-meaner her skirt was tucked into her knickers and she was mortified into silence. The mismatched stations pushed me even further out of sync but I was part-heartened that things could go tits-up in such a well-run city.

I close my eyes and drift back to home in my head. When things go badly amiss there I take up as little space as I can, make as little noise as I can. I tamp down my actions and live by Allen's. If I shrink and hunker and recede, the going will be easier. Easier than being out and thinking about what might be waiting for me at home, easier than coming home in dread. I have to watch myself then, that I don't lapse into a cleaning frenzy. It's easy done; the danger is in taking up the cloth in the first place. Times I've found myself hours later still polishing and finding new surfaces to shine, surfaces that aren't dirty. Mostly I let things lapse in the house, shake off urges to control the dirt. When I've forgotten to take the clothes in off the line on a wet day, every beat of raindrops on the windowpane is a thump of guilt in my chest. That's an added guilt I don't need; I stuff the clothes in the dryer and to hell with the environment.

I've enough guilt thinking about how this is affecting the kids. I try not to worry about them, but sometimes the bulk of the future weighs heavy on me and I wonder when I'll find out how much we've fucked them up.

When things are bad, I enumerate, catalogue, chart who lives near. I walk nights, plotting local friends' houses on my mental map, wondering what help they could be in a crisis. I calculate how close I am to the friend plus how close Allen is to that friend, combined with how close in miles they would have to live for me to contact them in the feary wee hours. I need an algorithm or equation of these factors: the ratios need to be just right. But when the awfulness starts up again, there is nobody. Where to begin to describe something unspeakable.

When things are bad, I have that sense you get in a bus or train when the driver slowly pulls the brakes: you're being pulled forward and it feels like forever, this drag, but you need the train to come to a stop before your body can be jolted backwards and let go of the tension, unclench and relax. Or when a powerful piece of road-work equipment is used, not necessarily noisy, but something you feel in your waters and you need it just to stop.

Times I'd be taken over by chest-shakes, my heart scudding faster and faster until I was sure something would tear asunder and give way.

In times of absolute crisis, I leap in. I dive in, I jump in, I throw myself into it like a sport – somewhere between a bursty sprint and a dogged endurance event: a 1500-metre race, we'll say. I can't be distracted from my goal, which is to make him better. Then, gradually, he begins to improve. Maybe not improve so much as stop thinking of ways to kill himself *all* of the time – our bar is fairly low. Improvement comes from a not-doing, a not-thinking, and it doesn't come from me, no matter how much I try. It's so gradual that by the time I notice he's going up, I'm seesawing down. It's as if good humour is leeched out of me and absorbed into him and I'm left with a lack, a nothing feeling. He falls dramatically asunder; I slide gently downwards. Christ, this is a fucking playground of an illness, seesaws and slides and swings of mood.

The knock-on is vicious: tell me how to be happy when you share a bed with someone in the pits and I'll call you a fool or give you a medal. My down is not so violently self-erasing as his, I'm just depleted from worrying and trying. Trying so so so *hard* to keep everything with the kids going, to keep him from harming himself, to keep some level of normality in the house. When he recovers, I start to droop and he's annoyed then that I'm not in the same happy place he is – shouldn't I be glad he's better? When he's up he wants me up and when he's down he wants me down, but I aim for the position of the Grand Old Duke of York's men: only halfway up, and neither up nor down. I try telling him if I followed and matched his moods we'd be screwed when he's down: I must keep to my own moods. The way I see it, there's no space in the house for concurrently depressed parents, no room on suicide watch for two.

Near the port, the train line opened out overground and climbed at a slant like a rollercoaster, squeezing in between office blocks where I could see people working. Men and women were so still at their computers that nothing could convince me they were living, breathing humans; it was as if they'd been put there for my viewing and didn't exist in their own right, giants in a normal-sized Wunderland. I'd gotten as bad as Roy, seeking out miniature figurines – comparing reality to its miniature rather than the miniature to reality. What else can you do when reality comes up short?

The train lulled me into a half-doze. It seemed like a feat beyond my capabilities to open my eyes and take in the surroundings, plot my disembarking. I stayed behind my eyelids, behind the present. My mind was tugged back again to the shape of things at home.

In all of this, the main gist and thrust shouldn't be how *I'm* dealing with it: it should be about his brokenness. And it was, at the start of it, it was. It's the saddest thing to see the person you love most being broken into misshapen shards by an unseen malady. But this malady would damn near take hold of me if I didn't insist on rattling on heedless. You have to brace and gird and steel and buttress yourself; if you don't engineer protection around your own mind, it will cave. You have to consider yourself first or you will get drownded, lost, tugged so far down you will use all your life force struggling to find a way back up again. And so, when it hits, I take in the breadth of it, the tumult of it, the tentacling into all of our lives, and try to come up with something of a solution that will keep me tethered to the floor with some semblance of normality for the kids. I bring them on picnics, day-trips, walks, outings; if Allen is halfways functioning I insist he comes too. Might as well be miserable in a different setting.

And so, it makes you vaguer, this disease. It shows you the ludicrousness of seeing things clear-cut, of assuming situations are as people say they are. It shows you the pointlessness of making plans and promises; despite the greatest of intentions, all of these will be uprooted on the strength of a rogue humour, the unspoken threat you glean from a dip or spike in mood. It makes you question everything because you can't take anything as it's fronted. It makes you overthink everything, from hints of moods to words spoken in jest. It puts the frighteners on you when phone calls are not answered, messages not responded to. Fridays I feel the lowest –

in work, others make plans around me; I smile vaguely and say 'We'll play it by ear'. Whose fucking ear, though?

He's at an advantage; he knows whether he's just in bad humour or thinking about hurting himself. I'm at a loss. He knows his suicidal status; I don't. I try not to be the obsessively nagging, worried wife, but I behave like a petty sleuth, watching for signs. Everything becomes steeped in significance; things that have no meaning at all and are pure circumstance or coincidence are fraught. Sometimes it's hard to know if he's just down in a normal way or depressed; if we're having a mundane tiff about something minor or if this is fraught with deeper dissatisfactions.

I wince at notes left on the kitchen table.

I balk at an unlit house.

I dread celebrity suicides. I can hide newspaper details of method, note, circumstances; I can't hide the internet.

Everything becomes fraught with misplaced meaning.

I seem to be always thinking and planning and worrying and what-iffing and trying to not-think but then thinking that the shock would be keener if he did away with himself and I hadn't thought about it to prepare myself.

After somebody kills themselves, the left-behinds talk of *the signs*. If only they'd seen the signs or read the signs (as if they were tea-leaves or palm markings), they say, they might have been able to prevent it. But what do you do when your new normal *is* the signs, when the signs come thick and fast and are ever-present?

Roy

Putzfimmel = obsessed with cleaning

Roy rushed back up the stairs to the Wunderland after his break. He wasn't supposed to leave the premises at break time and he took fright when he saw Inge standing at the top of the stairs waiting for him, looking anxious.

'Hi, Roy. I heard the manager talking with the engineers about the figurines. He sounded angry.'

'Oh?' Roy's heart began to scud around his chest. 'But aren't the visitors always taking them?'

Inge shook her head. 'No, this is worse – not just stealing them, destroying them. It's terrible, breaking the miniature people, why would anyone do that?'

Roy shrugged, trying to look casual.

Inge stared very hard at him, as if she could see through him. 'He said he was going to find the culprit. He said he was going to be angriffslustig about it.'

'That doesn't sound great.'

'No, it's not great, it means he's going to be aggressive about it.'

'Oh.'

She started to walk away, glancing back over her shoulder. 'I hope it's nobody I know.' She looked for a second too long at him; he kept his eyes on the floor and walked on.

Roy moved quickly, skirting the walls so he wouldn't be noticed, to the cleaning cubby and put together his supplies. He was to clean one of the workrooms, where the figurines were painted and fixed. It was like cleaning Santa's elves' workshop. It involved a lot of bitty work, delicate work, using fingers coated in a cloth to get into small corners and areas between figurines. Occasionally he got an urge to swoosh all the broken figurines onto the floor – wouldn't it be better to just start afresh? He spotted a couple of headless figurines that he'd sent plummeting to their deaths and a hoofless deer in the tray waiting to be fixed. He shuddered. They were taking the meaning right out of it, removing the creatures from where he'd so deliberately planted them – it was as if he'd had no effect at all.

Roy stabbed his duster at the desk and turned to sweep the floor. The leavings from the figurines were scattered around under the tables and he wondered if they were miniature waste products from miniature digestive systems. He forced his mind away from what Inge had said – it was too ominous to dwell on – and away from the removed figurines. He swept over and back, to and fro, allowing his mind to relax. Once you got your brain into the right place there was something calming about cleaning, but the problem with the job overall was that there was no glory in it. There was a certain prestige to cooking a meal or setting a clump of spring bulbs or planting a washed child in its pram, but cleaning was drudgery unthanked. People only noticed a lack; they never noticed the actual hygiene: clean was the status quo and anything that deviated from that was abhorrent and his fault. But overall he liked the work. He liked that it was a one-word self-explanatory job. He knew what was required of him when he went into work every day. There was no corporate wank-speak of triangulation and going forward and reaching out and diarising and bandwidth and idea showers and blue-sky thinking and drilling down and touching base and circling back and joined-up thinking and playing hardball and parking projects and running ideas up flagpoles and quick wins and actioning projects and hitting the ground running and moving the goalposts and verbing up nouns that should never be verbed. In a cleaning job there were no bullshit meetings in which people pretended their faces off, there were only honest sweepings and brute mess. Instead of something that needed doing and not knowing what it would take to get it done, there were things that needed doing and were done.

But there were also days when he was sweeping public areas that he wondered if every visitor had brought a bag of biscuits or pastries and shaken them intentionally over the floor, as if scattering breadcrumbs for ducks at a pond. There were days when he reckoned whole cities could be powered by the sweeping motions of his brush. Today, however, he was too irritated by the way his version of the Wunderland was being overridden to bother cleaning, so he downed cloths and mops and went to the toilet. He locked himself into a cubicle and pulled out his notebook. He peeled back the pages and began writing a list of the miniature lands. He wanted to map the Wunderland, in order to recreate it in miniature for his Wardrobe Wunderland, even if his version would be miniature doubled. Exponentials were difficult to wrap his head around.

Gert

Weltschmerz = world pain = melancholy

Schlump wasn't going to happen. They were carrying out works, I gathered from the announcements. There were bus transfers from other stations to Schlump but it all seemed a bit much like work for an aimless holiday gallivant. I stayed on the train. The morning was fucked sideways anyway with my head where it was at; may as well sit this one out. I knew I should be thinking about Roy, thinking about how to handle this current situation in this present-day city, but my head kept dragging me back to the past in a different country. Maybe being removed from a problem makes it louder in your ears. And the Roy situation seemed so utterly unsolvable, depending as it was on his willingness to communicate. No, my mind pulled me backaways, back to the beginning and end of things.

When the Allen I knew disappeared and was replaced by an unpredictable interloper, life became unrecognisable. Things that had come easy before suddenly required a lot of forethought and strategising. I learned to lie and to lie well – I had to get out of things with a credible excuse that the kids wouldn't give away. I cancelled events I'd been looking forward to, feeling like a sulky child when I couldn't do the things I wanted so badly to do: missing dinners and pints and holidays, making excuses for not attending parties or for bailing out of visits I'd arranged to the house, saying that something's come *up*. And something would have come up right enough: this beast from the depths, rearing up after a spell of hibernation, although I'm not sure whether his illness invents or unleashes the beast within.

So I pack suitcases and take out their unused contents a couple of hours later. I buy presents for birthday parties I don't attend and reuse the presents for people whose birthdays land in calmer times. I lose full-price airfares and deposits on hotels. I muddle through and try to throw from my mind the treats that pass us by.

Cancellation is a pattern I try to deviate from. I vary my excuses to stop them getting old and empty; I cancel at either very early or very late notice to stop people expecting it. My lies, like an addict's, are very convincing. I try so hard not to cancel the kids' plans: I try to provide one-sided parenting and cheer and shout for two at matches; I try to be mother and father – cuddles I can do but fun is a struggle when my mind is in a slough. It's a strange thing, cancelling on something you wanted to do in order to sit in a house with somebody who doesn't want you there. It can seem like a pointless task, but it serves several purposes: it stops him harming himself; it breaks up his mull-hours, however irritating he finds my prattling and meal offers; it saves me having to show a smiling face in public when all I want to do is sob and roar. Easier for people to think you're an unreliable flake than to find out what they don't want to know.

When I'm chided for pulling out of a girly night out that I cannot muster the high-pitched zeal for, an urge rises up my gullet to say, 'I'd love to but I've to keep watch over the knives in case my husband slashes his wrists.' What little they know of how much I spare them! I feel like a cartoon character walking around with my speech bubbles saying one thing and my thought bubbles thinking the opposite. Sometimes, like right now, when he's in remission (if that phrase can be used for a mental illness), my life feels normal. I do the things when I say I'll do them, no bailing, no excuses. But I can't count on this; I can't ever know that this will last.

So I live a two-pronged life and I envy ferociously the people who live simple, honest one-pronged lives, who do the things they say they'll do at the time they said they'd do it. My original life has cracked, fissured, ruptured someplace along the way. No point looking back to spot the tear: it's the upward plod I must focus on. Times I feel like Humpty Dumpty put back together all wrong.

I gave myself in to the train journey. I didn't want to budge out of the gently rocking cocoon. I couldn't stop the memory-gush even if I wanted to; scenes were appearing thick and quick.

Sometimes it feels like there are hundreds of tiny flies in my eyes. Sometimes it feels like shards of metal instruments were left embedded in my internals after surgery. Most times I make dinners and ask how school was and wash up dinner plates and make lunches and check homework and try to stay focused on conversations about after-school activities. Children ground you, they say, and it's one cliché I can get behind. Times I think I wouldn't survive this if it wasn't for them. Not only ground me, they root me, turn my feet into tree roots and draw me right down. There's no chance of going awaft when I've to figure out why Sophia didn't want to sit beside Hazel in music class or why Adam didn't pick Benjy for his dodgeball team in PE and try to temper my murderous urges towards Sophia and Adam.

The thing you want most, the absolute best-case scenario, is that he doesn't kill himself, and when that happens, after these threats and ventures into the night to do just that, it's pure relief. But after the relief settles comes the realisation I look a fool, a melodramatic, apparently needlessly worrying fool who has some explaining to do. Do I weigh each episode equally? Does the threat increase or decrease with repetition? Do previous episodes accumulate or are they discrete risks? Are there mathematical equations to decide these things? How do you quantify that kind of risk? And who would do it; is there an actuary or a risk analyst or a psychiatrist who could tell me? There must be some kind of equation, some perfect formula to help me plan this life. It seems so arbitrary whether suicide happens or not. He didn't drown himself in the river one night, he told me, because somebody chanced by. I'd like to think his reason for staying in the world had meaning, that the kids or I featured in this reason, but the reality was more happenstance.

Making a decision to leave the house when he's low, even for the speediest errand, is fraught. Some families look to the weather forecast to plan their activities, to decide whether to hang the washing out on the line. I keep an unofficial suicide forecast. It's not about putting on the TV after the news to look for rain-spatter and fried eggs on the map. It's more a case of peeks sneaked at his moods, unwritten tallies kept of the lengths of his silences. There's a certain sweet spot of lethargy that makes me think we're safe: he hasn't got the energy to end himself.

Times I used to think, *Right, universe, you've dumped me with enough shite, now off you go and fuck up someone else's life for them, stir some poison into their perfect lives*, but no. Now I realise that, in the same way that managers dump the most work on the most agreeable, competent employee instead of on a slacker who'd screw it up, the universe sees the likes of me as practised at wading through shite and adds more.

Our life together is based on the hope that he won't do the thing he most wants to do. Hard to keep a together-life when he wants out of it so badly and resents me for keeping him in it. He's as well as he can be now, but that 'now' is all I have to go on with. 'Well' is within the context of serious depression: once this beast has possessed him, it may never fully release. A kind of cautious equilibrium is the most I can hope for. Even at his best, depression has changed him, he has pulled further back into himself. I've learned to cope with his sulks and silences but I find out things about him when other people are around. Same questions I'll have asked previous, but when they're asked by different people, farther removed people, he will produce different answers. He tells of his plans, and inwardly I soar; plans have a future tense, plans do not contain deliberate death. Outwardly I nod as if this is no big deal.

I got out at the town-hall stop when it came around again. I suppressed the urge to press the red SOS button in the train station and ask if they knew a cure for the wrong life. When I get off trains in a daze I mostly follow the feet of the passenger in front of me, regardless of which exit they're taking. It's like my feet and my brain are unconnected, like my feet have their own little toe-brains to obey. I have to fight this urge if I need to be somewhere, but that day I was drifting aimless so I gave into it. The passenger I was following took the exit for the church so I headed that way. There was a model of the church in the porch. I had no interest in going into the actual church to look around, so I stayed in the porch examining its miniature. Like flying over a graveyard or an airport car park, things you wouldn't give a second glance to in full size are magical in miniature.

In the model of the church, a tiny legless monk was peeking out a door. There were miniature statues of the four gospel lads in white marble – I was tempted to walk around the outside of the real church and look for the full-sized versions, but if they weren't there, what then? What if reality and miniature fantasy didn't compute? I'd stick with fictional life in miniature: there was less scope for disappointment.

When

*When you've done everything right. When you've done the gentle exercise the mild exercise the moderate exercise the strenuous exercise. When you've eaten the nuts the seeds the berries the fish the sprouts the plant oils the kale. When you've cut out the alcohol the meat the dairy the wheat the caffeine the sugar the smokes. When you've set lofty goals challenging goals doable goals don't able ones. When you've kept your chocolate dark your coffee decaf your breathing deep your meditation transcendental. When you've tried the tai chi the qi gong the chakras the acupuncture the Bikram. When you've screamed your way through therapy laughed your way through yoga considered LSD to reboot your brain. When you've reached out to others been present in the moment kept a gratitude journal asked pleaded begged for help. When you've talked to therapists counsellors doctors psychiatrists family friends priests. When you've kept your silence because they likely will judge and surely won't understand. When you've tried hypnotherapy behavioural therapy psychotherapy psychoanalysis. When you've tried cognitive therapy mindfulness whatever's hot right now whatever was hot back then. When you've read up endless online lurked in chatrooms for tips deleted cookies for fear of being sectioned. When being sectioned sounds like being quartered after the hanging and the drawing, even then a relief of not living. When you've read entire self-help shelves in the library, the staff avoiding your eyes, the pages jinxed with tears. When you've tried: you've pushed you've pulled you've dragged (your heels to work your mind to sanity). When you've tried the Lexapro the Effexor the Zoloft the Prozac the Paxil the Cipramil the Xanax.
When none of it's worked, what then: what then?
When what's working now stops working, what then?*

Roy

Schande bringen = to bring shame = to disgrace

During the split in his shifts, Roy walked back to his apartment and let himself in. When he closed the door behind him, there was a silence so thorough he knew Gert and Stefan were out. He went into his bedroom (how could Gert have made so much mess in so few days?) and went over to the wardrobe. The figurines were as he had left them. This was almost a surprise – he often expected them to have moved or rearranged themselves in some way. He stared at the figurine in the middle, the one hunted out of the circle. His face seemed to be furrowed deeper in shame – maybe he was anxious that his boss would find him out. Roy moved the figurines into a line formation and turned the lone one in the middle around so he was facing away from the others.

Roy looked fondly at his figurines. They needed this dark, secret home, away from the prying eyes of the Miniatur Wunderland, where they could be part of a little population that would be tallied into a census, where they were safe from banishment or rejection. He stroked the head of one of his figurines – Gunther, he thought it was – and he reminisced about taking his first one, much as parents remember the birth of their first child or hunters their first kill. He had read that 3,500 figurines were kidnapped by visitors every

165

year, but he believed them to be liberated, and he assumed it was by people with the same purity of reasoning he had. And some figurines didn't belong where they had been placed in the Miniatur Wunderland. Roy would set them to rights.

Gert

Schäferstündchen = *the little hour of the shepherd* =
to meet for courtship or sex

I left the church and walked back to the flat. I couldn't be
doing with more trains that day. I'd hoped that the movement of my legs would take me out of my head but the seep
of circular thoughts was unstoppable.

I don't know for sure if Allen has acted outside the marriage – I don't know how far his flirtation with his 'sound'
colleague went – it's something I try not to dwell on. I do know
that when he was low, he was attracted to other broken specimens, lost floundering souls – maybe in the hope that a double
negative makes a positive instead of an exponentially negative
disaster. When he was high, he sparked off more confident
women. There was so much focus on what Allen wanted and
needed from our relationship, I hadn't given much thought to
my own needs. I'd doubted my attractiveness after being told I
was so lacking, but one night, after I'd put the hours into making myself attractive to Allen, I felt a surge of resentment at all
the effort I'd felt compelled to make. I didn't bother suppressing the Sure-I-deserve-it and Why-the-fuck-nots and went out
one night on the lash. I found myself drinking alone with a
male friend after our other friends had left. 'One for the road,'
he'd said. Neither of us wanted to end the night. Neither of

us seemed too bothered about the future-tense hangover, or the present-tense spouses and children at home. Somewhere beneath his words I sensed a gap: and it was through that gap I slunk in. It was, literally, a one-night stand, or more accurately a three-minute stand, or more correctly a grapple up against the gable wall of the pub.

When the pub closed, he had hugged me goodbye, a hand lingering just that second too long on the small of my back. The night grew larger in that one gesture. If we were in a court of morality and I had to explain what happened, I'd say I *initiated proceedings.* I took a notion for the ride and stuck the face in so's he'd no choice but to respond. I performed all the unzipping and tugging open of clothing to get to the necessaries. It felt like being back at work, undressing patients for their baths; the man in question was the most passive participant this side of a hard cock, but that part he managed just fine. Maybe the passive role absolved him from any responsibility – he could blame me for initiating. The angle didn't suit me; it required too much bobbing and jigging which is hard on the knees, and it was a struggle to gain purchase on him. But the dark suited me; I didn't care how red and puffed my face was or how ripply-jiggly I was from this angle or how utterly daft we looked, at our age, when it should have been a glass of wine in front of the *Late Late Show* – or the *Oireachtas Report* if we really wanted to make a night of it – and there we were lorrying into each other like teenagers. It felt good, though, fucking on my terms, exceeding expectations rather than failing to meet them. Afterwards, there was an awkward gesture some place between a kiss and a hug and I had to stop myself from saying 'Regards to Anna and the kids'. I walked home damply smug. Easy for me to screw my way around the outskirts of my marriage; I'm the one doing the laundry – my stains won't be caught.

The next morning, I felt neither guilt nor satisfaction. There was no moral quandary or shame, just a slight fear of catching something off him which would catch me out. I felt like I'd stepped into a sideways universe. I'd always considered myself an honest person and here I was banging another man guiltless. It struck me then, if my eighteen-year-old self could see me now, how disappointed in me she'd be. Hell, she probably wouldn't recognise this updated and ill-worn version. It also struck me, when you hear tut-tuts about people who've had affairs or left marriages for other people: how can the gossips be so *definite*? How do they think they know what went on or didn't go on in that relationship? And if they judge so mercilessly, so monochromely, surely they're suppressing similar desires to up and leave themselves? I tamp down these exit-urges all the time but at least I don't leap in and add my stone to the castings.

And so, that night gave me a taste for it. I hadn't realised what I'd been missing out on but now I found myself panging for a banging. I initiated, then, what would technically be called an affair. It was deliberate, and *affair* is the right word because it felt like a business arrangement. Both of us were married; neither of us were looking for something the other couldn't offer. I used to think marriages broke because of affairs; now I know some work because of them. When every marital fuck is so fraught, it's easier to leave well enough alone and seek elsewhere. The man I sought out was not exactly the stuff of fantasies – he had all the charm of a partially sucked sweet – but he was there and he was keen and he was discreet. He was also known as a ladies' man, and as far as I can see, ladies' men, men who fuck extra-curricular like it's to earn points on their FitBits, either love or hate women, but I couldn't figure out which category this man fell into.

Coming at someone's body anew in your middle years is a different thing. Certain parts of the body are more than they were; certain parts are less.

'I used to be thinner,' he said, 'with more hair.'

'Ara, we can all say that,' I said.

Sex is not the spontaneous high-jinks of youth; you have to mind not to cramp or pull a muscle or go too hard on a bockety hip. The soundtrack is noisier than youthful sex; your joints wheeze and creak and answer each other. I probably should have felt timid about my dry-sucked dugs or my sag-stretched belly (he usually fucks younger women) but this didn't seem to be about the quality of my skin. I spent years tormenting myself about my body when it was smooth-skinned perfection, and now that it's more blemish than smooth, I've stopped caring.

The first time we met I decided to get drunk, to make the going easier. I overdid it on the whiskey, though; no sooner had he started pumping away than my head went on the fritz.

'Will you take it handy?' I said. 'All that thrashing around is making me queasy.'

'I will,' he said, but he had his eye on the prize now and there was no stopping him.

Every time I closed my eyes the room spun, so I kept them open and fixed his face with a stare to anchor me to a point.

'Jesus,' he said, 'will you stop eyeballing me like a dead sheep. You're putting me right off my stroke.'

'Ah, you seem to be managing just fine,' I said.

I turned my gaze to a point on the wall, but that was no good, because the point I stared at was stationary and yer man's head was still going a-bobbing in my peripheral vision. With his body going a-hammering and mine going a-lepping, my head was half a beat behind, and it was that half-beat was the problem. Somewhere between me retching silently – whose convulsions he mistook for an early orgasm – and vomiting over the side of the bed, he came. *Damn*, I thought, that's how niche fetishes start; next thing he'll be wanting every woman he rides to puke on him.

'Don't mind it,' he said when I went to wipe the puke, 'it can wait.' But I persisted. I didn't want his only memory of my body to be the sour stink of regurgitated whiskey. I slept with him another few times, but it fizzled out when I couldn't be arsed making such efforts to hide where I was going. Small towns aren't built for affairs and I wasn't keen enough to drive to a hotel a few miles down the dual carriageway. And it didn't make sense to risk being caught for someone whose funeral I probably wouldn't be bothered attending.

Roy

*Um den heißen Brei herumreden = talk around
the hot porridge = beat around the bush*

Roy gathered his cleaning supplies for the evening shift from
the cubby and sat down. He had napped after tinkering with
his Wardrobe Wunderland, and then when Gert had come
back, they'd walked to the Wunderland together. He felt nervous and excited, as if she was meeting his child for the first
time. The woman at reception had stared at Gert so curiously
he'd felt compelled to introduce her as his sister. He was a
few minutes early for work so he took out his notebook. He
hadn't enough time for his Wunderland mapping idea now,
so he decided to come up with a to-do list. Buying buttons
was number one. He wanted to make his figurines feel more
at home and they could perhaps use buttons as dinner plates
or frisbees. He wanted to visit the shop in Hamburg that used
to sell only buttons but now, disappointingly, sold clothes as
well. Roy loved buttons; his favourite were the four-holed
ones but the two-holed ones were just about tolerable. Three-
holed buttons were a rogue rarity and an abomination as far
as he was concerned. He considered buying bags of buttons
in haberdasheries but it seemed a cheat, like buying the single
Top Trump or Garbage Pail Kid card you needed for your
collection online instead of happening across it in a packet

or swapping to get it. Or, worse, like buying purple Quality Street in bulk instead of rooting and conniving against your family to get them. He bought second-hand clothes and ripped off the buttons. Roy liked shops that sold only one thing. Specificity of trades appealed to him; there were too many shops selling all these clothes and food and electronics and toys in one building. If he didn't hate clowns so much, he would visit the shop in Hamburg that sold clown accessories, and some day he would visit the one that sold only umbrellas and stayed open late on rainy days. How did the staff plan anything in the evenings – did they check the weather in advance to see if they had to work late?

He flicked back through his notebook to a list of his favourite flower words in German:

Gänseblümchen = goose-flower = daisy

Osterglocken = Easter bell = daffodil

Schneeglöckchen = little snowbell = snowdrop

Löwenzahn = lion's tooth = dandelion

Schwertlilie = sword lily = iris

Stiefmütterchen = little stepmother = pansy

Inge walked into the cubby, dropped her bucket by her feet, and sat down. She stretched out her legs and wriggled her ankles in circles. Then she folded her arms over her chest and sighed, but when she saw Roy looking at her, she smiled. He smiled back. This must be what people meant when they talked of a connection; soon he would ask her for a drink. Roy usually waited for Inge to initiate conversation, but today would be different.

'There's a hole in my bucket, dear Liza, dear Liza,' he sang, splashing his words into the silence of the cubby.

Inge peered into his bucket. 'There is a hole?'

'No, I was just singing the children's song.'

'Ah yes, it's German, Heinrich und Liese.'

'Everything's German.'

She smiled. His conversation had made a woman smile; this was big. He wondered where to go from here, whether there was something to be said that would prolong this amiability.

'Inge, if you were to pick a button, would you go for a four-holed, three-holed, or two-holed one?'

She looked surprised but thoughtful. 'I guess four-holed buttons – they have a pleasing symmetry.'

Roy smiled the smile of a man who's been read right for the first time.

'Oh, Roy,' Inge leaned forward, 'did you hear there's going to be a meeting?'

'No?' He dug his hands in his pockets.

'Yes, management have called an urgent meeting about the damaged displays. It's going to be the day after tomorrow.'

'Oh? I thought you said it was urgent?'

'Yes, but meetings take time to organise – we can't rush into anything.'

'No, no, I suppose not.' Roy tried to arrange his face in a calm expression and got up. He and Inge walked together in the direction of Mittel Deutschland, Roy preoccupied but forcing conversation about the weather to hide his discom-bobulation. Inge hurried to keep up with him and gave a little cough. Roy looked surprised to see she was still there.

'Roy, are you sure you don't know anything about the missing figurines?'

'Of course not, what would I know?'

'I don't know.'

She looked troubled, Roy thought, a troubling of thoughts, but Roy took the lead from her discomfort and said sternly, 'We must work now.' Inge nodded and walked off to

Knuffingen. Roy let out a long breath and stewed silently. Inge seemed to doubt him – what kind of friendship was that? (Collective noun: a suspicion of friends.) He took the duster out of the bucket and surveyed the miniature land before him. Visitors were pocked throughout Mittel Deutschland but it hadn't gotten busy yet. A miniature car was smashed into a tree, and a figurine was being carried away on a stretcher. He knew you could say stretchered off, but the *off* sounded vague and ominous – to the hospital? Morgue? Funeral home? A herd of brown cows was being led down a road, one of them pink. Roy looked over both shoulders – nobody watching – and ripped the pink cow quickly from the road and put it in his pocket, hoofless. He wondered if he would include animals in his census or whether he should have a specific animal census. He took the pink cow out of his pocket and peeked at its ears; there were no tags. The creatures had no identity so he would have to create a separate filing cabinet for animal birth records. He put the anonymous cow back into his pocket and skimmed the duster over some figurines recycling bottles; green, brown, and transparent bottles were being put into separate containers. If he was a figurine-maker and he had the power to devise magical worlds where anything could happen to any creature, he knew for certain he wouldn't have miniature humans sorting miniature bottles into differently coloured miniature recycling bins. He would have miniature humans smashing differently coloured miniature bottles on the heads of the miniature humans who rejected them.

He moved on to a crowded amphitheatre showing *Romeo and Juliet*. A green alien was sitting patiently on the steps watching the play. Roy stared at the human figurines – why weren't there hundreds of green aliens sitting in the seats and one human on the steps? Why were humans still the majority in

a magical universe? He stared at the mass of miniature human-
ity and waited for the lights to dim before crashing the duster
down on the heads of the crowd, despising them in the way
that he despised people who all faced the same way enjoying the
same thing. Why was nobody looking at the alien? Why were
they all so smug and passive and empty? He started thunking
their heads, hoping to batter some curiosity into them, but not
hard enough to break all of them. An entire audience of broken
heads would be hard to explain to a newly watchful manager.
He contented himself with sawing his duster across the tops
of the heads, breaking only a couple in the middle where they
might not be discovered, and stuffing the heads into his pocket.
A part of him wanted to do as much damage as possible before
the meeting in case he was uncovered as the culprit; another
part advised caution and abandoning his project.

He flicked the duster over a forest. A man, covered mostly
by trees, was having sex with a woman. Even though the figurines were a few centimetres high and utterly still, they gave off
a sense of vigour and rigour and gut brutality that unnerved
him. When he looked closer, he saw a man in the bushes
with binoculars watching the couple, and then his eyes lit on
more men watching them. What *was* it about peeping Toms
in the Wunderland? How could there be so many miniature
perverts so desperate to watch miniature sex acts? It added
another layer of disgrace that he would prefer not to exist.
Why were so many people determined to watch, to sit and
judge and assume they knew what it was they were seeing –
how could the watchers have such ferocity of conviction? If it
had been only his accusers who believed the rumours they'd
started (if they even believed it themselves – he sometimes
thought it was pure spite, for the sake of causing mischief,
they'd started it), he would have been able to prove himself,

but there were enough watchers who wanted something to watch that wasn't there, and when it wasn't, they invented it. Roy gripped the metal bar around the exhibit hard, the bones of his hands bulging into webbed claws that he relaxed only when his breathing returned to normal.

He waited for the lights to dim again and made sure nobody was around, then he leaned over, using his duster as a cover, and tried to pull the man off the woman, curious as to the mechanics of miniature sex, but they were stuck tight. He put both figurines between his fingers and thumbs and pulled until one came off in each hand. Then he snapped off the heads and replaced the heads where the bodies had been. Now the peeping Toms were spying on two bodiless heads. He would continue with his project, despite the risks of being caught, to save the figurines from spying and gossip and protect them in a cosseting closet. He picked up the bodies and added them to his pocket – a peculiar kind of convention he was hosting in there, with miniature heads and bodies that didn't match.

A surge of anger burbled up his gullet and he yanked the peeping Toms up with two hands. He rammed the figurines into his pocket and headed off on a sexual cleansing rampage. He slunk around groups of visitors standing at various miniature woods and streams where the peeping Toms were hiding, waited till the visitors had moved on and the lights dimmed, and reefed the miniature leery monks out of their standing and into his pocket, leaving the couples having sex to get on with it in peace – well, as much peace as they could have with so many full-size humans watching them. He had rarely felt so good and useful. His pockets bulged and rattled with figurines, and he realised that mixing so many perverts in with non-perverts wasn't fair, so as soon as he got back to Mittel Deutschland he turned out his pockets.

He put all the monks back into his left one and the torn-off heads into his right.

Further along the forest, another herd of cows stood in a field, as if they were waiting to do a group activity. They looked so peaceable that the word *herd* did them no justice – a rumination of cows would be better, or if they were acting up, a bother of cows. He would like one or two for his Wardrobe Wunderland but that would be a purely selfish act when they were so obviously happy here. And he feared the pink hoofless cow in his pocket might be bullied by the regularly coloured cows so he moved on to a stopped windmill. A still windmill looked so wrong; it was as if the world had ended or a three-handed clock had stopped. He walked on to a market and festival. These miniature figurines seemed to do nothing but go to festivals and circuses and theme parks and playgrounds and county fairs – when was the work done? A market sold antlers, clothes, puppies, swords, violins, and buckets; he liked the randomness of the goods on offer. He kicked his own bucket along the floor and dusted the forest until he got to the fairground. There were rides and amusements and a food tent filled with delicious things. Something about all this pleasure-seeking made him feel hollowed out; he couldn't help but feel excluded from these good things and wonder when his chance would come. A ghost car was stuck in the trees. Roy dusted the car vigorously and thwacked it, hard, until it tumbled out of the trees and into the big reveal, he was sick of things being hidden that should be seen and things being seen that should be kept from view.

At break time, Inge was nowhere to be seen. He nodded to the two other cleaners there, who chatted to each other in German, ignoring him. Roy knew he should check his phone or text his sister and see how she was getting on in the Wunderland, but he wanted to maximise his him-time. He dug into his backpack, took out his train timetable book and opened it on a random page. He'd landed on Sweden. He could get on a train at Hallsberg at 08:15 and be in Herrljunga by 10:56 – that sounded about right. Or he could hop on at 06:12 at Varberg but, no, that's no use, it took just over an hour to get to Boras; if he waited for the 08:44, he could go all the way to Uddevalla, which sounded like a peaceful valley a rumination of cows would wait to be milked in. He closed the book and opened it again at random. He had hit on Poland. The Łódź to Krakow train was leaving at 08:48 and would get there for 12:14. How beautiful, how rarefied, how exquisitely specific that he could know, in a different country, down to the precise minute when a train would pull into a station hundreds of miles away. He looked again at the word Łódź. In just four letters, there were three accents. Roy knew he could try every combination of sounds available to his tongue and he might never get to the right way of saying that place name.

The page-knowledge of what time a train would pull into a station hundreds of miles away was like seeing what time it was in a city thousands of miles away from the clocks in a hotel lobby. He had an urge to set multiple clocks around his apartment to different world times so he could tell exactly when in *his* Hamburg day trains of other cities would be departing and arriving, but Roy's clocks would not be of the usual Tokyo, London, New York, Paris variety; his would be the time zones of small European cities and towns. He would start with Mostar, Ballina, Margate, Lyons. Or maybe he should have a second-city clock sequence or a commuter-town clock sequence or tidiest-town clock sequence. If he followed through on his clock plan, the walls and ceiling would be covered to an inch in clocks – he would have to use square clocks in order to fit more in. Also, if he just stuck to Europe, the time difference would be on a minor scale; maybe he should press out to world times and –

'Are you going to travel somewhere?'

Roy jumped. Inge was standing behind him looking over his head at the train timetables.

'No, I was just looking.'

'Yes, it's good not to rush into things.' She sat down and looked curiously at him. 'Anna at the front desk said that you brought your sister to the Wunderland?'

Roy nodded. He wished she wouldn't keep posing statements as questions, questions so open-ended as to be seriously daunting. And it was dishonest to act as if they were friends now that she suspected him of wrongdoing (collective noun: a misgiving of friends). 'Yes, she's visiting now.'

'Why aren't you with her? Aren't you interested to show her around?'

'I'm working,' he said curtly. 'And she's an adult, she can show herself around.'

Inge said nothing, only stared at him.

'Speaking of which, I'd better get back to work,' he said, stuffing his timetables book back into his backpack, leaving Inge to arrange her own thoughts. And, if Inge was anything like Gert, there would be thoughts.

Gert

Wunderkammer = chamber of wonders = cabinet of curiosities

Roy had dithered something awful before going to the Wunderland. It seemed a strange kind of a way to go about things, but we had looked at the bar graphs on the website before we'd left; they were highest for the morning and lowest for the evening.

'At home,' I'd said, 'it'd be the opposite. When I bring the kids to the zoo, we go at the earliest possible time to avoid the crowds, and here you go late to get the place to yourself.'

He'd looked almost interested and grunted in reply.

We'd walked the few hundred yards to the place, Roy looking happier with each step. He couldn't even conceal his joy at being rid of me soon – good preparation for my kids becoming teenagers and being mortified of me, I suppose.

'It used to be a coffee warehouse,' he'd said, as we reached the door.

'Oh,' I'd said, 'that's why there's such a buzz about the place.'

He'd glanced quickly at me, nodded at the attendant at the door, then said, 'This way,' and bundled me up the steps. I was just glad he didn't make me queue with the regular visitors – it's the smallest things I hang out for in gratitude. It was strange to see Roy out of context, dealing with his colleagues and not in such a *schlump* as he is at home. I thought he might get me in on a discounted rate, but he's scrupulously above board about such things and I didn't like to ask. Even to joke about it might have spoiled the evening, he's that spiky. I expected him to help me translate when I was buying my ticket, but after saying 'Allo' to the cashier, he wandered off leaving me to transact alone. She dealt with me polite and slow but also curious, staring at me as if trying to read the family secrets in my forehead. Roy joined me once I had my ticket. I put my bag in the locker and walked through the gift shop. He stopped briefly to chat to a security guard; well, when I say chat, I mean the security guard said something to him and he replied with a *Genau*. *Genau* he says to everyone and he says it so well. I'd looked it up when I first got here. It means *Exactly* in English: *Precisely*, but in context, *Right*. A precise word for a vague concept. Roy has learned off the tone of it, the perfect inflection, but there's no follow-through: he can't get beyond the Genau.

Once we got to the start of the exhibition, Roy left me to go to his cubby. There was a screen showing visitor numbers from different countries. Ireland had well over three thousand, but Gabon had two, Guyana had nine, and Guinea-Bisseau had two. The G countries weren't doing so well. Antigua + Barbuda had one and it made me wonder which of the two islands the tourist was from but I knew not to save the question up for Roy: it would infuriate him. 'Why?' he'd ask. 'What difference does it make to your life where they're from?' It often seems my wonderings aren't placed so highly in his esteem as his own.

Before the Wunderland started, there was an assembling and repair shop where you could watch the men working through windows. I could see the glue and kitchen roll; I liked that commonplace items were used to make magic. These workmen's in-tray was not full of letters and papers to be filed but broken figurines and scraps of wire. I skipped the tableaux of the history of the world summed up in perfect glass cubes. It gave me melancholy to think of all the lives taken and spoiled by war, neatly arranged like something glamorous. And it tired me to think of whole centuries enclosed in a perfectly cubed box when I couldn't fit an afternoon of mine into one. How do they choose what to put in and what to leave out? It pissed me right off that history was decided by the big figurines; it's the figurines so tiny and unimportant as to be invisible that I want to know about. Never mind the elected deciders who will history up the books for generations; what of the lives of the countless unknowns who wrote history in pencilled Xs on their ballot papers? They're the ones I'm interested in.

I entered the model railway exhibition at Switzerland. The first thing I thought of was how Allen and the children would love this, but then every mother travelling without her cubs would say the same thing so I pushed that out of my mind: it's important not to live in clichés. The overhead lights had dimmed and little lights had come on in the train station and buildings and in cars. I leaned over the metal bar and adjusted my eyes to take it all in.

It was all Roy had talked about – miles of train track, hundreds of thousands of figurines in miniature lands. It was so impressive, but I couldn't stop thinking about all the things those engineers and designers could be doing out in the real world, making real homes for full-size homeless people instead of making believe in a wonderland. I moved on to where a small crowd had gathered. There was a Lindt chocolate factory, and when you pushed a button, a chocolate came out of the machine. A tall chubby boy was crouched by the factory, holding his hand in front of a hatch. When he picked out the chocolate, he pushed the button again and repeated the gesture.

There were murmurings from the children behind him, but none of them did anything. He reminded me of the child Roy befriended too hugely, and just look at the hell of a bother that caused – Roy wouldn't be here if it wasn't for the fallout from that. I did so much thinking about that misjudged friendship, so much analysing and ruminating and overthinking that my brain has switched itself off and decided on innocence.

I marched over to that child and shouted. 'Move!'

Up close, the child looked younger than I'd thought. He straightened up and met me nearly at eye level.

'OK,' he said, then he shrugged and moved off slowly.

It was all just too small. Too many figurines, too many buildings, too many ordinary scenes crammed into a small space. I couldn't bring my eyes away from the backs of the scenes, the grass that was obviously a sheet of green material, the wires, the grey cotton wool for sand in the beach-volley-ball scene, the sense of it all being for show and nothing real, no substance, no depth. It all smacked of one-dimensionality; there was no sense of continuity. I couldn't understand how they chose what countries and eras to miniaturise. The weight of the centuries they didn't show and the countries they left out was crushing me – how to decide what to include and what to exclude? It'd be like being told you had to choose to save one of your children.

There were magical creatures – dragons and trolls – mixed in with real ones – dinosaurs – which to me are as magical make-believe as dragons because they existed too long ago to be real. It was the ordinariness of the figurines I couldn't get my head around. They were going to the toilet and recycling bottles and waiting for trains and going to weddings. If you could create a magical land, why not create new mundani-ties and have your figurines perform those? Why not recycle bottles from which genies spill out of, why not go to a toilet-cum-hovercraft in the middle of the lake, why not have water suspended above the lake, why not have a mass wedding of all combinations of brides and grooms and only two guests? Why do they keep the same order of life as in the real world, and if that's the magic involved, then I'm missing it.

A miniature girl in a blue top was either crowd-surfing at a festival or being carried out of the concert by security, and I really wanted to know if she was having the best of fun or was being rescued from being crushed. Some of it spoke to me: I liked the woman mowing the lawn in the miniature rooftop garden and the figurine hanging miniature clothes on a miniature line. I liked the bold colours of the prams, buggies, wheelchairs. I liked the rivers and ponds that had a jellied rubbery quality.

But I was spooked by the same figurines that kept appearing in different lands. A family in old-fashioned garb at a train station also appeared up the mountains. It seemed as if they'd followed me; if I ran back down to the train station, would they be there or had they left? The whole thing tricked my mind. And the clocks: throughout Switzerland there were several clocks, all set to different times; my head was fucked six ways from midday. One clock said 4:55, another said 8:04; another said 4:00 – which is it? I wanted to scream. And in Switzerland too, of all countries: it should be the same precise time down to the second. Further on, under the airport scene, miniature men were trying to drag real-life full-size tools using ropes and pulleys. Spatially, my head was all over the place. My miniature magical world was colliding with my real normal-sized one until I couldn't figure out which one was more real and which one I lived in, whether I was extra-large or they were extra-small. There were workmen sat supping beer in a cosy makeshift cubby with a crocodile, the crocodile belonging to the scene every bit as much as the workmen. There were thirteen miniature figurines piling out of a tiny stunted-looking car, stooped and rubbing their heads; if I stood watching long enough it seemed that more would emerge – that's how messed up my head was. I liked the haunted house with dragons chasing a man who was running straight for the grim reaper, talk about frying pan to the fire; I reckon I'd take my chance with the dragons. And that was my problem right there. My logic had skewed so thoroughly, this seemed a reasonable choice to make.

The lights would dim in cycles, fifteen-minute cycles Roy had said, and it felt like waves of darkness that you could almost touch. That was the best time, those minutes when people were still because little walking was done when darkness swelled around feet. I envied Roy the silence of it when the buttons weren't being pushed, and noise and flashing lights and movement didn't flaw the quiet.

I liked the miniature bride in a wedding dress sitting on a rock in a sluggish-looking stream surrounded by a dead tree and bits of scrub and shrub, all death and decay. These likely weren't the photos the bride was dreaming of, but maybe wedding photographers could learn from this: it might be best to photograph the freshly married in the worst places – in graveyards and mortuaries, next to burnt-out cars and comatose drunks in doorways. Then things can only improve after the wedding. Worse when you're photographed next to pagodas and perfect lawns; the only way from paradise is down.

At the edge of a miniature village with brown chocolate-cake houses, there was a quarry with a dinosaur skeleton at the bottom. My head addled further – time zones bumped and collided for me. Miniature women hung washing on neighbouring clothes lines: all the clothes were white – how in hell did they keep them so clean? I liked that the houses had miniature satellite dishes, that the miniature figurines were not subjected to poor TV choices. I liked the flea market further on; it made me wonder if the miniature people had to do as much sifting through shite to get to the good stuff and whether miniature figurines haggle. Christ, it was getting in on me. I walked through the entire Wunderland from start to finish – no sign of Roy; I wouldn't be surprised if he was deliberately hiding from me – and it never got going for me the way I thought it would. Seeing the trains run around the tracks made me sad, so sad, that Roy's obsession with train timetables didn't bring him anywhere beyond his bedroom. He could sit all day reading timetables and muttering about which timed train would bring him which place, his head more comfortable in the page than in the reality of an imperfect train station. The figurines, the little plastic people in the trains in the Wunderland, they've more life in them than Roy.

The figurines dying in strange ways – smashed to shit at the bottom of a canyon, a child dead in a swimming pool, a fairy drowned in a large sea, all the mutilated figurines squashed and limbless – gave me heart-sink. I couldn't understand why these saddest of things were shown in a magical wonderland – if you can kill a child or a fairy, you might as well end the world. These grotesque deaths reminded me of Mam and her martyrs, the weirder the death the better. Our family home had pictures of dying martyrs so realistic I'd thought for most of my childhood they were photos, pictures of torment and agony and death so violent it's a wonder the three of us didn't turn into serial killers. Go up to the toilet and St Perpetua and Felicity were writhing naked with a placenta trying to escape a wild cow; go outside to hang the clothes on the line and St Cecilia's botched beheading was spewing blood in a stream next to the clothes pegs in the back kitchen; head into the kitchen to do your homework and St Cyriacus's limbs were being yanked from their sockets. St Mercurius was hung from two poles in the first of four pictures in a tableau outside Roy's bedroom, then stabbed with nails, burned, and finally beheaded. To add a bit of romance, above our parents' bed was a picture of St Valentine being clubbed and beaten with stones until he was finally beheaded.

I stood at a miniature scene not taking it in, thinking of a full-size scene at home. Something in my stomach clenches tight when I think of our parents now. The ordeal with Roy, the rumours that reached their ears – it damn near sunk them. They were always the ones doing the talking and now they were the ones being talked about. It didn't occur to them to ignore the gossip: to them, gossip is news and fact and truth. There are events in elderly people's lives that can hurtle them full throttle into the downslide of old age – a son or daughter dying, a bad fall – but this kind of reason you never hear of. I've seen elderly people being checked in to the nursing home, despite having thought they had years of independent living before them, on account of a single pivotal incident. Last time I knocked into Mam and Dad's house, it took ages for them to answer; the doorbell is a pitch above their ear-reach. I let myself in these days and find them half-awake. Their waking seems to blend in with their sleeping – it can be hard to tell which it is they're doing, even though they always insist they're wide awake. The TV is on loud, it never strays far from the Irish channels. Two news bulletins are watched every day: the six one and the nine o'clock, along with hourly radio updates in case something happens in between.

In my parents' kitchen, the glasses were cloudy, there were clumps of dried egg on the fork tines, the plates had scraps of food on them. Bits of crud clung to cereal bowls; grime rimmed the saucepans (they furiously resist our offers of a dishwasher.) The kitchen surfaces were sticky, cooking smells clung to the kitchen curtains, there was a general demeanour of dust and grease about the place. I didn't know whether their eyes had begun to fail them or things like keeping a kitchen and its contents clean had started to feel like a pointless task, but it didn't seem my place to clean the surfaces of the house I grew up in, surfaces my child-hands had dirtied a few decades back.

The living room was full of mechanical parts. Since Dad's retirement, he has taken to looking up the second-hand websites and driving around the county paying out small money for used engines and parts for machines he doesn't own. This is no contemplative tinkering in a shed: this is stockpiles of useless metal, some of it flaking rust, clogging up their house. When I visited last, he sat in the living room with his metal parts, a job of work to do before he could begin to make them run, while Mam sat in the kitchen reading the deaths in the paper. She reads the deaths for the *Suddenlys*. The *Peacefullys* suggest an elderly person dying in their sleep in a nursing home, peace made with the world, goodbyes said to the family, but the Suddenlys have more excitement, Mam says. Within the Suddenlys are the Tragicallys, which, while rare, are the most thrilling. She says she feels cheated by apparent Suddenlys that on further investigation reveal the deceased is more than ninety years old. Mam also gets annoyed by 'after a brief illness' when there's no mention of how brief is brief; if we're going with proportionate, then surely two years is brief for a ninety-eight-year-old. Mam wants her death notice to be under the heading *Roaring*. She puzzles over the death notices for clues like some people analyse crosswords, latching onto signs of how the Tragicallys died (donations to suicide prevention charities or addiction treatment centres in lieu of flowers please). If I chance over to the house in the middle of the deaths-reading, she'll beckon me over to point out an alternative family arrangement, a bereaved son and his 'partner' (a man), or a bereaved son called Rex which turns out to be the mourning dog. Makes me wonder how Allen's death would be received. Would there be a new-found pang at the Suddenlys and Tragicallys?

I was to meet Roy in the restaurant at the Wunderland. I made my way quickly through the rest of the exhibition, with trains running under me and all around me and buzzers buzzing and sirens blaring and lights flashing from buttons constantly being pushed. It felt like I was in some kind of electronic maze or amusement arcade. It was a relief to come out into the blinking bright and to sit down, even if it was on a train seat. I looked at the menu. The Wunderland must have got in on me because I found myself wondering whether there was enough food on the menu to feed all 260,000 figurines and whether the portions would be minuscule. As well as the usual cakes and muffins, rice pudding and jelly were on the menu. Jello they called it, like the Americans. I don't know how Europeans choose which bits and pieces of English to take from British-English or American-English – all I know is nobody's choosing Irish-English.

I looked around at the other booths: it was mostly families. I was getting used to the feel of myself with no children, but it was strange to have the brain-space to not think about defrosting mince and scraping mud off football boots. I'd become so used to measuring other women by the number of humans connected to them – husbands, children, babies – but here it was different. Roy appeared while I was mid-mull, interrupting wherever my head was taking me, and sat down opposite me.

'Well?' He looked expectant, an expression on his face like when the kids show me a drawing and wait for my reaction.

'It's great, it must be a great place to work.' My voice was a whole dose of decibels short of cheer. Roy must have noticed because his face slackened, so I pasted on a smile and added some shrill. 'I liked America the best – what's your favourite land?'

'I prefer parts of Europe, the trains are better, but did you notice the skeletons of mules at the bottom of one canyon, and Snow White leading the seven dwarfs up another?'

In truth, I'd skipped as fast as I could through the Grand Canyon; it was the colour of old blood and I couldn't stop thinking of one of the children cutting themselves.

'Yeah, yeah, what a place!' I was entering vagueness out of necessity – America got barely a glance from me. 'What's your favourite part?' I asked.

He was silent for a minute. 'I like all of it. Except for the birthday party – too much clown.'

I nodded at him, my eyebrows stretched upwards, trying to encourage him to keep talking, but all I could think of was a birthday party he'd had when he was seven or eight. Until that year, Roy had never wanted a birthday party, but he must have read about one in a library book or seen one on the TV because he knew exactly what he wanted. He wanted a clown, he wanted balloons, he wanted a cake with his name on it. We made the cake, we blew up the balloons, his classmates all came, but there was no such thing as hiring clowns for parties then, and surely no money to pay them with even if there were, so our father got himself a pair of stripy pyjamas and stuck pieces of cardboard on his slippers to extend them. He had a proper clown's plastic red nose and, for a wig, our mother had cut the gusset off a pair of tights and put it on his head with pieces of red wool stuck on. Roy had looked wary when all his classmates started arriving and downright annoyed when they played with his toys or rubbed the balloons on their clothes and stuck them to their hair. He was disgusted by the cake we'd made and by the way his name sloped and slanted to the edge when the end of the cake came before his name was finished – Gráinne and I ran out of space and shrunk our letters to fit – and complained about not having shop-cake. But when Dad came in in his clown suit, juggling apples, oranges, and golf balls – he thought to juggle an Irish flag of spheres, make us more patriotic – Roy ran off to his bedroom and has refused to celebrate his birthday since. He had the vocabulary of fun, and we provided the artillery, but he couldn't understand the spirit of it. Fun was something to be ticked off his list, after homework and household chores.

'I like the festivals too,' he said, 'but more the county fairs because I like the dragons—'

What followed then was a list, an itemised list of the figurines he liked, the situations and locations he liked the figurines in, the lands that had the highest densities of train tracks. Roy could list facts and figures in his sleep – he has the ability to store packets of statistics in different shelves of his brain, but he can never assemble those packets into a theory or an opinion that's wholly his own. He can retain large bodies of information but what use are they, these facts, what good do they do him when he can't put them together to make sense of the world around him?

'—the birthday girl was a spoiled brat so she got punished, and the—'

'Let's eat!' I said quickly, with a slew of words about what we could eat. 'There's all sorts of sausages and good desserts – let's order now.'

I'd grown as bad as him with my lists of words, food-words to gloss over awkward family-packs of history. Roy called a waiter and ordered. I didn't have a chance to say what I wanted, but he seemed to be happy with the responsibility of ordering so I let him at it.

'I liked the miniature Santy climbing down the choco-late-factory chimney,' I said.

A familiar smug expression appeared on his face. 'How do you know it's a miniature Santy; do you know what size a life-size Santy is?' He smirked in that infuriating way.

'Fuck off, Roy.'

'What colour were the dwarfs?'

'What?'

He moved closer to my face. 'In Amerika, what colour were the dwarfs wearing?'

'I don't remember, all kinds of colours. What is this, a test?'

'Red, they were all wearing red. What else was unusual about them?'

'Christ, Roy, I saw hundreds of thousands of figurines – how am I supposed to remember everything?'

'They were being watched, by a peeping Tom.' He leaned back in his seat.

'That's a bit creepy,' I said.

'Did you not notice any other peeping Toms in the exhibit?'

'Yeah, I noticed a few.'

'Oh,' he sat forward and looked expectant, 'where?'

'I can't remember where, in some of the lands.'

He looked a bit crestfallen then and I couldn't tell if he was disappointed in my failure to notice or in the existence of the miniature peepers. I glanced around for our food. I wasn't prepared for an interrogation about pin-sized figu-rines; it was difficult to take seriously. Roy was studying me, as if the lines on my face contained the answer to the riddle of the universe.

'Did you not like it, Gert?'

'I liked it fine – I'm just tired, that's all.'

'Tired.' He said it like I had invented the word and it was a disgusting thing.

'Yes, tired, Roy, tired from worrying about you and trying not to mention the fucking elephant in the room.'

His eyeballs flung themselves around in their sockets and finished somewhere around my chin, a mutinous set to his jaw that I well knew.

'What about all this mindfulness crap you go on about? Why couldn't you just focus on the present in the Wunderland and stop thinking of other things – isn't that what you keep telling me to do?' He sat back in his seat, smug look on his face, the clever prick; he'd got me rightly this time.

I took a deep breath. I wanted to flatten him but now was a time for mending not breaking. Reply softly and he'd be shamed into unprickling. 'It's OK, Roy, I liked it, I really did.'

'OK.' His face lost a portion of its sneer.

'It reminded me of the Magic Faraway Tree – you know the book Hazel loves? With the different magical lands at the top that keep changing and you have to be careful not to be stuck in one when they change.'

'Right.'

We sat in a near truce of a silence until the food arrived: sausages and chips and jelly and creamed rice.

'It's nice to be able to imagine you at work, Roy. At home, when I think you up, it will be good to know how to situate you.'

He nodded but didn't look appeased. He was staring far off beyond my eyes.

Roy

Ich verstehe nur Bahnhof = I only understand
train station = It's all Greek to me

He went to the toilet and left Gert eating her jelly. He locked himself in a cubicle. If he mashed the palms of his hands over his ears and tapped his fingers against the back of his head, lightly and slowly at first, then working harder and faster to a crescendo, it felt like a jackhammer or a train was coming or something, something terrible was about to happen. Gert didn't like the Wunderland. Gert didn't like the Wunderland. Gert got him here, Gert arranged this job, this life, and Gert didn't like it. He shook his head quickly to rid himself of his thoughts. The Wunderland was his place to like or dislike, his world to like or dislike, not Gert's. Who the hell did she think she was?

Gert

Heidenangst = scared as hell = jitters

The jelly was so sweet, it cloyed. The metal spoon felt wrong; it clacked against my teeth because they didn't have enough food substance to deal with – such a solid implement to be used against such a wobbly, insubstantial foodstuff. Roy had gone to the toilet. He was gone a long while and I got the panics and thought maybe he'd run away, when he came back looking flushed and uneasy, Saturday-afternoon-Ikea stressed, a low-slung dog in a large crowd. But no matter; he came back.

Roy

Zähneknirschend = gnashing teeth

Gert didn't like the Wunderland.

Gert

Fix und fertig = totally exhausted

'Let's go for a drink, Roy,' I said to him when he came back. *Take the edge off,* I thought to myself. I'd spent the four hours of his shift walking the exhibit, afraid to leave early for fear of offending him, and I could do with a pick-up. He looked about as enthusiastic as if I'd asked him to lay out the clothes he wanted to be buried in, but he came anyway. We went out through the gift shop, and I bought a train for Benjy and a teddy bear for Hazel. Allen and I tried to give them each toys for girls and boys, to stay out of the princess aisle of the toy shop, but turns out you can't lay your gender-neutral preferences at the feet of your children: Benjy wants to be a train-driver, Hazel a princess. Roy was too embarrassed to use his staff discount so I grudgingly paid full price. Asking for things that are well within your rights comes hard to my brother. He sees it as a long arm coming down from the sky and pointing at him in judgement. We came out of the Wunderland in darkness and crossed canals and roads to get back to the street we were on the first night. Some of the boats docked in the water had names of faraway places that tease with their promise of heat. *Buenos Aires. Goa Dreamer.* I was glad we weren't there to witness sunset. It's the turn of time I dislike: day to night, the turn of the clocks at autumn and spring. Makes me think I should have crammed more in, should be in a different setting to where I am now.

'Do you know any cosy pubs near here?'

'Bars,' he said, 'not pubs.'

'Do you know any cosy bars near here?'

'No.'

'Well, let's find one.' I needed a feed of spirits to keep my own spirits up. When the only other person in your immediate proximity is pulled downwards to the glums, it is fiercely hard to not be pulled down with them.

And so we walked, Roy and I, we walked the night city. Shops were closing around us, shutters pulled down, traffic thinned on the roads.

'This one?' I'd ask as we passed a bar. 'Or this one?'

'No,' came the answer, 'not that one.'

And on we walked. The bar was never this one, or that one or the other one; there was no bar in the entire city that would fit the two of us it seemed. We walked past shops selling expensive goods, the kind of shops I turn my head from for fear of seeing a reflection of my plain face surrounded by beautiful things. It being February, the shops had pink and red decorations, hearts and roses. It depressed me, the contrived nonsense of clichéd romance. Coming downstairs one morning to find that Allen had glued a wayward sole back onto my stinky old runner and propped the leg of an armchair on the shoe to keep pressure on it: that's romance to me. Doing something that needs doing, or wants doing, without being asked – never mind your hearts and flowers and ta-da! moments.

'Roy, isn't it funny the way the shops turn red for Valentine's Day?'

'I suppose.'

'And they turn green for St Patrick's Day, pink for Mother's Day, yellow for Easter. We need a celebration on the blue end of the spectrum.'

He looked at me to see if I was serious then thought for a moment. 'Blue for Chilblains Day?' he asked.

We walked past places that looked like they served food or drink or food and drink, but for some reason were not the kind of place Roy would go to. I stopped my feet in the footpath.

'Where do you want to go, Roy?'

'Home.'

'All right, let's go home.'

He would wear out your heart, this brother of mine, he would shove your patience in the nearest rubbish bin, which he would then correct me for saying and insist I use whatever word English-speaking Germans used. Dealing with him is like trying to tug cling film and tear it without it warping in on itself or wrapping around your hand in a cloying bandage. We walked in the direction his feet proposed, we walked the legs off ourselves, and eventually the port appeared. It was only when I knew where we were, when I could place us in relation to the flat, that I began to feel tired and count every footstep until we reached the warehouses. I felt like a used plaster at the bottom of a swimming pool. Roy let us into the flat and went straight to the bathroom. I went into the bedroom and shut the door, no niceties about goodnights or who would use the bathroom first tonight. I got undressed and looked out the window at the moon, a semi-circular gape of a smile in the sky. Sometimes it's hard to tell if the moon is half-hidden or if it has been sliced cleanly in two.

I think dealings with my brother are not unlike dealings with my husband. In both relationships I brace myself and try to force conversations about realities, but both men obfuscate, distract, disengage. Hard to know if it's me that's the problem, if there's someone out there who Roy would talk to, who Allen would talk to.

Anyway, there must be a better way to live. There must be a way to live that doesn't involve so much secrecy, so many half-truths and avoided truths and twisted realities. Allen has concocted different versions of our recent past in order to keep going and not dwell on how awful it was for me and the kids, but it leaves me with secret realities that can't be uttered for fear of damaging him. I understand it's important to protect his pride, his sense of self, but where are my protections? How many of us are living like this? How many half-lives are spent watching over people who don't want to be watched, hiding the truth to protect the watched?

I used to think tough times improved your character, but they've narrowed my mind, focused me inwards. When I hear of a terrorist attack in a city, my first thought runs to people I know who live there, and my first feeling is of relief when I know nobody. After that comes compassion for strangers, but it's a delayed second.

How to live with something this big and this secret? The impressions people get of us are so wrong, so morbidly inaccurate, I get weary thinking of how to correct their assumptions. When I turn up at an event not in the best of form but trying my utmost, sometimes people say I'm a bit off. I want to tell them a bit off is a lot better than burrowed indefinitely under the bed-covers. My *off* is higher functioning than your *on*, I want to shout. The effort required to get to *a bit off* is colossal. You live with the possibility of your world stopping, and most people don't know. You rehearse what you'll say to the children if their father goes missing again. He has gone missing a few times since that first episode but, boomerang that he is, he always found his way home.

I keep a tension index for things we do go to. I remember not what I wore or who I talked to or what music was playing; I remember what mood Allen was in and how well he was hiding it, or, if I was attending alone, I'll remember if I ripped home early to find the consequences. I'm often told how lucky I am to have such a fun, sociable husband by people who clearly think I'm a misery guts. If they could just see what I'd experienced in the hours and days prior to his current sociability, they might not judge me so harshly.

I know I shouldn't care what people do or don't think of me. I should focus on me and what I've done or not done. I succeeded in not thinking about Roy while life was at crisis-point with Allen. Much like a cow with four stomachs, my brain has several compartments. I put Roy into one and locked it until worries about Allen eased. Once I let myself think about it, I felt wretched about how I had handled, or not handled, the Roy issue. Getting rid of him may not have been the wisest option – maybe I should have tried to help him stay and fight the rumours. It seemed too big an ask, though. Gráinne and our parents turned their eyes blind to it – an understandable if convenient way of dealing with it – and there was only so much I could heap on myself.

It's the squeeze of it. If either my original family or concocted family could sort themselves out, I might feel a bit more like I could get a handle on the world. Times I feel like a heel of bread stuffed into the toaster, pushed unwillingly down to the furnace.

I turned this way and that in the bed, trying to find some ease from the thoughts pinging around my brain.

I shouldn't have sent Roy away, I know that now. It was a suggestion at first, a suggestion that grew legs and became a decision. I let him down by not confronting it myself. In order for me to defend him publicly, I would have had to fully believe he was innocent, and that was a thought process I didn't want to engage in. When I allowed myself to think about it, though, when I put all the thoughts and feelings together on one page, I concluded that he was innocent. It's easy to quash suspicions when you decide to. My focus turned to finding him a place in another country, hoping a different language and different structures would accommodate him better. I had hoped he would fit into a country with more definite ways of going on, but that hasn't happened. He has taken his oddities and translated them into a language that doesn't exist; no country could accommodate them. My eyes burned with tears behind eyelids closed for sleep that wouldn't come. Oh, Roy.

DAY 5

Roy

Erbsenzähler = pea counter = obsessed with details

Roy set to work on his morning shift, something not right rattling him. He felt as if there was a foreign object stuck in the far recesses of his mouth that he couldn't quite get at with his tongue. He set his bucket in front of a miniature construction site in the land of Hamburg. There were lots of cranes, which he ran his duster over. Lattices were very unsatisfactory surfaces to dust; there were way too many holes. He dusted a coffin being buried in a graveyard and looked quickly over his shoulder, not waiting for the lights to dim before yanking it from the men lowering it. He prised and peeled and plied but the coffin wouldn't open. It was glued shut. Roy placed the miniature coffin on the floor, picked up his sweeping brush and slammed it down onto the coffin again and again until he put a dent in it. Inside was indeed empty. Roy felt empty too. He felt as if he'd been lied to, as if the Wunderland was part sham. Maybe Gert could see the lies behind it and that's why she hadn't liked it. He took out his phone and looked up the word *sham*: Heuchelei in German. He wrote that on a page in his notebook. Then he looked up *funeral*: Beerdigung. He wrote that on the page. Then he looked up *There is no corpse*: Es gibt keine Leiche. He wrote that on the next line and put his phone away. He put the smashed pieces of the coffin back in the cemetery and flattened the men so it looked as if something had dropped from the sky and smashed them all into smithereens. Then he leaned his sign against the church so that full-size visitors could see they had paid to be fooled.

A giant (well, a miniature giant – maybe there was a compound German noun for giant in a miniature setting?) pig came out of the train station. Roy seized it, liberating it from its trotters, and put it in his pocket. A trotterless pig would surely be friends with the hoofless cow; they could be the first animals on his animal census. He moved on to a miniature pool-hall. A clown was surrounded by bunny girls; a monk stood in front of a slot machine. He pushed a botched birthday party he'd been given as a child out of his head, a horror of a day with all sorts of unpredictabilities and let-downs. Then he beat the clown to tiny pieces with the butt of his brush and left the mess where it was, to hell with it.

He polished the glass then moved on to the football stadium, covered in Perspex. He remembered being taken to Croke Park to see his county play football when he was young. His father had screamed blue fury; Gert gave as much as her lungs had; Roy stayed completely silent. He had grasped the fundamentals of the game and was happy when the ball had gone under or over the bar, but he couldn't muster the levels of fervour his father, and most of the spectators, were showing. He kept forgetting to follow the ball, preferring to examine the different coloured shirts, count the flags, watch the train pass through the gaps in the stands. His father became impatient with the tilting of Roy's head towards things that weren't the game at hand, and he felt his father's shame deeply. There had never been pressure put on him to play a sport and excel at it, but it was believed that watching it could be a good way to spend time together. Gert was more of a son to her father than Roy ever was.

Roy tossed his family from his head and looked at the miniature Hamburg in front of him. He liked cleaning a miniature version of the city he was living in and being able to compare it to the full-size city and find the flaws in translation. He peered into the miniature city hall to look for a miniature genealogist but there was no such figurine and no desks or filing cabinets that could hold records of births, marriages, and deaths. Surely there must be some census records – otherwise how did they know there were 260,000 figurines? You can't just create a quarter of a million people, toss them into life, and not keep records of them; you can't just expect them to know where they come from. Who was the overriding hand behind all this, the person who deemed there should be 10,000 festival-goers in Switzerland or eight firemen in Hamburg or a recurring pervy monk in each of the lands? And if he found the census records, what date of birth would be on them? The figurines were handmade, but would the date of birth refer to the day a figurine was finished or the day it was conceived in the inventor's imagination? If all these figurines had birthdays, there would be constant cake crumbing about the Wunderland, approximately 712 happy birthdays sung a day on average. There could be a rolling, roving birthday celebration that could move from exhibit to exhibit or, better yet, an exhibit devoted to Birthday-land, where the celebrating figurines could be brought every day. Roy shook his head at the inadequacies of proper records and moved on to the miniature Miniatur Wunderland.

He leaned over the bar and stared in the window of the Wunderland, wondering if he could see himself at work, or the latchkey kid or any of his colleagues, but he couldn't make out face details. It stranded him, this layering of worlds. He took the window cleaner out of the bucket and sprayed it at the windows.

Then he wrapped two fingers in a cloth and pushed through the glass, which gave a high-pitched *squickle* and shattered inwards. Inside the broken pane, he could make out a miniature family – mother, father, and two small children. He dug his fingers further in and flattened them. It felt good to raze whole families to the ground, but he needed something more.

Outside the Wunderland, miniature trucks delivered goods and a queue of miniature visitors waited. They all looked so expectant, so happy to be there, so certain everything would work out, it galled him. Roy looked around him for watchful eyes, then scanned the ceilings and corners for cameras, but he couldn't see any flashing lights. His heart started racing, but some things just needed to be done. He felt almost resigned to being caught and the phrase *might as well be hung for a sheep as a lamb* came into his head. Except here it would be *might as well be sacked for a massacre as a murder*. He upended his duster and laid it flat atop the tiny visitors' heads like a long, low cylindrical cloud before bringing it down sharply. Once the bulk of the queue was knocked, he grasped one end of the duster like a rolling pin, grabbed the other end in the middle, and rolled forward and backward, forward and backward, with crude might. Miniature heads crumpled, miniature bodies split into pieces, miniature fingers came undone from miniature hands. When all the figurines were smathered, it felt good and clean, but he still wanted more.

He peered inside the miniature building at the miniature model train – it looked disgustingly perfect. A miniature of a model train was a double confusion of sizing, messing with his head. There was something coiled and pent-up in its bearing, like a dog hovering on its back paws waiting to spring, and it bothered him. It bothered him hugely that objects had more confidence in their workings than he had in his. He poked his fingers through the glassless windows and pushed at the train until it began to tip. Roy peered over his shoulders before poking his fingers through another window and shoving the train. He still hadn't found the middle, the sweet spot for imbalance, so he moved a few windows along. Now he put the fingers of two hands through the windows and gave an almighty push, trying to winnow all his strength into four fingers. The train objected slightly before giving in and toppling off the track. It felt good to derail a train, even a miniature of a miniature.

He flicked the duster around the opera house and a zoo, with a dinosaur that looked so perfectly at home that Roy had to think whether dinosaurs were real and zoo-able. He leaned over and pulled the animals out of their cages and pens, starting with the most vicious, setting the lions and tigers and gorillas on some of the miniature visitors. Then he plucked some other human figurines and set them inside the cages and pens, eating slop from troughs.

'There,' he said, 'see how you like that.' He wondered what the full-size visitors would make of their miniature counterparts getting mauled, or whether they would even see the correlation.

Roy found himself at the end of miniature Hamburg just as a group of visitors came round the corner. It was always a sad thing to find yourself at the end of a land, even if it was an imaginary land. It felt like he had run out of space in the world, like there was nowhere that would fit him or contain him.

Gert

Das Fernweh = distant ache = yearning for freedom of travel

He was gone to his morning shift when I woke, and I had to use all my power to dredge myself up. Lucky the bed was so uncomfortable, else I'd be more likely to spend the day in it. When we were young, Roy would lie in bed thinking up thoughts that could do him no good; even from a young age, his head was in the coffin. Some people daydream about what they'd do if they won the Lotto; my brother lay there thinking of the people he'd have on his visitors' list if he went to prison. He'd found out that prisoners in Ireland are allowed up to six visitors and, depending on how much we annoyed him, he'd move us up and down the list, sometimes off it entirely. He always had a problem filling the two other spaces; he never could make a friend long enough to last more than a few days on the list. He'd throw his whole self into alienating people in the most imaginative ways. He once told a vegan friend that he didn't really like meat, he just ate it to keep the animal population down.

Last night in bed when I couldn't sleep, I read short stories until I was dazed, glutted with too many lives intensely lived. I passed a terrible night with disturbingly vivid tea-dreams – I shouldn't caffeinate before bed. The stories I'd read entered my half-conscious mind and bled with my dreams in an ominous way. I woke, or half-woke, to see a small creature tugging at my breast. Before the thought could reach my brain and tell me it wasn't real, I felt a gut-pang like one of my kids needed me. I try not to think too much about them while I'm away for fear of guilting up but they creep into my dreams at night, their faces under shadow. I feel a sense of vague unease or unspecified urgency, as if there's something I should do before it's too late, like turning off a gushing tap before it floods the bathroom.

I had heard Roy rising and shuffling to dress in the dark wee hours. He moved around the apartment with mouse-stealth, so quietly it was as if he didn't want to leave an imprint of himself in the carpet, and when he left, he pulled the door softly like he was taking the weight of it upon himself.

I scraped myself out of bed because nothing is gained from rumination. Our mother uses the phrase *Least said soonest mended* a lot, but I also think *Least thought soonest mended* should be in use. You don't see ants mulling long-winded about life: they scuttle about heedless, and heed is something we pay too much of.

I got up and showered, hot as I could bear it. If my skin doesn't ping with the heat, if my lower back isn't shivering with the pelt of sore-hot water, it's not hot enough. When things are bad, I do my crying in the shower. There's water coming at me from above; there may as well be water dripping from my eyes. Hard for anyone to hear me over the whine of the electric. On good days, the hum of the shower is the roar of a football stadium of fans; on bad days it's the buzz of a chainsaw coming for my throat.

I tugged my clothes on, sensible clothes. I wished I'd brought something a bit showier. Where to start with showiness at my age, though, which bits to show off and which bits to hide. When I went back to the bedroom, the dark and bareness took hold of me, lowering my mood, so I grabbed my bag, stuffed some magazines in it, and left the flat. There was a squirt of light coming from Stefan's bedroom but I wasn't going a-knocking to check if he was there – I just pulled the door behind me and hoped it wouldn't get robbed. I went to the café by the station, the kind of place you wouldn't be overly stilled by. I was hoping the sense of coming and going would inflate me a bit. Child-ache had set in: I missed them more than I could think about; I missed them so much it was physical. With Allen, it's different. I hold some part of me back from missing him because I feel constantly on the edge of losing him to someone or something.

I ordered coffee and pastries because pastries are what we eat for breakfast. I'd prefer cake but cake was not served until midday.

I took out one of my magazines and flicked to an interview with a female celebrity who was all bubbles and froth, a one-woman hen party, the kind of person I avoid in real life, but in print, her punctuation was cheering. She seemed to have been born with her finger on the exclamation-mark key, which kept me nicely in the shallows. When I try to hide the worst of Allen's moods in front of the kids, I live lies for them and serve up exclamation marks aplenty to keep up the jollies and cover over fissures wide as sinkholes; it's only when they're in bed that I allow myself to droop.

This woman was talking about her life choices. I don't know why so many celebrities bang on about their life choices, as if where we end up is under our control, as if it all just works out after picking a certain path from a checklist as a teenager. In my experience, you choose a direction, then you spend the rest of your life scraping the worst of the shite off your decisions.

I turned to the problem page near the back. A woman was asking for advice on how to make love to her husband so that he wouldn't be tempted to stray. The answer was a load of sweet-sick muck about commitment and feeling, with lots of eye-gazing; if I was the agony aunt, I'd say, 'For starters, if you're making love you're not doing it right.' Agony aunts in advice columns seem to give advice based on hypothetically perfect lives. They advise the maritally problemed to leave their imperfect unions and Live! Your! Best! Life! They say that it's best for both parties in the relationship, and for any children involved, if the unhappy person leaves the problematic situation and finds first themselves and then somebody else. What utter cock! How many marriages would survive this advice? What about the reality that all relationships go through tough times and maybe, just maybe, sticking at it might be worth it?

I moved onto the next magazine. There were endless style tips to take you from desk to dinner or from office to bar – what wank-speak! It sticks in my gullet this assumption that every woman works in an office. Where are the outfits to take you from nursing home to local pub, from dole queue to house party, from bar to busman's holiday? I feel unspoken to in these magazines, the annual Christmas-party-dress feature disowns me – it assumes I have glamorous places to go to socialise with similarly sequinned and velveted women. Next there was an interview with a celebrity about how she spends her weekends. How is it that in all these 'Day in a Life' columns, the interviewees seem to spend their Saturday and Sunday mornings practising yoga or tai chi before strolling around a farmers' market and then having a leisurely lunch and strolling around an art gallery. How much fucking strolling can you do in one day? Why aren't they tearing around Tesco or racing to get their kids to football matches on time? How is it that these celebrities are so busy having leisurely lunches with friends on restaurant terraces they don't end up horsing Big Macs in McDonald's, hoping they wouldn't be spotted coming out under the golden arches by the hipster vegan-mom squad? And as for their evenings – it seems every celebrity loves nothing better than to cook a simple meal (prepared from their farmers' market haul, of course – locally sourced, ethically produced, fair trade, low-plastic, zero carbon emissions) and share it with friends. If they're all so busy hosting all the time, who actually attends their dinners? The world needs guests as much as hosts. There's something so unbearably smug about their lives that I can't help wondering what mass-produced realities lie under the curated perfection.

I sidled up to the counter for a coffee refill and another pastry, one with something in the middle this time because too many flakes felt unsubstantial and I needed to be grounded by gooey centres. My mind drifted back to the doughnuts we have with the kids every week, the simple sugared ring doughnuts that over time have evolved into ones with more and more elaborate fillings, the kids' dissatisfaction growing in direct relation to the amount of choice.

After the children were born, I ditched my office job and minded them at home for some years. The circular, endless days were comforting for a while; we looked inwards, like being inside an O. When the O began to bulge at the seams, I decided to go back to work. I wanted a job that wouldn't have me tethered to computer wires all day so I did the carers' course and went to work in the local nursing home. The days pass quickly there, though the chatter is mostly the same. I read the summaries of *Coronation Street* and *Eastenders* online so I can keep up the chat with the patients. Conversation swings better for me since I had children. It's a predictable pendulum that's easy if dull. I'm part of a club unintended –

even if I do find it dreary listening to the other carers' tales of their children, I have something to contribute now. It's a kind of cycle of outdoing us mothers have – whose child is the cleverest, tallest, most advanced; whose husband is the most useless, grumpiest, laziest. We do up our children and do down our husbands.

When I'd dragged out my second coffee as long as I could, I paid and left the café. If I'd known how much time I'd be spending alone, I'm not sure I'd have come to Hamburg. I had imagined more time with Roy. I somehow thought I'd have managed to penetrate his sulky armour and force a conversation. It hadn't occurred to me he'd be going to work as usual and leaving me to my own bleak wanderings.

I walked towards the port, the pull of the water at me like a whiskey-hankering. A ship was parked, or docked maybe. It was a museum ship, by the looks, with tourists gawking around it. I climbed the steps, walked the metal gangplank onto the ship, and bought a ticket from a woman who handed me an information sheet. I was reluctant to leave the warmth of the little ticket office so I looked around at the items for sale. There were ships in bottles and messages in bottles and maps made to look old and lots of nautically themed curios and objects that bore no relation to the sea but had the Hamburg city arms printed on them and so, it had been decided, they were souvenirs. A thimble was for sale, *Fingerhut* it was called in German. Finger hat – what a beautiful translation. When I had worn out my looking, I left the office and stepped out onto the boat, reading the information sheet: 'Her crew consisted of the captain, two steersmen, a cook, a carpenter, a sail maker and a donkeyman, eleven able seamen, three ordinary seamen, and four ship's boys.'

I wanted to know the difference between able seamen and ordinary seamen and how you'd move from ordinary to able, and whether ordinary is unable compared to able. I peeked at the sailors' bunks and the officers' quarters and the pigs' and hens' quarters below deck. I couldn't help wondering whether animals get seasick and puke so hard they'd rather be at the bottom of the sea. I was going to look this up on my phone but realised that the answers to the things I want answered are not on this device, nor on any other device that I know of. Here are my questions:

How to not get sucked down?

How to not become bitter?

How to not fuck up the kids?

How to get through the day?

When things are at their worst, how to get through the next four minutes?

I left the ship and wandered the stretch of shops selling St Pauli merchandise and generic seaside tat. Each of the shops seemed to be selling the same items at the same prices and I wondered how businesses could stand their wares out from the other sellers. If I was a shopkeeper here, I'd go rogue. I'd sell items with seaside pictures from all the port cities around the world except Hamburg.

I realised I was thirsty, even though feeling thirsty in this cold seemed as incongruous as feeling an itch in an amputated limb. I went to a riverfront restaurant and ordered a coffee and sat facing the waters. A shame about the grey weather; when the sky and water are the same drab colour the world starts to close in on me. It was the end of February, soon time for the clock change. That should have filled me with joy, the prospect of an extra hour of brightness, but all I could think of was the hour's sleep I'd lose and the effect it'd have on Allen. The equinoxes come down hard on him. I wonder if there could be something planetary about him, some way he's attuned to minuscule seismic shifts, like an animal sensing an earthquake. Has he some sensibility the rest of us don't have? Is that why he reacts badly to life? The spring equinox is tough: the disconnect between the promise of longer, warmer evenings and the reality of hail and sleet, so common in recent springs that unseasonal has become seasonal.

But the autumn clock change is the worst. I dread the turn of the sun. I used to like the dark evenings, but since Allen took sick, they weigh heavy on me. Winter used to be my season of choice with its stew-promise and sofa-potential. I liked going for bundled-up walks in the dark evenings around the town when few were about and people bared their décor to the world with an open-curtain policy, but now, when Allen goes to bed, I sit watchful, long after he's been given mental health clearance. The ceiling seems to come down a ways on top of me; the dark closes in, and the house wraps itself around me, like the clutch of a too-tight coat under the armpits. It's worse watching out for an adult than a child. I can set them to rights with cuddles and nightlights to guard against demons. Lights bring on Allen's demons; better for him to be safe in full dark.

Just after a crisis, when things were bad but not frighteningly bad, I took to carrying my passport around as a fantasy escape route. Deep down I knew I would never take off, but it was a comfort to have the burgundy rectangle flush against the inside pocket of my handbag. Where I'd go, I didn't know. The destination didn't matter so much as the possibility of fleeing. A *flee*, that's the word I wanted, an escape with connotations of a fling. I got as far as the airport a couple of times, feeling giddy to be there unplanned and alone, and every time, I would get the bus back into the city with all the returned holiday-makers (I prefer holiday-maker to tourist – it gives off the bang of effort). I'd feel a mixture of envy and relief, relief at not having to make a decision more than anything.

I still feel guilt at the thought I could do that to my children, especially as they were so hard-got. Or maybe that was the problem: want something so much for so long that you switch off some part of yourself in order to preserve yourself if you can't have them. I've seen the opposite extreme, the parents who spoil their hard-won miracle children. It's the pit of extremes we live by, those unhealthy edges of love that the life-comes-easy brigade don't have to deal with.

Even though I'd put the Roy worries aside, they still managed to seep out when I was at my lowest. No matter how much you blockade your fears, just try and stop them creeping in when your defences are on the ground. The thoughts can be stemmed, but the feelings burst through. Knowing there'd come a time when I'd have to meet his situation head-on in Hamburg – well, that was a fret I couldn't take on.

When things are bad, I cry nights; I cry sobless so as not to wake the kids. I want to roar, I want to bellow, I want to squirt pure murder from my lungs, but I sniff up and gulp down the grief. Grief which I'm not officially entitled to because nobody has died. Yet I'm felled by the stuff, floored by it, even though there's no coffin in the corner of the room, just the dying of a man's mind upstairs.

Times after I've done a fuck-load of ironing, after I've shelved and drawered and hangered all the clothes, I want to sweep them all from the shelves, wrench them from the drawers, yank them from the hangers, and hack them shred them tear them rent them rip them fuck them into a pile on the floor and stamp on them. Times after I've wiped the kitchen counters and swept the floor, I want to take every dish every plate every cup every glass from the cupboards and smash them on the floor kick them at the walls and fuck me if I don't lay a flying kick at the walls themselves while I'm at it. Times during Allen's first failed medical intervention – followed by the weaning off the first batch of drugs, followed by the three-week wait for the new tablets to kick in, followed by that weaning off, followed by the third successful dosage – times then I had thoughts of taking the children to a different country, starting them off anew. Times I have thoughts unbidden, thoughts that careen unchecked, when I mentally piece together all the pills in the house – the sleepers, downers, painhitters. It's a comfort to know I'm covered: if I could just get the number right and be sure of it. My desires are not like Allen's. His is a violent elimination from the world; mine is a gentler fantasy of not-being. I'd be blamed entirely, of course. There was always something a bit funny about her, they'd say, something a bit off, something you couldn't quite put your finger on. Small wonder he suffered from his nerves, they'd say, those poor children, how could any mother leave her kids like that. Unnatural, they'd say, selfish, they'd say, nothing like that ever happens round here, they'd say, and if I did it during the day they could say *and in broad daylight too.*

Small blame on me, but still, if those children knew how close their father and mother came to ending it all, they would never knock a night out of their own bedrooms again.

But I don't do these things; I won't do these things. I help the children with their homework, I bring them to mass occasionally so they know the priest's name for their grandparents' questions, I turn them up at birthday parties washed and dressed and carrying an age-appropriate present. I behave impeccably, as always.

Roy

Aufs Glatteis führen = to lead someone into black
ice = to lead someone astray, to deceive

Roy headed for Scandinavia and dusted a candy-striped con-
fection of a circus tent. He swiped his cloth at a group of
hippies in a treehouse (collective noun: a dreadlock of hippies) and knocked one of them out to the ground, pinching
the dreadlocks from his head. He moved on to the sea, to the
(relatively miniature) huge white suspension bridge, a den-
tal comb or harp of a bridge, the Øresund Bridge. Roy had
written the name in his notebook, his first O with a forward-
slanting slash through it that he thought he could pronounce
correctly if he said *Ugh*, like he was disgusted by something.
Vowels were a bit unwieldy to learn because speakers sludge
them together; when their accents took hold of their speaking
it was the vowels that varied the most. Roy wanted precision,
and for that reason, he was more of a consonant man. He had
read that there can be no language without vowel sounds and
he wondered if it followed that a language made up of only
vowel sounds was a superior one; maybe if he could find the
right group of people they could devise a vowelly language
and *Uh* and *Ee* at each other all day.

He surveyed the Øresund strait. A miniature giant crab
attacked a human scuba diver, which seemed only right –

didn't giant humans kill and eat small crabs? Maybe it was time for restorative justice. A dead man was tied to a rock at the bottom of the sea holding a sign saying 'Blubb Blubb'. So, Roy thought, drowning people say the same thing in German as in English, not even an umlaut in the difference. He looked at the miniature keeper in the miniature lighthouse on a miniature island and thought of his grandparents' house on the south coast of Ireland. When he and his sisters stayed in the house during the holidays, the light from the lighthouse swept the room once, twice, three times in soothing flashes that he counted himself to sleep with. The last time he'd stayed there, the lightbulbs had been replaced by energy-saving ones, and the light was so weak, it was discernible only if you concentrated on a particular point in the room. This filled him with more loss than when his grandparents died.

After he'd polished the glass, he stood up and reached his duster over the bridge. Specks of dust settled on the surface of the water, which looked so pristine underneath, so perfectly still and unhurried, that he felt the need to defile it to make it flow, to introduce some kind of current. He looked quickly around but nobody was watching him – nobody ever noticed the cleaner – and he spat into the water. It was unsatisfactorily temporary but it would have to do.

He moved inland to a forest and swiped his duster at flying miniature fairies and a frolicking unicorn. Then he plucked one of the fairies and dunked her in the water where he'd just spat. He picked up the unicorn, leaving one of its hooves glued to the forest floor, and placed it on top of the bridge, about to jump. Nobody would expect to see a suicidal unicorn – it would spell the close of the world when the purest of beasts wanted to end themselves. Roy moved on to the Christmas snow village, either ten months early or two months late. He wiped the ice hotel, a nativity scene, a snowman carousel. If birthdays were a disappointment then Christmas was the anticlimax to end all unfulfilled party promises. The build-up was extreme, the presents poorly thought out and unsatisfactorily executed, the day itself a bore and a relief to be gotten over with. If bad things were on your mind, then Christmas was a time they festered intensely.

The same rector from the other lands was rushing into the church with his bag; maybe this one was late for the Christmas service. Roy reached in and tugged the doctor's bag from the rector's hand and put it in his pocket – the miniature clergyman would have trouble giving his sermon now without his notes. He dusted an elephant ice sculpture and considered taking it to add to his animal census, but decided that a miniature ice sculpture of an animal is probably too far removed from a census-able being. He dusted a family of penguins waiting at a station platform with their suitcases and a pet dog. Penguins appeared in many locations throughout the Wunderland – hanging out with a sea lion, a pet dog, among nuns. They really got around for flightless waddlers. Roy picked a couple of penguins from the middle and pocketed them; they seemed amiable and capable of getting on with the hoofless cow and trotterless pig. A miniature woman beat a red rug on a frame with a paddle, the same figure he'd seen before. It was unsettling, this feeling of déjá vu that had been intentionally planted in his mind by the designers and engineers, the same figures recurring. The Wunderland felt haunted by creatures repeated, figurines doubled.

A camel ridden by a silver man pulled children on a sled. This was the kind of exhibit he liked, a sun-rathering camel landed in the snow, something ill-suited and incongruous and just plain wrong. Under this Christmas scene was a huge miniature mine with tunnels and shafts. The room hopped with the clanks and groans of machinery, and every so often a stomach-juddering crash, and Roy tried to time his cleanings around the worst of the noise.

The snow scenes looked so falsely, dreadfully optimistic that he felt the need to tear them down a peg or two, bring them back to reality. He waited until a moony-eyed couple had moved on to giggle at an exhibit further down Scandinavia before snatching the snowman and the nativity scene and the camel. He'd been accused of ruining Christmas before: let him really ruin it this time.

He checked his phone. Gert was probably out of the apartment by now; he could sneak back on his break and tend to his wardrobe. He rushed from Scandinavia, passing other lands but ignoring his co-workers, and tore back to his apartment. He hunkered down at the wardrobe and deposited the couple of penguins, setting them down in their own circle with the hoofless cow and trotterless pig. He tried to figure out a hierarchy of animals and wondered which creatures would come out on top. Probably the cow, based on brute strength, unless the penguins could be wily and the pig cunning. Then he put the doctor's bag beside the lone figurine in the main arrangement, set his Christmas figurines in their own little circle near the edge of the wardrobe, and stamped on them until they were mostly smashed. There: Christmas ruined again.

Gert

*Backpfeifengesicht = a face in need of a fist = a face
in need of a good slap*

That afternoon we went to the city's boneyard. It was the one thing
Roy suggested, and I didn't want to discourage him by refusing.

Some tourists visit zoos to see other living species; my
brother prefers the dead of our own species. I was waiting for
him when he finished work. He was looking a bit more comfortable with me now, not so much a jumpy stray as a slightly
nervy pet. His tongue was moving in his mouth like he was
worrying a mouth ulcer or easing a bitten tongue.

'Hey, how was work?'

'Fine, fine,' he said, distracted.

'All set for the graveyard?'

'Cemetery,' he said, 'it's not connected to a church.'

'Cemetery,' I said, adding cold to my voice, but it makes
no odds; he doesn't notice small vocal sulks. I tell myself he
can't help it, I tell myself if it's the one thing that makes him
feel good, let him have it, but I can't do it with good grace. My
anger is not so much at his attitude or his responses; it's anger
at myself for not anticipating or pre-empting his responses
and taking steps to avoid them. It's like physical pain: the
problem is not the pain itself – the problem is when you forget the pain and go about as normal until you're suddenly
felled by it. My rage abrupted over and came out in a shout.

226

'Why do you correct everything I say? Why does it *matter* that everything I say be spot-on perfect?'

He looked shocked by my splurt. 'Why would you want to speak incorrectly?'

'Ah, fuck's sake, Roy, give me normal conversation. Stop bloody telling me things you've learned from books.'

He looked surprised – and small wonder when he doesn't know my frustrations have been building for days – but said nothing and increased his pace. We walked in the speediest of silences to the train station. Strange how it felt local now. This felt like my station, even though after tomorrow I may never see it again. We walked up the steps and stood waiting for the train. I wanted to ask how many stops we were going and if we had to change lines, but when I composed these questions in my head, they were never anything but dull and would lay me open to being ignored or insulted. A child stood on the platform opposite, clutching a cone and wailing at the remains of an ice cream on the ground. I wanted to remark on the strangeness of a child eating an ice cream outdoors in this weather but that would be classed as a predictable comment and that would aggrieve my brother.

'There's nothing sadder than a child's ice-cream cone fallen splat,' I said.

'Except maybe genocide,' he said.

A further silence erupted, this one deliberate and pent-up boiling. When the train came, I followed Roy on board. We were possibly supposed to be sulking at each other so I pointedly stared out the window. I spotted a billboard advertising the buttery spread I'd bought in the supermarket – it felt reassuringly familiar, but it's a sad situation when you're clinging to spreadable butter for familiarity. The train squeaked and rattled and I was glad. I like a thing to act and sound like itself – too smooth and you forget you're on a moving object and neglect to notice the stations; on a bockety one, you've no choice but to get involved. I'd give Roy another go at a polite conversation – the silence shouldn't be for keeps.

'I like German U-Bahn and S-Bahn stations,' I said.

Roy looked at me, full-eyed, hopeful. 'Oh?'

'Whenever I've visited London, I've been stressed by having to put your ticket through the machines to get in and out of the stations, and the rush of people coming at you from behind.'

'I see,' he said, deflating a little.

'Hamburg is calmer, I don't have to constantly think about swiping on and off.'

'You don't so much like Hamburg trains, then, as dislike London trains,' he said, looking at me like I'd put dirty feet on his clean sheets.

'Ah, go easy on me, Roy,' I said. 'I was just making con-versation.'

He puts the making into making conversation, my brother, and the effort he puts into undoing what I make still stuns me. I turned back to the window. I couldn't be up to him this hour.

I kept my eyes out the window of the train. Cities must show their worst sides to train windows – the dirtiest, most graffiti-strewn buildings, the unpainted backs of houses, the roofs coated in bird-shit. I waited for Roy to speak, and when he did, it was to say 'We get off here'. I followed him off the train. It was soothing, after years of leading a child-pack, to follow and be shown and be led. Independence is overrated at times. I like package holidays and journeys that require nothing from me. I like long-haul flights: the air stewards decide when your bedtime is and when your wake-up time is through lighting and mealtimes. Your stomach might think dinner but there's breakfast on your tray.

We changed train and got on a colder train that headed out through the suburbs. We passed a long, low-slung building that surely must have been a nursing home – a familiar shape outside any town, the look of a lengthy death-wait about it. I closed my eyes because keeping them open and waiting on conversation was a pain in the eyeballs. When I felt Roy moving, I opened them.

'We're here,' he said.

'OK.'

It didn't cross his mind that I hadn't uttered a word, not so much as a vowel, in an age, but I tried to put gloomy thoughts from my head. I need to keep my spirits high when I'm visiting dead places.

'It's the second-largest cemetery in the world and the largest park cemetery in the world,' Roy said, reading from a leaflet.

'Oh?' I tried to appear interested without frightening him off with too much interest, skittish beast that he is. 'What's the largest?'

'What do you mean?'

'If this is the second-largest,' I said, 'what's the largest cemetery in the world?'

'Why would you want to know that? What does it *matter* what's the largest? Why, whenever there's a list of biggest, brightest, best, and you name the second or third, does everyone want to know what came ahead?'

'Human nature, I suppose.'

He snorted. 'That's what they say when humans behave like fools.'

He talks as if he's not a member of the human race. We walked on in silence.

'Iraq,' he said, after a silence wide as a cruise ship.

'What?'

'That's where the largest cemetery is. There are one and a half million people buried here, compared to five million in that cemetery in Najaf, Iraq.'

'Have you been?'

'No, not to Iraq.'

'Have you been here before?'

'No.'

He reads things, stows knowledge from books, he knows so much about things from online research, but he never *goes* to those places, he never *sees* these things unless he's brought. Even then he manages to act superior; I envy him that.

'There are 230 gardeners looking after the place, it covers almost 300 hectares, and there are 17 kilometres of roads.'

Ah, numbers, Roy, you fly your numbers in my face but what do they mean? I can't take in 17 kilometres of roads with my bare eyes, I can't imagine what 300 hectares looks like, I don't think I know 230 people in the world. Everything is researched, not lived; everything is considered, not done. If he lands smack into old age with a tower of books read and a power of facts gorged on and little else, it'd be a right waste of a life.

'Are you happy, Roy?'

'What the hell kind of a question is that?'

'OK, I'll narrow it down. When are you happiest?'

He thought for a while. 'When I've recharged my phone and cut my toenails.'

'That's it?'

'And when I've topped up my travel card.'

Jesus, it was like he'd climbed into his coffin already.

'Let's walk,' I said. 'You need to get out of your facts and into the trees.'

We walked in and around a muddle of tombstones. I liked the silence of the internal graves, not the outskirting ones that faced the road. Visiting a graveyard near a busy road, it feels rude to be alive.

'There are over 200,000 burial sites,' he said, 'nearly the same as the amount of figurines in the Wunderland. Maybe Hamburg tourist office just likes that number and rounds everything up or down to it.'

I'd lost the patience to humour him so I grunted and took a glance at his brochure. It said 'The World's Largest Existing Cemetery Park'. I liked the word 'Existing' in the context of a death-garden and I liked that the *cemetery* seemed to be there only to qualify the word *park*, a kind of incidental word, as if it was mostly a park with a few corpses thrown in.

Roy walked ahead, weaving in and around the rows of crosses and stone slabs; when I caught him up he slowed to a dawdle that was too slow to match so I pressed ahead and now he walked behind. He was more interested in dead strangers than living family members. I turned around. 'Roy, how many dead people are there in the world?'

He came closer, an unfamiliar expression of interest in his face. 'Well in *2001: A Space Odyssey*, Arthur C. Clarke said there were thirty ghosts for every living person, but now it's more like fifteen dead to one living.' He took out his phone. 'Yeah, 107 billion dead people estimated since Homo Sapiens began.'

'So if they rose up now, we'd be for it.'

He looked around the cemetery. 'I imagine only the local dead would rise up, so that'd be one and a half million from here.'

I looked around. 'Well, there's nowhere near that many living people wandering round – we'd better hope they'll rest easy so.'

I've come to realise that the only way to continue a conversation with Roy is to keep it some place between reality and fantasy. We walked on. The tombstones that had seemed so ordered now seemed to have been placed directly in my foot-line. I kept stumbling and cursing, Roy walking on heedless. There was nobody famous buried in this graveyard which was disappointing.

'Gert?'

'Yes?'

'If I was buried here, do you think the other corpses would speak English or German to me?'

This was beauty to me, this putting of questions to me, this trust in my opinion – he has hardly asked me anything he truly wants to know the answer to since we were children – but I disappoint. My mind is so fogged from worrying about him, worrying about Allen, I find it harder to turn it to hypotheticals these days. Nothing I could invent would sound plausible; he has long outraced my brainpower. Damn. Damnit. Damn it all to hell. 'I don't know, Roy.'

I picked my way among the graves and saw a photo of an elderly woman behind a small square of glass. It seemed unjust – that's not how she would have seen herself. In her mind she was likely in her twenties and still got mirror-shocks up to her death.

'Roy?'

'Yeah?'

'What country puts the name of the living spouse on the grave in red ink and then removes the ink when they die?'

'Japan.'

'Oh. It'd be a bit creepy, wouldn't it, seeing your name on your husband's grave before you died?'

'No more creepy than making a will. Cheaper too, getting all the engraving done at once.'

'I suppose. I can't imagine it – dying I mean. It doesn't seem real to me.'

'It seems more real to me than some parts of living,' he said.

We fell silent. I couldn't think of a way to extend the conversation or ask him which parts of living aren't real to him. Someday I would like to find the word-potion that would unspool his tongue or his brain or whichever part between the two is clogged.

I began to walk faster, but uneven ground and lines of tombstones like toy soldiers didn't allow for hurry and hurry seemed misplaced in a graveyard – sorry, *cemetery*. Roy was ambling behind; he seemed to be reading every inscription – why? How many of them could he possibly take in? And if he took them all in, where did they go and how would they come out?

Graveyards don't usually hang heavy on me – on the contrary, I find it reassuring that we'll all be dead someday – but this one was different. This one had shades of my brother and my husband and the wreckage of our lives. I felt uneasy about feeling low, like when you read a sad book and feel weighed down by an imaginary grief you can't rightfully lay claim to. I didn't really know why we came – the dead are dead in any language: they have no nationality. Any effort to find something different – apart from German names on the inscriptions – was as pointless as trying to find commonality with my brother. I walked by some huge ornate crypts, pimped and bejazzled for the rich and vain, and went down the steps of one to knock on the door, but Roy had caught me up and stopped me, either out of respect or for fear we'd wake the dead – I'm not sure which. I shook him off.

'Why is it that you care more about the dead than your living sister?'

He said nothing and walked back up the steps of the crypt.

'Roy, will you please just talk to me? Please.'

I upped my pace but he had gone off in a snit of a speed-walk, heading for the exit, Roy in the lead, me huffing behind him trying to keep up. A man working with a leaf blower was dressed so

233

snug against the cold he was like a beekeeper in a hazmat suit. A woman walked by hatless, her hands clamped over her ears to warm them. Other visitors were pinched and huddled against the wind, which carried hints of sleet in it. This cold would gut you and skin you alive; it was worse than pain, this cold, but it was appropriate for the setting: it should always be winter in a grave-yard. I sniffed; there was no smell. Nothing smells of anything in winter. I looked at my sulk of a brother and changed tack.

'Roy, do you remember playing Graveyards when we were small?'

'Yeah,' he said sombrely, 'I remember robbing plastic flowers and trinkets. The loot from the new graves was best because the colours weren't as faded.'

'And how we fought tug-of-war over that red and yellow wind-chime from the children's plot?'

'Yeah.' He smiled then, a genuine smile. Strange kind of family who can only bond over robbing children's graves.

I decided then to go with the way his brain veers, to ease conversation along rather than make it. 'Roy, do you reckon the dead speak a universal language?'

He stared off aways ahead of him. 'Probably. I mean, they've more in common with each other than they have with their living equivalents, don't they.'

The 'don't they' was uttered more as a sentence, but I was sure as hell going to take it as a peace-offering question. 'Yeah, they do. And what about animals? I wonder if their owners' accents or language affects the sounds their pets make.'

'I don't know. I know that German humans write animal sounds differently to us, but I don't know if that's because the animals themselves are making different sounds or if German ears hear different things than we do.'

'German dogs don't say *woof*?' I asked.

'No, hold on, I made a list.'

'How did you find this out?'

'Stefan left a comic open on the table. A speech bubble from a bee's mouth said something that wasn't *buzz* so I went online to check.'

'Oh.' I had hoped this had come up in an actual conversation but he's still computer-dependent for knowledge. He took out his notebook, that bloody notebook he carts around a world of useless facts in. He flicked through the pages and then creased the left side.

'Here it is.' He tried to pass me the notebook.

'No, you read them to me,' I said, else I'd go home having barely heard his voice.

'OK. So they have *wuf wuf* like our *woof woof,* but I'm not sure if they pronounce the *w* the German way, as in *vuff vuff.* Then the bees don't *buzz* here, they *sum.* If you say *sum* and hold the *m,* your lips fizzle and tickle and it does sound like the hum of a bee so I can't disapprove of that one.'

'Fair enough,' I said. This was his version of fitting into a culture and who was I to mock it.

'Hens say *gack gack* instead of *cluck,* their husbands say *kikeriki* instead of *cock-a-doodle-do,* which sounds more like a children's rhyme than an animal sound so I'd favour *kikeriki.*'

'Sounds about right,' I said.

'Pigs don't *oink* here, they *grunz,* but neither of them sounds right to me.' He pushed his nose upwards and snorted like a pig. 'How would you spell that?'

I felt like I was in school and if I didn't get this question right, there would be consequences. 'H-N-O-C-K?'

'Yes.' He nodded. 'I like the *hn* but we're squeamish about those letters together in English. I don't know where the Germans get their *r* in *Grunz* – it's a blatantly *r*-less sound.'

'Absolutely.'

'Cows don't *moo* in German, they *mmuh*, which is an improvement. The double *oo* is too perfectly formed and rounded in English, and we all know cows don't round off their sounds at the finish.'

'Oh, everybody knows that.'

He glanced at me, doubtful of my seriousness, but I bigged up my eyes all innocent and he continued.

'Then there's frogs. Frogs in English say *ribbit*, but German frogs say *kwaak*, which means a German frog has more in common with an Irish duck than with an Irish frog.'

'Huh, interesting,' I said, trying to stay the right side of enthusiasm: too much or too little and he'll clamp up.

He looked at his list again. 'The German sound I find most disappointing is the wolf's. Ours howl *owOOOOOOOOO*; German wolves just say *huh*. It's an anticlimax of a howl, as if they really weren't that hungry in the first place.'

'True,' I said. '*Dracula* wouldn't be quite so scary if the packs of wolves just shrugged their paws and said *Huh*.'

He looked quickly at me to check if I was mocking him but I was right on his side, more on his side than anyone else I know. At the same time as I frown on his lists, I envy them for their seekingness, their attempt to make sense of the world and control things that aren't controllable. I used to make to-do lists, but at the end of the day I'd have to decant the tasks onto even bigger lists, few items ever fully ticked off.

'What sound do steam trains make in German?' I asked.

'What?' His face tautened in my direction.

'It was just about the trains, Roy, wasn't it? He's into trains too – that's why you—'

'The trains,' he said, his voice pursed. 'Yeah, trains.'

I nodded. 'I thought so.' His face had grown pale, his lips had taken on a bluish colour. 'Roy, I'm sorry. I believe you, honest I do.'

'Do Mam and Dad?'

'They will.'

He looked away. 'And Gráinne?'

'Not yet. Soon.'

He blinked a few times and dropped to a seated position on the stone lip of a grave. I sat beside him.

'Jesus, Roy, we'll catch consumption sat like this – it's fucking freezing.'

'You're turning into Mam with your old wives' tales. How are they?'

'Same as ever. The saints and martyrs still follow me round the house when I visit. The kids knock some craic out of them, though. How come we weren't brave enough to get a rise out of them like that when we were young?'

'Because we'd have got a clatter or a shkelp if we did.'

'True,' I said. 'The TV volume is on the highest setting now, and they still think the newsreaders are whispering. Mam reckons she can outsmart the weather by checking the forecast on different news channels until she finds one that suits her. Still won't use the dryer, so the weather has to be fine to get a load of washing out.'

Roy smiled.

'And Dad's collection of parts is starting to take over the house. Maybe he's building a kind of a Jacob's ladder to the heavens, boost him up a few rungs. They're grand. They say they love looking after my two, that it keeps them young, but any afternoon I leave them with them, they've aged centuries and have the door open and the kids bundled out before I even get out of the car. They miss you. The kids, I mean.'

He nodded.

'You'll have to babysit some night when you're back.'

'I will. I'll be here another while yet, though.'

'Do you want to come back, eventually?'

He looked at his hands, clenching and unclenching under his gloves. 'Yeah, some day. I've things to do here first, though, unfinished business to sort out.'

Not for the first time since I'd come, my stomach tightened. I couldn't ask what things; I dreaded knowing what things. To preserve my mind I'd say nothing and say nothing well. I got up quickly and put out a hand to pull him up. 'Come on, let's go. Let's head to that café over the crematorium. Do you reckon they use the same ovens for pizzas and corpses?'

'Gert!' He looked aghast but not completely disgusted and took my hand to pull himself up. It's the small slits of hope: I'd find my way in through that chink.

Roy

*Erklärungsnot = explanation poverty = the need
to explain your actions*

He gathered his bucket and accoutrements from the cubby
for his evening shift and set off for Amerika. There was something about spelling Amerika with a *k* that made it seem more
American (Amerikan?) than America with a *c*. The *k* signified
a kind of buy-yourself confidence. The *c* was too quiet, too
subtle, too shade seeking rather than limelight craving.

Roy liked the seaside resort; there were see-through panels underfoot so you could watch the trains pass beneath. He
skimmed the duster over a space shuttle and crouched down
on his hunkers to watch a shark chasing a scuba diver under
the surface; every time he looked at this scene he expected the
shark to have closed in on the diver and grabbed a toothful.
He stood up and dusted a dolphin show, trying to figure out
how he felt about dolphin shows and whale shows and cap-
tive animals in general. Some people were so certain in their
beliefs that such things were wrong, and wouldn't life be easier
if everything was so definite. He moved on to the miniature
Las Vegas with its replicas of the Eiffel Tower and a pyramid
and Sphinx, surrounded by miniature high-rise hotels.

The layers of make-believe began to wear at his brain;
this always happened in the Vegas section. He was looking

at a miniature replica of a real city that contained miniature replicas of real buildings in other continents. Why couldn't the Wunderland designers make miniature replicas of the actual Eiffel Tower in Paris or the actual pyramids in Egypt rather than replicas of replicas, where flaws were bound to multiply and unlikenesses proliferate and eventually the thing would be so far from the original thing as to be unrecognisable. And children would grow up thinking the pyramids and the Sphinx belonged in either Hamburg or Las Vegas. The deception tripled reminded him of Gert's attitude towards him in the cemetery. She'd seemed to be fully on his side but then she'd asked him what his friendship was about. Now he wasn't so sure.

Vegas was impressive when the lights went out – the lit-up strip looked glamorous in miniature, not seedy or garish as he'd heard it was in real life. He had heard tell of hotels so big they had full-size trains to deliver guests to their floors, which was incomprehensible to Roy – he couldn't wrap his brain around that kind of giganticism. He checked for anyone watching then dug the butt of the duster into the pyramid, making a gaping hole, turning the pyramid into an angular volcano. Fire coming out the jagged hole would be an improvement, he thought; that's an element the Wunderland lacked.

The Eiffel Tower loomed next. He had been up it with Gert and Gráinne and their parents a couple of decades ago. He hadn't been bothered with the view. If he didn't know a city, why would he be interested in picking out landmarks? He'd felt nothing but contempt for the couples gazing from each other to the view through the wire mesh – he felt like an animal trapped in a cage. His sister Gráinne had taken photos from every angle, but what was the use of photos of buildings you don't know and would never know – what do you do with them? Surely photos taken and unexamined held some sort of live spirit inside that was yet untapped – if all the unexamined photos that remained on digital cameras or phones or undeveloped in old cameras joined forces and rose up, the world would be taken over by flat 2D outlines of low buildings taken from higher buildings and the same sun coming up and going down. Roy looked at the miniature Vegas version of the Eiffel Tower before him. It was the layers of fakery that bothered him, the untruths tripled. Gert had said she wanted the truth, wanted him to talk to her, but in reality, nobody wanted the bald matt truth. If she only knew how much he was sparing her, not letting her know everything that was in his head.

Roy waited for the lights to dim, checked for visitors, leaned in further, yanked up the Eiffel Tower, and lopped off the bottom section with a *hiyaaaaah!* of a karate chop. Now it looked less like a capital A with an I on top and more like a lanky armless person with a pin for a head. It was still a little too recognisable as the Eiffel Tower so he went at it again, lopping off the middle part with the side of his hand. Now it was just a latticed pole, surely nobody would recognise it. He put the smashed tower parts in his pocket and moved on. His fear about being caught had turned into a blatant two fingers to management – this was the first time he had rebelled in his life and it felt good. He had gone along too willingly with what other people wanted of him: bosses, family members, Gert. She had arranged for him to come here for his best interests, she'd said, but it seemed after their chat in the cemetery that they were her best interests after all. Why didn't people say what they meant?

Roy shook himself and moved on to dust a freeway accident. During the day, the male visitors horded around it – something about sirens and accidents and airplanes drew adult men gaping in awe, a piece of masculinity he was mercifully free of.

He swiped the duster over a sign for a motel which made him lonesome for the road trip he would never take, the diners he would never eat in, the motels he would never sleep in. Whatever way his life moved, he was fairly certain there would never be anyone he would want to share those experiences with. He couldn't drive so a solo road trip wasn't possible, and anyway, cars didn't follow timetables or act with timetabled precision. He pinched the motel sign until it crumpled and moved on to the Grand Canyon. Skeletons of mules and horses lay at the bottom of it, like large bone-shrubs. The remains of an airplane and its seats also speckled the bottom of the canyon. There was so much loss and destruction it seemed pointless to dust it. Roy dug the handle of his duster into the rocks until he dented them and crouched down, trying to imagine what it would be like to be at the bottom of a canyon looking up – would the awe be less than being at the top looking down? And which was better, to look down from cliffs or up at mountains? Was more poetry written from one angle than the other? A billboard showed a 'Just Married' couple with the words 'Family Planning', which seemed a bit unromantic and overly practical. If he had his way, his family would have been planned so well that one of his sisters wouldn't exist.

Next, Roy looked at the miniature Area 51, with its spaceships, green aliens (some of them playing basketball), amorphous jellied green blobs, and pickled animal specimens. Why were aliens a source of fear for people? He liked the idea of being taken to another planet, of starting again completely anew. He moved on to a river, where three miniature men were about to throw another man in. He pulled the three men up and threw them in the river, breaking off the fourth man, the intended victim, and placing him (now delimbed) on the riverbank. Roy wasn't sure whether the man would thank him if he was real and life size – he'd heard saving a person from drowning could be a thankless task, and if it was jokey horseplay, then Roy had needlessly quadruply amputated a man who wasn't in any danger at all.

A miniature woman lying on her front in a blue swimsuit was reading while the same peeping Tom from other miniature lands watched from bushes with binoculars. Roy yanked up the pervert and snapped him in two – it took a couple of goes but his rage narrowed to a point in his fingers. He replaced the halved figurine near the miniature bushes, took out his phone, and typed *peeping Tom* into Google Translate: *Spanner*. Then he wrote SPANNER in capital letters on a piece of paper and put it in front of the monk. It was important to shame the people who needed to be shamed. He plucked a clump of feathers from his duster and covered the woman (the voyee?).

'Roy?'

He jumped out of his standing and turned around.

Inge stood watching him closely. 'What are you doing?'

'I'm just fixing something – one of the monk figurines seems to be broken.'

She stared from him to the figurine and moved closer. Roy moved to block her progress, the metal bar digging into his back. He would have to make conversation, any conversation, to distract her but what, what could he say?

'Inge, do you like perverts?'

'What?' Her whole face creased into a question mark.

'The monks, I mean, the Spanner-monks in the Wunderland – how do you feel about them?'

'I hadn't really thought about them before, why do you ask?' She started to move again nearer the monk.

'LOOK OUT!' he roared.

Inge ducked and cowered. 'What, what is it?'

'Sorry, I thought I saw a fire.'

Inge straightened up slowly and looked at him. 'Is everything all right, Roy? Would you like me to call your sister?'

'Everything's fine,' he said, 'I'm just tired.' Tired seemed to get you off the hook for any kind of behaviour.

'OK,' she said, 'I will go back to work.'

He gave a cheery wave and said, 'See you later.' Inge nodded slowly at him and walked away. Roy took out a cloth, sprayed some polish on it, and rubbed at the metal bar until it was mirror-shiny.

As he polished harder and harder, he felt something bubble up inside him. Rescuing the figurines his own way would be too time-consuming, particularly with this meeting coming up. He would be outed as a thief and a vandal but it was purer than that – who would understand what it was? His mind drifted back to the fire he'd mentioned to Inge. How pleasing it would be to watch the plastic faces melt, the miniature buildings bend, droop and ooze, the miniature roads warp and crack. The figurines he'd liberated were safe in the wardrobe – they wouldn't have to endure smoke inhalation in their miniature lungs. How satisfying to see the faces of the visitors change from excitement to horror. If the security cameras caught that expression change, it could be a whole new video genre – or maybe it had already been invented, like a mass snuff movie for miniature figurines. There was surely a German compound noun for that: Expression of Shock on Face of Person Who Witnesses Figurines Annihilated By Fire.

Gert

Zu tief ins Glas schauen = to look too deep into
the glass = *to drink too much*

I had a quick nap after the graveyard trip and got up before I
could succumb to horizontal ruminations.

It was chillier that evening and when I went to look in
Roy's wardrobe for an extra fleece, I saw something glint-
ing at the bottom of the hanging compartment. I crouched
down and saw a scene, a miniature scene the likes of which
I'd be hard pushed to describe. There was a row of figurines
at the bottom of the wardrobe, many of them smashed up
or missing body parts. A model train at the edge of the circle
looked like a runaway train about to plough in and destroy
this bizarre set-up. There were intact figurines – a mother,
father, and two children, a man in red and white vest and
shorts, a group of nuns, and some climbers in harnesses –
but everything else was destruction. There were uniformed
prisoners without feet, a pink cow without hooves, a pig
missing two trotters, and a couple of penguins with no feet.
There were severed heads, a lone arm, bodies of a headless
couple having sex, and the figurine of a woman who looked
happy despite having no feet. There were unidentifiable
shards from various buildings or exhibits and a man with
what looked like a smashed briefcase in front of this line of

245

figurines – that briefcase must have contained a miniature bomb, else why such desperate destruction? The miniature briefcase was resting on a miniature red towel surrounded by tiny flowers – was it a bomb and its commemoration all together in one scene? I had chanced upon the aftermath of a miniature disaster. There was a smashed-up Christmas scene that stank of wanton annihilation – if you decimate Christmas, what hope is there? The sense of destruction and needless suffering put the bleaks on me, even though the sufferers were neither real nor life-size.

In a corner of the wardrobe was a miniature filing cabinet made from matchboxes sellotaped together. I prised it open and inside were twenty or so fingernail-sized pieces of paper with minuscule handwriting on them, unmistakably my brother's. I had to squint hard to read them and eventually I saw that they were birth certs for the figurines, presumably the ones he'd taken. I sifted through them: there were different birth dates for Gunther, Hans, Katherina, Inge, Dieter, and others. How did he know so many German names? In the bottom drawer of the filing cabinet was a smaller sheaf of miniature papers held together with a paper clip. I peered closely at them. These were death certs for other figurines – presumably the ones he'd already smashed to shit. A wire of ice lanced through my body – oh lord, the fear. This was what he spent his time at; this was how he lived his days. When would he stop – the birth certs and death certs were only begun? Was he going to kidnap and mutilate every figurine from the Wunderland? A sense of menace seeped from the miniature filing cabinet and I stood up and closed the door of the wardrobe quietly, as if my measured movements would delete what I'd seen from my mind. This was why he didn't want me to go near the wardrobe. I should have known something was amiss. Was this what he meant when he'd talked about the unfinished business he'd wanted to sort out before he came back to Ireland? I sat down on the bed and stared at the wardrobe. An innocuous-looking piece of furniture suddenly seemed ominous. I didn't know how to process this new information. I didn't know what way to go about dealing with it. How the hell had he got away with destroying so many figurines already – it was surely only a matter of time before he got caught. I felt wretched, regretting the toast I'd guzzled before my nap, which seemed about to resurface. What would happen if Roy was fired for theft? Would I have to bring him home or how the hell would I organise another job here? Our chat in the cemetery hadn't solved anything. And I felt foolish for even thinking that anything could be solved with Roy, Roy who thrived on the spaces between truths, silences between words.

My problem is, when I'm surrounded with so much disordered thinking, I lose the ability to discern logic and normality, whatever that is. Allen has on many occasions tried to convince me that I was overthinking or overreacting to his actions, and maybe I was – do enough eggshell-treading and your own mind is not to be trusted. Oh, Roy, what is it you're at now?

There was too much miniature death in the flat; I needed movement and voices. A sad mind in the midst of bustle is a happier thing – and outdoor scenes would take my mind away from indoor wardrobe scenes. I made efforts to fling what I'd seen from my mind and decided to take a port tour. I wanted to see how the parts all worked into the whole, how the system of containers and ships in and out happened. I left the flat and walked quickly, trying to outpace my unease about Roy. I forced my mind to focus on the movement of my feet. At the port, I checked my phone before turning it off –

a simple action for most people, but one that was hard-got for me. I can only turn it off when I'm as sure as I can be that Allen is stable and the kids are safe. I doubt my own mind on such things; it's the doctor's word I take, a relief to shunt responsibility to the medical system. I like being offline and out of credit or reception, reminds me of taking an old-school phone out of its cradle and off the hook, and it does get me off the hook at times.

The port felt someways familiar because I'd looked on it every day since I arrived, but mostly from afar; like returning to a book I'd left half-read with the pages before the book-mark forgotten. It was only when I asked one of the tourist reps that I found out that port tours don't run in the winter months. I was deflated; after not getting to Schlump the other day it felt like all my intended destinations were going to be thwarted. But despite the disappointment, I felt a twinge of relief at failing at something that wasn't due to my own lack of effort. I felt like a sign at a closed tourist site: 'Due to circumstances beyond our control, this facility is closed. We apologise for any inconvenience caused.'

I wandered around. Wandering seemed to be all I did lately. I'd lost all sense of time and dates and routines. The lines I made through Hamburg were hazy and warped; the lines I make at work are straight and clean. I waste no milli-seconds or millimetres taking wide loops around the rooms in the nursing home: I aim like an arrow and fire myself point to point. Today in Hamburg, however, on a day of small shocks, I needed a point to my meanderings, so I took the streets near Roy's flat: up one and down the other. I needed to feel that I was completing some ground cover. I went to put a chewing gum wrapper in a nearby bin, but there were so many differ-ent slots for rubbish and recycling waste and instructions on how I might treat the various rubbish items before discarding them that it daunted me to hell and back. I stuffed the wrapper in my pocket to bring home and bin in Roy's flat; better to be shouted at for messing up by someone you know than by a stranger. I went to an ATM to take out money because I could do with a successful transaction, something to have achieved on my walk. I tried to take out €200 and the machine gave me several denomination options:

3 €50 + 2 €20 + 1 €10

2 €50 + 5 €20

All very civilised, but it felt like one more decision on a day my mind wanted a rest so I closed my eyes and hit an option – who the fuck cared what denomination I got.

I considered visiting the Speicherstadt museum nearby, about the people and traders who lived in this area before they were deemed ungentrified and removed. I felt an urge to cling to facts and knowledge that would keep me in the here and now but realised that museums leave me in a snit. I can't take it all in, I will never retain or remember all the information, so why bother even reading it? Number facts and percentages and money figures and dates are the first to leave my mind. I'll remember the cake I ate in the Louvre café but I won't remember any detail of the *Mona Lisa*. I'll remember the replica chopped-off ear I bought from an unofficial seller outside the Van Gogh Museum but I won't remember any details of the *Sunflowers*. Never mind museums, I'd take to the pub – sorry, bar.

It felt deliciously illicit to be drinking alone during the day. I ordered beer, even though I don't like beer, because it's Germany and I should learn to like what they make the best. Roy was probably right shunning cereal and choosing dark breads, but I'd never tell him that. The barman held eye contact for a second longer than he needed to and skimmed my finger when he handed me the glass. I felt momentarily excited until I remembered this was his job. A younger man who looks like that doesn't flirt unintended with an older woman who looks like this. Times I envy those wealthy older men their egos, the ones with beautiful younger women – I envy them the ability to convince themselves these women would love them without their power or wallets or powerful wallets. I smiled back at the barman but I'm so out of practice at spontaneous flirtation, it would be grotesque if I tried to respond.

I sat into the bar stool. One pint of beer is about the height of it that my bladder can take so I moved on to whiskey. I don't know my once-barrelled from my triple-casked so I squinted for the cheapest-looking label and asked for a shot of that. We made no pretence of me having German, the barman and I: it was all done through English. I got fed up beckoning him and feeling I should be putting chat on him when all I wanted to do was lapse into home-thoughts, so my single shots soon progressed to doubles. I wanted a hangover. I wanted a tangible excuse to feel like shit.

When I stop Allen drinking, when I make eyes at him on a night out that maybe he's had enough, I'm looked on by our friends as a nag. (Nag, see also: Virago, Fishwife, Hellcat fury, Harpy, Spitfire, Battle-axe, Bitch, Vixen, Harridan, Scold.) They don't know the low the alcohol brings on later. When he's a certain side of depression, Allen is where the party starts and ends. Our friends don't know that after the giddy buzz comes a plunge into such deep mind-sludge it's a horror to get him out. It might be that the people who are most fun at parties are the hardest to live with, like a cottage that looks pretty and quaint from the outside but is dark and cramped inside. If those friends saw the contrast between the before and after, they might help me take the pint from his hand. I'm no teetotalling judgemental shrew. All I want is to drink the pub dry, empty kegs of stout down my throat, hold the bottle of whiskey over my head and scald my throat with it, fall asleep and forget. If there were no children, I could. But there are children, these children who believe their father has headaches, strange headaches that put him in bed for days; I must keep my mind.

Even though Allen is stable now, I can't fully let my guard down. I live life at a flinch, one blink away from catastrophe, because the depression may rear up again any month, any week – I try not to think any day because that gives me no time to prepare. If I thought he was cured I could move on, as all the advice columnists advise, *move on*, as if it was just buying a bigger, better house and forgetting about your old one. If I fully moved on, when the depression hits again it would shock me as hard as the first time and leave me flailing to react. Even when he seems well, it might be temporary, it might be an all-clear or a remission, or it might be the calm before the suicide. Can I ever fully trust his moods, his intentions? How can four lives spin on one thing, one thing that might never happen? I live in the half-knowledge that he may end everything as we know it. I live in the uncertain spaces between mental health and sickness.

My life has grown narrower.

A feed of whiskey dampens my mood and makes it harder to stave off the glums. Thoughts creep into my mind of the fuck-ups I've presided over. My mind squirms back to the scene in Roy's wardrobe I found earlier. There was something so deliberate about it – so posed and intentional – that it spooked me. For a man who doesn't engage with life in any meaningful way to put so much effort into an imaginary world, well I found it odd. Looks like I made the wrong decision sending him away. I thought I could protect him, protect my parents from the accusations, but keeping him here on his own can't be good for his mental health. He might have had some sort of chance if he'd stayed at home with his family around him. Christ, how can it be that the best of intentions are so fraught with failure? I can't help thinking I've got the wrong personality for this; I'm the wrong woman. I used to see myself as practical, full of get up and go and vim and vigour. But these last few years have flattened me, floored me, damn near expunged me. There are fantastic women, practical kinds of women, who birth five-a-side teams of children and rear them dogged to perfection, all the while laddering up their careers and organising play dates and charitable events and not just maintaining the upkeep of their faces and nails and hair but acing it. These women just keep moving moving moving, no mulling; they *do*, they don't think; they *act*, they don't ruminate; and isn't it the better way to be? Allen would probably have fared better with a woman like that. This may not have hit so hard if I could have pulled him up out of it, if I was a nifty powerhouse of a woman, not a mediocre plod-along.

The problem with depression is that your world has gone into a washing-machine spin cycle but it's all happening – or not happening – in private. If Allen had been diagnosed with a serious physical illness, people would be told, there would be masses said and mass cards sent. There would be shoulders to cry on, people asking how you and the sick person were doing. There would be frank conversations with the children, their teachers would know, their friends' parents would know. People would step in and step up and I would not be entirely, appallingly alone. A potentially terminal illness with no clear-cut terminus is a special type of hell to live with.

There's neither start nor end to this thing. There's no finding a lump, no memorable scene in a doctor's office with a firm diagnosis, no date etched onto the family calendar signifying the beginning of a new medically intervened way of being. There is no timeline with midpoints of treatments, no narrative we can form based on a doctor's revelation of a diagnosis. There is only a blur, a murk. Trying to pinpoint when the depression started would be like trying to figure out the precise moment a headache starts or a rainbow ends. Instead of a medical professional explaining to us what was wrong, there was *me* trying to explain to them what was wrong with him, Allen silent all the while, the unwilling patient. I never knew whether the doctors fully believed me, whether they thought me a hysterical wife, dribbling Munchausen's by proxy, creating dramas, inventing crises. I tried so hard to piece together the timeline, to see if there was any one thing, or collection of things, that drew out this creature. Was it always there dormant inside or did it just suddenly appear?

I clung onto my bar stool like a life-raft. My mind whipped from thought to thought, over and back disjointed.

A few months after his first suicide attempt, when the kids were at their cousins overnight and Allen was in uncharacteristically chatty humour, I asked him. I managed the tone just right, asked him what it was exactly he was thinking of when it came down to it. I managed it in a non-accusatory way. He said when it came to the moment, the crucial will-he won't-he moment, there was no conscious thought, something else came over him. But before that, in the planning stage, he said, he believed – no, not just believed: he *knew* that the kids and I would be better off without him. Sadly, financially he's correct: he's worth more dead than alive, and so he can use that to justify ending things. What a fucked-up way to organise our financial life; I didn't know what those insurance and assurance arrangements could signify when we made them. I've tried time and again to show how our lives would be in smithereens if he left us but his logic is this: he's such a terrible person we'd be better off without him.

Selfish, they say, when someone ends their own life. I want to tear the larynx from their throats when I hear that. I want to grab two fists of hair and yank so hard I'll be left with hair-spools in my clawed hands. *Selfish*. If they heard at close quarters the sound of someone hating themselves, they wouldn't say selfish. Heroic, they might say, for lasting so long. But how can you explain that to people who live life on an even stretch, who don't dip too high or too low beyond the horizon, whose best plan for curing depression is to Just Buck up and Put Your Best Side Out and Why Don't You Do Something Nice for Yourself. That's like telling someone with an ankle-bone bursting through their skin to Just Breathe Deeply. It's the Justs and the Why Don't Yous that give me the dry heaves.

I leaned back too far and just about stifled a wobble off the seat. The bar stool was not such a good idea; it was very far off the ground. The barman was eyeing me but not directly, his efforts at touch had decreased a lot. I was trying to look straight ahead, like I was on a ferry, eyeballing the horizon to stave off seasickness, but all I could see was my face in the mirror and it was doubling up, swirling at the edges, as if I was being blurred out, vanishing. My eyes and stomach didn't match up. I waved my hand and the barman brought another double but reluctantly, as if he doubted my capacities.

'I can handle it,' I said, but my words disobliged me. I lost a couple of syllables along the way. I put my head in my hands; it was easier to hold up that way.

I couldn't make out if Roy was in trouble and needed help or if it was my help that had got him worse into this mess. My mind whirred into ever-worse scenarios of where Roy could end up, and they mostly involved him handing his clothes over to a uniformed attendant. 'Don't forget the belt and laces, sir.' The scene in the wardrobe couldn't be the actions or a sane person, or could it? Roy was always into model trains and make-believe, wanting to be anywhere but where he was. Could this be just another world he's created of his own, a kind of deranged hobby?

When you're mired so deep into something you doubt everything and everyone; times I couldn't make out if it was me or Allen who needed help. I was depression, he was depression, we were depression, it was depression. We were the noun not the adjective, there were no commas no punctuation during this time, we used up every fucking pronoun, singular and plural, depression engulfed us like a heatless, smokeless invisible-flamed soul-sucking fire.

The line of how much I'm willing, or able, to take keeps shifting. If this situation had appeared before me when I was twenty-five, full of eggs and beans, I can't say I would have willingly stepped into it, this quarter-life full of jolts and fears. I sometimes think, if we could see the results of our poor choices and ill fortune, if we could look ahead to the grim future we've arranged for ourselves or had the misfortune to have happen to us, there wouldn't be rope enough in the hardwares or paracetamol enough in the chemists' for the volume of suicides.

I took an ill-judged gulp of whiskey and it went down the wrong way, scalding my windpipe and making me cough. The barman raised his eyes in my direction and I raised my glass confidently. 'I'm grand, sir, don't be worrying.' He looked like he might be worrying.

If I was asked to describe my relationship now, I'd call it a truce. That might sound bleak to some couples but it was hard-got, this truce. Some ways we'll never recover, no chance. Something cleaved in me that first suicide attempt and it never fully mended. Some ways we're better than before. We'll never be love's young optimistic dream again: we're love's middle-aged cynical nightmare. That first serious conversation about suicide paved the way for lighter ones, if that isn't the greatest fucking oxymoron of all times: *a light-hearted conversation about suicide.* I ask him on a scale of one to suicide how he's feeling. He tells me his new medication is a cheap generic brand. We joke about yellow-pack depression and pun about cut-price suicide prevention. Terrible taste, but if we didn't make appalling in-jokes that seem cruel to those outside our context, we'd be in a permanent weep.

I was about to order another double, but the barman made a show of taking my glass and placing it in the dishwasher. A professionally made hint: I'd take it. I paid him a lot more than the bill came to, but it seemed worth it, and I'd spent feck all of my holiday money. I managed myself off the bar stool, waved at the barman, and walked very deliberately to the door. A taxi was easy got, the address of the flat not so easy, but we got there, the taxi driver and I, and he got another wedge of my holiday money. Never was a bed so gratefully gotten into.

DAY 6

Roy

Geisterfahrer = ghost driver = wrong-way driver

Roy almost slept through his alarm he was that tired. The beep shrilled through his sleep, and he sat up confused, his brain rattling for certainty. When he saw 4:15 on the screen, he spent a fug of a minute trying to figure out whether it was 4:15 in the morning or afternoon – that was the problem with working split shifts. He had pretended to be asleep when Gert clumsied in a couple of hours earlier. She was muttering to herself and the stink of alcohol was so ferocious he burrowed his nose further under the duvet. His heart had beat extravagantly. He didn't like when people drank too far away from themselves; he couldn't piece together who they were.

The meeting about the missing figurines was this morning. Today's task was cleaning Switzerland, but after dumping his bucket in that land, Roy took a walk around the entire exhibition to survey the damage he'd done. In the miniature Miniatur Wunderland in miniature Hamburg, the tiny windows he'd broken had been replaced, the figurines he'd taken or smashed had been replaced. He felt sick. He hadn't made so much as a dent in the land. It was as if he'd never been born. As he walked around, he soon realised *all* the figurines he'd taken from all the miniature lands had been replaced, *all* the windows he'd smashed had been fixed, *all* the infrastructure

259

and modes of transport he'd broken had been restored to exactly what they'd been before he disturbed them. This gave him gut-fall: he'd had no effect, nothing he'd done had lasted, his mark would not be made here. He walked back to miniature Switzerland, past the other cleaners who stared at him. He looked at each of their faces and realised he didn't know any of their names, except Inge. Or he might recognise their names from the roster in the cubby but he couldn't match name with face. None of them looked particularly pleased to see him, some looked hostile, a couple looked downright suspicious. He hadn't thought there were so many cleaners. Roy looked at his boots and hurried along.

Inge called out to him from miniature Hamburg, something about going to the meeting together, and he ignored her. He returned to his bucket, picked up a cloth, and began to shine the metal bar surrounding the exhibit. He shone up silver fury, he put both his elbows into it and his shoulders as well, he pushed and shoved and pounded the bar until his fists gave him red hell. What was the point, what had all of this achieved if the figurines he'd rehomed had been just replicated and replaced, as if they were not unique, as if they were just off a conveyor belt, never mind handmade? And if each figurine needed a birth cert, how could you make new ones for identical figurines? And his census – how would he manage it? Human census-takers wouldn't have to cope with the issue of cloning – yet – but he would have to decide whether to count the hoofless cow in his Wardrobe Wunderland or the newly hoofed cow in the Miniatur Wunderland. It all seemed too much to sort out, and there was nobody he could ask for help. Gert would just say something soothing but useless; nobody he knew would get it.

His cleaning frenzy showed no sign of abating. He lashed into the work with a power of energy that could wear down metal or erase paint. He needed somewhere to put his anger; there was no point taking it out on surfaces.

He dumped his bucket and ran out of the building, to hell with rotas and rules, and sprinted back to the apartment. Gert was still asleep – he could hear her snoring from his bedroom. He grabbed a box of matches from the drawer that Stefan used for his pipe and ran back to the Wunderland. The sun was no closer to coming up, the morning as dark as it had been when he first got up. He made his way to the miniature Hamburg, the city hall with no records, what the fuck *point* to all of this if there were no insides, no interior, no substance, no NOTHING. The Miniatur Wunderland figurines that had been replaced stood proudly again; this was a sickener. He walked back to his section and tried to steady his thoughts and his shaking hands.

'Roy!'

He jumped. Inge was standing very near him.

'What?'

'Let's go to the meeting – if we go now, we can get a good seat.'

'Oh,' he said, 'I need a minute.'

She looked concerned. 'Are you OK? You look a little stressed?'

'I don't feel very well. You go on to the meeting – I just need to go to the toilet first.'

Inge's face puckered. 'Would you like me to get the boss for you? Maybe you should go home?'

'No no,' he almost shouted, 'I'm fine. You go on and I'll be fine.'

She looked a bit scared. 'OK, I'll see you later.'

She walked away, looking over her shoulder a couple of times. Roy waited until she'd rounded the corner before sneaking back to miniature Hamburg. His heart thudded and scudded somewhere around his ears, it felt like.

He leaned over the miniature city hall and struck a match. It didn't take. He looked around and found a figurine clutching a miniature newspaper and he held the match to the paper. This one took. All the joy of his life had come to this: the fire *took*. He watched as the single flicker took courage and announced itself. It was a slow build. Roy watched as it grew more flames and spread slowly, horizontally. A rogue flame tried to leap vertically but gave up, following its sibling flames along the miniature town. With a slow *whoosha*, the fire wrapped around the nearest buildings and took off towards Amerika. The flames were now tumbling, bumbling along, pulling one another forward and whispering, snickering, faster and faster in a cheerful yellow-orange race. An alarm sounded, the slow rise of the smoke alarm lowing like a birthing cow and then taking hold at a higher pitch, keening its warning, followed by footsteps in the distance. Roy quickly set another match and flung it at one of the lands. He couldn't wait for the full billow and engulf, nor the anticlimax of hosed water, so he ran, ran, ran, past all the cleaners who were beginning to gather and wonder if this was a true fire or a miniature false alarm, and out of the Wunderland. He ran back to the apartment and into the bedroom without knocking.

'Gert, get up, get up, we have to go.'

The stink of drink in the room was a shocker. She lifted her head from the pillow and stared at him puff-eyed and bloodshot. 'What the fuck, Roy? What time is it?'

'I've done something, Gert, we have to get out of here.'

He ran to the wardrobe and pulled out his backpack, stuffing the figurines and the model train and the miniature filing cabinet in while Gert watched him, blinking. Then he ran out of the room and took the train timetables book from the shelf, grabbed his passport and wallet. He ran back into the bedroom but Gert hadn't budged.

'Get *up*!' he roared. 'It's not a fucking joke – we need to move.'

The look on her face then, the sheerest of fear, but she still made no move. 'Roy, what have you done?'

'A fire, Gert, just a small fire, but they'll probably overreact.'

The look of confusion then. 'Is anyone hurt, Roy?'

'No.'

She threw off the blankets and rose out of the bed. 'One minute,' she said, and started pulling things out of her bag.

'No, Gert, you're supposed to pack not unpack.'

'Relax, Roy, I'm just getting dressed, give me two bloody seconds.'

He left her and paced the sitting room with his hands cupped over his ears, tugging the short bits of hair surrounding them.

Gert

Katzenjammer = discordant clamour = hangover

Oh, my head, my head. The hangover I wanted, well, I got it, and a fair bit extra as well. I could have done without Roy banging in and bellowing sparks and flames. He had me mithered into trying to pack my things with a head like tight-packed studs. A fire, he'd said, a small fire. Nobody was hurt, he'd said. That's what I wanted to hear, truth or not. My brain was half a beat behind my ears so processing what he said was a problem, but the more he said, the more I thought, fuck it, let's just go. Time enough he made a plan that had me in it.

Roy

Streichholzschächtelchen = blow wood box = matchbox

They moved quickly through the apartment, swooping things into their bags before rushing out the door and down the stairs. Strange not saying bye to Stefan, strange he'd never see him again. Would he notice his matches were missing? Would he link his possessions to the fire?

'Where are we going, Roy?'

'The station,' he said.

They heaved their bags shoulder-wards and moved at a half-walk half-run clip across the canals, picking their way in the lamp-lit gloom. At the station, Gert panted up the steps; Roy raced ahead.

'Which direction?' she asked.

'Hauptbahnhof,' he said, 'Poland. A train leaves at 09:57, arriving in Łódź at 21:41 – we'll make that one.'

'This is just like a Bond movie,' she said, 'or maybe a Jason Bourne one. Bond is too posh for ordinary trains.'

He stifled the urge to admonish her. He'd need to hold his patience for an eleven-hour-forty-four-minute journey.

Gert

Schnapsidee = a decision made while drunk =
a really bad idea

A mystery, this high-speed international flee, probably a bad mystery, but if I close off my mind it's a soothe to be led, to be told where I'm going. I might be still drunk. I'm going on a trip with my brother – who'd have thought it? My stomach doesn't feel great, my head feels as if it's attached to a swing-ball, I wonder if Roy has packed the aspirin.

Roy

Zugzwang = move + compulsion = to be forced to make a move

She moved too slow. He tried not to shout at her. She didn't seem to understand the urgency and was enjoying the fun of the jaunt, muttering giddily to herself. Maybe she was still drunk. He didn't look over his shoulder; if he didn't look back nothing bad had happened. The U-Bahn came, the one in the direction of the main station, and they stuffed themselves on, poured themselves into seats. Gert looked out the window –

'Keep the head down, will you?' he hissed. 'This isn't a fucking joke.'

She turned. 'That's twice you've said *fuck*, Roy, things must be serious.'

They rode like that, silently looking ahead, his face set grim, hers working up to the makings of a smile.

Acknowledgements

An extract from *Wunderland* previously appeared in *Reading the Future: New Writing from Ireland*, edited by Alan Hayes. The author gratefully acknowledges financial assistance from the Arts Council in writing this novel. Thanks to the Rooney family and the Lannan Foundation for the recognition and money that paid for childcare. Both were invaluable to finish the book.

To my brilliant editor, Emma Dunne, for putting some serious shape on an unwieldy novel and for her compassionate ruthlessness about killing tens of thousands of dud words. To Aoife K. Walsh, who showed insight, generosity and dogged good grace during the whole process, and all at New Island Books. Jo Walker for her beautiful designs. Ger Nichol for years of support.

To Greg Baxter for the Some Blind Alleys writing workshops which got me thinking I could write in the first place, and for being so tough on cliches.

To everyone at Boston College for providing refuge in the form of a desk in a pandemic. To the staff at the National Library, and the staff at various cafés in Dublin for turning a blind eye to a woman putting her laptop ahead of her coffee.

To the crèche carers who mind my children with kindness and fun – without that, I couldn't have rested easy enough to finish this book.

To the women I work with in Housekeeping in Trinity College for their curiosity and support, especially the cleaners in the museum building, the Long Room Library and the arts block. Also to my supervisors for being supportive and understanding about taking leave to write.

To Sinead Crowe for a sofa to sleep on in Hamburg while I researched the novel.

To the incredible friends, non-writers and writers, who listened to me moan about rejections as well as celebrated the good news and showed up at launches and various events. You are too numerous to mention and I'd be kicking myself if I left somebody out. To my neighbours and my parents' neighbours and friends. To anyone who asked after my books or took the time to send good wishes, thank you, it can be a lonely business.

To the late Geraldine Purcell, who was continually supportive of my writing and excited for any successes. To the wider Purcell and Hannon families, the Lally and Morrissey extended families.

To my parents, who gave me Friday babysitting during maternity leaves to get out of the house and write, or not write. To my sister, Sarah, and my brothers, Stephen and Mark, and sisters-in law, Nuala and Louisa: we will buffet breakfast again one day. To Brian for every kind of support and more. To Alice and Joe for day-to-day wild joys and demolishing any kind of writerly notions I might have.